MW00718310

HOMEGROWN...

...Back in the Day

By:

Mikki Rogers

Initially edited by J. Keith Aikens

Thanks to many very special friends; the final edit was completed in the eleventh hour:

Bridgett Phillips, Eric & Bronwyn Norman, Linda Reece, Carolyn Grillier, Marlene Seaton, Terrence Williams, Robin Hunter, Andrea Townsend and GOD who was definitely on all of our side to make this work…

Thanks to all of you for giving me the support encouragement and the strength to make this happen.

FOREWORD

There is nothing more majestic than the changing of seasons, the birth of a baby, the soft sweet perfume of Casablanca lilies and the strength of friendship that began in the beginning and has no end...

Friendship that is defined by puppy love, dumb love and no love...

Friendship that only gains in strength, in spite of, rather than because of...

Friendship that is so deep, that while you may not remember the circumstances of your first encounter, you recall with zealous clarity the first exchange...

the first experience and all that follows.

you remember with precisioned recall the conquests...the defeats...the successes...the failures...

And, like every good griot, you tell the story accompanied with a generous dose of loud and rancious exaggeration that are not tolerated, but celebrated with laughter so loud, all others must leave.

This is such a tale of glory that is found in spending a life together...

A life borne of five lives...

A life that can only be defined of five lives...

A life that on its own accord can only survive through true energy and expressions of the five lives in celebration...

TAYLOR, SIDNEY, AARON, TREVOR and KELLY were

HOMEGROWN...and, ...**Back in the Day**

...there was once upon a Great Time.

...From a true life long friend,

Valerie C. Ferguson

ACKNOWLEDGEMENTS

When I think about my own up bringing in Cincinnati, Ohio I can only thank God that I was loved and protected by my parents Mr. & Mrs. Sylvester & Nina Reece, JR. My father, Sylvester Reece, Jr. passed away in September 1995 and I cannot tell you how much he is missed. He was the tower of strength and the anchor of our family. In the days that our parents raised us, to say it was difficult for them would be truly putting it mildly. They struggled to make ends meet, fed and clothed me, my three brothers, William, Michael, David and my sister Linda. They introduced us to and helped us form a relationship with God. They taught us how to be decent human beings. I still remember some of the old sayings that were drummed into our heads daily: 'Love the Lord with all thine heart', 'Pretty is as pretty does', 'Good things come to those who wait', 'Patience is a virtue', 'Cleanliness is next to Godliness', 'Treat others as you want to be treated', 'You get out of life what you put in to it', 'Never wear out your welcome', 'God bless the child that's got his own', 'Always keep yourself nice to be near'. These were just some of their words of wisdom and I find myself even at my age still remembering and living by most of these things. I have tried to instill the same values in my two wonderful children. These words makes you stop and think, don't they? Thanks mom and dad. While it was a much different time then, the family should mean the same today.

I love with all my heart and thank my husband, Gregory Rogers. He has been supportive to me in any and everything that I undertake. Without him most of my accomplishments would have come with a much higher price tag.

I thank my sister, Linda Reece and her beautiful children, Nina, Josh and Hope for loving me and sharing their lives with me. I thank my brothers, William Polnett, JR, his wife Dorothy, Michael Reece, his wife Andrea and David Reece, his wife Kim who have all been strong for me and our family.

I thank my wonderful sons Rodney and William. They have made me a very proud mother. And they have no idea how they have also helped me stay on the road to the straight and narrow over the years. Thanks young men for my beautiful daughters in law Marlene and Valorie and my grandchildren Tyler, Kayla and Aysia.

I thank my best friends, Linda Reece, Jean Haskins, Bennie Mae Doggett, Martha Bolden, Ruth Roberts, Carolyn Grillier, Jackie Rogers, Valerie Ferguson, Lynn Dominguez, Char Yates, Gayle Davis and others who have been both supportive and strong for me when I thought I had nothing left.

May the Lord richly bless you all.

A word from the Author:

This story is based on fiction. The story line is from the creative mind of the author and any references to any person or persons, places or actual events is purely coincidental. The purpose of the story line is to give the individual who reads this novel a sense of authenticity respective to the events that take place in the periods indicated in the story.

For the purpose of explanation, this story is being told in the first person and not by the author.

INTRODUCTION

Success is directly tied to the past...

A meeting of the 'Sisters' was fast approaching! We would all come together again to enjoy each other's company and to reminisce about our youth. When we planned this meeting, we figured that we would do as we normally would and cram a little of everything into the short period of time that we had together. But our expectations of this meeting were limited in the scope of how much ground we would actually cover this time. We usually kept this appointment, no matter what else was going on in our lives. Each time we got together, one or the other needed the rest of us. We realized years ago that life's ironies, big or small, had one or all of us in need of help, a shoulder or an ear at times. Life had its way of playing little tricks on not just us, but any and everyone at one time or another. So, we were always there to comfort each other, wherever we were or whenever it was needed. Little did we know, when we were children and young adults, how treacherous the roads that we would walk could become and how many close calls we would encounter before actually becoming adults. These roads would be heavily laden with happiness, laughter, heartache, racism, alcohol abuse, death, drugs, murder and so many other severe things, which would have our lives spinning out of control at times.

There were several of us that grew up together in Cincinnati, Ohio, but these relationships and this story begins with the three 'Sisters.'

CHAPTER ONE

It was decided that we would all meet again in Atlanta in the summer of 1995. It had been two years since we were all together. We agreed eight years before that no matter what was happening in our lives, we would get together for a long weekend at least every couple of years, if not sooner, just to enjoy each other's company. Three days of "PRIME TIME" was just one week away.

Morgan and I had much to do to prepare. Brenda, our housekeeper, was in one day earlier than usual to spruce up the house because the 'Sisters' were coming in on Friday, her regular day. Her schedule was to come every other

Friday to do a thorough cleaning because the house was much too much for me to handle. It was also part of her employment agreement that she would make herself available when we needed assistance with special affairs. We had a seven bedroom, six bathroom house with all of the up-to-date amenities and I had to make sure it was sparkling whenever we entertained. Based on my humble beginnings, this was now my signature and it had to be perfect each time. Brenda agreed three weeks earlier that she would be available to serve at the party that Morgan and I were having for the 'Sisters.' The party was scheduled for Saturday. Brenda really needed to work all the extra hours that she could because she was going through a rough period since her trailer had been burglarized, not once, but twice in the last six months. The first time was during Christmas last year when all of her children's toys, a VCR and many other household items were taken. We found ourselves in many conversations with her about it. Morgan often told her that it had to be someone that she knew, but she and her husband Ron couldn't figure it out and neither could the police. Brenda was visibly shaken about the first break-in, but the second intrusion in her life was devastating to her. I asked her to stop cleaning for a few minutes to have a cup of coffee with me in order to try to calm her down. We sat at the kitchen table for a short while just looking out of the window at the birds playing in and around the birdbath in the back yard as we chatted about this and that. Then, all of a sudden, it appeared as if a light bulb turned on inside her head. She realized, as we sat there chatting with time passing, she had two more houses to clean before the end of the day, so she thought she had better get a move on. I also had some last minute things to do, so I needed to get going too. But, nonetheless, she seemed to have collected herself a bit and I was happy about that. Morgan was also helping me prepare for the 'Sister's arrival and the party. He was going to the market to pick up some last minute items.

"Honey, please don't forget to pick up some fresh fruit for the fruit bowl and eight bottles of the Black Opal wine that they like and ten more bottles of champagne for the party. Whatever we don't drink tomorrow, we can serve at the party Saturday along with the champagne, okay?"

Since I had gone marketing a few days ago, I couldn't think of anything else. Besides, the party was being catered...no way I was going to try and handle all that by myself, especially with the type of work that I do everyday. When I am off, I refuse to spend my precious time cleaning and cooking, especially for a sizable affair. I would be too tired to enjoy the festivities.

"Okay," Morgan responded to me while asking, "are you sure you won't need anything else?"

"No babe," I said, "that will do it for me, I'll see you later."

"Good-bye babe...and I'll see you later Brenda," Morgan said.

"See you at the party Morgan," Brenda said as almost in a fog.

He left through the kitchen door. A couple of seconds later I heard his car start in the distance. I stood to make my way to the same door as I looked around at Brenda who was busying herself trying to finish. As Morgan was backing out of the driveway, I got into my car and started it. Brenda walked to the door to close it but before she did, she leaned out to wave goodbye. I let the car window down to give Brenda her last minute instructions. "Please don't forget to be here by two o'clock Saturday afternoon. We have to make sure that everything for the party is ready and goes smoothly."

I also said to her, "Brenda, try not to worry too much, the police will catch the low down burglars. Those dirty dogs will make a mistake and someone will notice!"

She said, " I really hope so Taylor, because the kids are afraid to go to sleep there now."

"I can understand that," I told her, "but they are kids and in time they will eventually forget it ever happened at all. I should know with everything that happened to me, when I was a kid."

Morgan promised to keep himself pretty much out of the way during
Friday night. It was to be ladies only night. He and a friend were going to hang
out too. I told him to stay out of trouble. Seemed as if every time we are out
together, the ladies were drawn to him and always flirted. He was a good looking
man with golden brown skin, about six foot-three with a medium build. He had
beautiful hazel eyes and wore a full heavy mustache. He was very handsome.
Although he was nice to look at, I certainly didn't marry him for his looks or his
brains and Lord knows he had no money to speak of when we first met.

He graduated from high school and attended a little more than a year or so
at a local college. He was hired by the local transit company in Atlanta when he
was in junior college and had been at the transit company for a little over fifteen
years when we met. Even though he wasn't highly educated, he had a good head
on his shoulders and worked hard. Morgan was a gentle man and always liked to
see me happy, as I did him. He knew how much this meeting with the 'sisters'
always meant to me, so he was all for it. He often mentioned to me that the
relationships I had with the 'Sisters' was something special and that I should
really hold onto them. He realized that not many people kept their friends from
their childhood, like we did. He also liked all of the 'sisters' alot, although he had
his comments from time to time. He had an uncanny ability to size people up
after only a few encounters with them. But, for the most part, they all got along
well.

Morgan and I had a very special relationship, so much so that we agreed
when we were first married that only one of us should try to climb the corporate
ladder. We realized that if we were both working night and day and on the road
for our respective companies, weeks at a time, we would never see each other.
We wouldn't be able to build a solid personal relationship needed in a marriage,
which was of the utmost importance to us. We wanted our marriage to survive
and flourish, so we agreed that he would be the support mechanism for

5

me, as I began my climb up the ladder in the banking industry. Besides, I had the potential to go a lot further a lot quicker in my industry, than he could in his. I started twenty years ago in the administration area of a local bank company. But, because racial prejudice loomed over most management areas of the banking business, it created a strong choke hold on hiring and promotional practices, especially as they related to African Americans. It was difficult to attain the promotions that I should have received, based on hard work. I was overlooked many times, but I refused to give up. I eventually became overtaxed with the situation at my outdated place of employment and moved, after all those years, to a competitor right across the street who understood my worth, at least monetarily. But there, even though I was making more money, some of the same nonsense was happening in their everyday activities too. But, because I was familiar with and able to identify some of the moves that upper management would make in certain situations, I was competent enough to outsmart them before they could me. Eventually, they recognized that I knew the politics of the business and after some of their more obvious indiscretions, they figured that I had to have a specific agenda of my own that I was working to combat their open disregard for what they knew was the right thing to do. They had to realize that I was much too intelligent not to have daily documentation of their underhanded actions, which could have them over a proverbial barrow if I ever took them to court. So, the way that I looked at it, they had to do the right thing by me. Besides, by that time they realized they had in me one of the best, brightest and determined individuals available and that I could add to the overall success of the organization when given the opportunity. Consequently, I began to get the promotions that started my climb to becoming a Senior Vice President with U S A Bank, a national banking partnership. So, the plan that Morgan and I had put in place was working and working well.

PART II

They were all due in today! My ride to the airport was fairly uneventful.
As I drove down the freeway toward the airport, I had my music blasting and the
sun roof of my brand new Lexus open, and my hair was blowing in the wind.
Aaron was coming in from Cincinnati, Sidney from Philadelphia and Trevor from
New York. Trevor had missed two of these mini reunions and swore to us a few
weeks ago that she wouldn't dare miss this one. Their flights were previously
coordinated, so that I would only have to make one trip to the airport. There was
one other member of the group who already lived in Atlanta. Kelly moved to
Atlanta about five years after I did. Today, she was at work and would join us
later in the evening.

These relationships began back in the late fifties, when we first started in
junior high school. Aaron was a year older than Sidney, Trevor and I were next,
then there was Kelly only a few months behind. Actually, we were virtually
running neck and neck, give or take a few months.

On my third circle of the baggage claim area, I saw Trevor. She looked beautiful as she stood there waving, so that I would see her. She was a soft spoken, very light skinned pretty girl with long, thick black hair. Looking at her I was reminded that real light skinned girls were big hits in junior high and high school. The boys always tended to favor girls who had light skin and if they had long hair too, they were highly sought after. So, she had to literally beat them off with sticks even starting from a very young age. Over the years she worked hard and applied herself and eventually made it to a Vice Presidency of the National Insurance Company with major offices all around the world. She has become a leading authority in the insurance industry and has broken all kinds of records with her ingenuity for new trend setting insurance issues and skillful people management, which catapulted her to one of the top spots in her field. She had a bright smile on her face when I first saw her standing there. As I pulled up to the curb, she leaned over to look in the window and said,

"Hey girl." As she approached the car, my heart began to race, because I knew we were in for a fabulous time! At least, I had done all I could to make sure it was a fabulous time.

"Aaron is still waiting on one bag and I believe Sidney went to the ladies room but I'm not sure, since she just disappeared."

"You know that Sidney will be the last one out of the terminal," she told me.

As I got out of the car we both hugged and laughed. You must understand that as we grew up, Sidney always moved very slowly, mysteriously and methodically.

"One minute she was there and the next she wasn't," Trevor said.

Obviously, we were used to Sidney's antics. By this time, Aaron appeared through the baggage claim doors and headed toward us. She was a slender woman, who was dressed to the nines with a look of wear and tear on her face. She was still a good looking woman even though she had experienced so much. She had been through a lot in her life and had done very, very well considering. Her story alone could keep us talking for hours on end. Her appointment to head all of the Social Service Agencies for the State of Kentucky had her pulled from one direction to another in America. She was a highly sought after speaker with speaking engagements most recently from the White House to the Congressional Black Caucus keynote opening session in 1994.

"I can't believe it!", she bellowed.

"What?", I responded?

"Sidney just disappeared," Aaron said in amazement!

"She'll be along in a moment, but she is still true to character," I spouted!

"That is a trait that is hers and hers alone!" said Trevor.

While Trevor was speaking, Aaron moved toward me to hug.

"How are you doing Taylor," she asked?

"I am doing great!" I said with enthusiasm.

"I am so jazzed about this weekend, I just know we are going to have a good time!"

This reunion really has me charged!"

"I can see that girl! Where's Morgan?," Trevor inquired.

I turned toward her, "Oh, he decided that he would see us later...he wanted to give us a chance to bond without him," I answered looking like a love struck newlywed.

"That's just like him, isn't it?", said Aaron?

"Yes, I do have a very thoughtful husband, most of the time, don't I? ", I said proudly.

We moved toward the trunk of the car to put in their bags.

"There are so many new things I want to show you all in Atlanta now," I said.

"But, most of all I want to do whatever you all have in mind. Because when we meet in your respective cities, I want to do what I want to do, you know what I mean?"

"Why am I not surprised about that?" Aaron said sarcastically.

"You have always wanted to have things your way most of the time," she said.

"Okay... here we go," said Trevor as a referee.

"That's not altogether true," I said defensively. "If I had my way, way back when, you would have had a much harder time penetrating the sisterhood," I answered pointedly.

"You both needed me and you know it," Aaron said with much more satire.

Just at that very moment a policeman approached us and asked us to move the car. He pulled out his book of tickets and told us he would have to write one on us if we didn't move right then.

Aaron said, "Okay, okay, we'll move it," with her regular tone expressing authority.

We all jumped into the car being careful to keep an eye out in the direction of the baggage claim doors to look for Sidney.

"I can't believe it, Sidney is still no where to be found," I said!

Just as we pulled away to circle, Trevor said, shaking her head, "There she is."

By that time, it was too late for us to stop to pick her up, so we had to continue with our plans to make the circle. As we approached the baggage claim area again, Sidney was standing there smiling with her eyes sparkling as they usually did with the sun cascading from her reddish brown hair. She was a pretty medium brown skinned girl, standing about 5'4" with an oval face and shoulder length hair. As I saw her, I thought to myself about the first days when we met and how she had always been very determined that one day her hard work in school and in the workplace, would pay off for her and she was right. She had always been so determined in everything she did. Her rise to be the top ranking female at the number one airline in America was a feat within itself. And, the fact that she was the only African American female to hold such a prestigious position in this lucrative field was used as a personal benchmark for many female executives around the world. But, the reality that she was one of the 'Sisters' who spent so many hours on the high school steps in Cincinnati, Ohio, daydreaming about and planning for her future, had her as excited about this mini reunion as the rest of us!

10

"You will always be the same," I said, as I got out to help her with her luggage. She said, "What ever do you mean?"

We all marveled at being together again as Sidney and I moved back to get in the car. We caught the eyes of several young men standing in the immediate area. They were virtually looking us up and down. Sidney's back was to them, so I gave her a little nudge so that she would turn around to do her thing. I knew it would be right up her alley to complete the circle and flirt with them too. We were all attractive ladies and the fact that we were a little older now didn't change a thing. When she was done making their tongues hang out, she tore herself away from their roving eyes and we jumped into the car.

"Hello sisters!" remarked Sidney, "Why did you drive off?"

"Well, it was either that or have the car towed," I said, as we all laughed again. I said, looking at Sidney through the rear view mirror, "You will never change. Always the last one out of anywhere!"

"What did I do now?", she asked with her eyes opened wide, and trying to look innocent.

"NEVER MIND!" We all said as we drove off.

"Where to ladies?" I asked.

Aaron said, "Let's take a driving tour first, since the Olympics are coming to Atlanta next year. Let's see what's different and then maybe a late lunch" We all agreed. We rode around to see some of the actual Olympic sites and the construction that was underway for some of the venues of the Olympics and where they would actually take place. Then to the Martin Luther King Center area and ultimately to several black neighborhoods, both urban and upscale and finally back to downtown. After cruising downtown for quite awhile, we stopped at Underground Atlanta, parked the car, got out to walk around. We casually strolled in Underground and enjoyed the sights. We came upon a quaint French bistro and decided that we would stop there for lunch. When we were seated, we began catching up on what was happening with each other. We spontaneously moved into a conversation about the latest news regarding the high school. Very few of the same teachers were still there, but we still had strong ties to the activities there. We talked about how different things were after so many years. In as much as Aaron was the only one of the 'Sisters' in or near Cincinnati, we usually kept up with all the particulars through her and another high school friend Bo. He was a boy that had a birth defect and as he got older, it got worse and now he is in a wheel chair.

Aaron and Bo told us who had gone to the pros, who all were big shots in their jobs, who all had gotten fat and had a house full of children, who had died, who was in trouble with the law, who was divorced or married, and all of that. And, if she couldn't find out about it all, Bo could and he kept her in the loop. All of the nay-sayers from the old neighborhood who talked about us all the time were our incentive to remain looking good and doing well. We were determined to make them all eat their words. After we had lunch, we strolled around some more looking at some of the kiosks in the mall area of Underground. Several of them had very interesting paraphernalia displayed in their cases as well as some very unique African American merchandise. We saw one merchant in particular that had several Black art pieces that were out of this world with out of this world prices too. Even though all of us were financially independent, we still enjoyed the possibility of purchasing bargains. Nothing gave us a deeper thrill than to get a bargain while shopping. That's just part of being a woman! We all believed in having the very best, but wouldn't just throw money away. We preferred to give to our favorite charities, rather than just blow it like that! We still thought about the days when it was very tough for us and we respected those days. As we walked, I told them about a club in Kenny's Alley, just down the way called Teddy's Live.

"Do you think there is anything going on there now, at this hour?" Sidney asked.

"Yes, I think so. They have a talent show going on, on both Friday and Saturday afternoons," I answered.

We decided to go in. The place was jumping. There was a live band playing music from the 60's and 70's, as we walked in. According to the lady at the door, one session of a four part talent show had ended and the next was to begin in an hour. This was perfect! I paid the entrance fee for all of us and we were seated at a table and started to settle in. There were several couples already there and as I looked around the club, I saw five or six guys that I knew, along with some of their friends. Of course, they started flirting with us and the girls being who are, beautiful and mischievous, wanted to play that game too. We were determined that we would let our hair down during this long weekend, starting with right now! They danced, drank, giggled and talked. It was great!

By the time we got to my house, they were feeling pretty good. We brought in the luggage and took it to their respective rooms, hung up their clothes, took showers and got into our bed clothes. One by one, we came into the family room afterwards. I had already opened up two chilled bottles of the Black Opal chardonay for us and poured each of us a glass. I was ready for a chilled glass of wine myself, since I was the designated driver for the evening. Our conversations began by talking about our respective positions and how things were coming along. We even discussed how much longer we wanted to work at all. We were sitting there sipping a glass of wine and chatting when the door bell rang.
"Is that Morgan?" asked Trevor.
"Well, I'm not sure, let's go see," I said, "but he should have his key, so he wouldn't be ringing the door bell, at least I don't think he would!"
We all went to the door together bunched up like a small band of the Keystone Kops.

We were acting pretty silly at this point. We peeked out of the window alongside the front door, only to find out that it was Kelly. Kelly was the only one of us that hadn't faired too well in a career . She was now a receptionist at the Atlanta Housing Agency and wasn't making too much money at it. She had a couple of good jobs over the years, since moving to the Atlanta area in the mid seventies, but for one reason or another, none of them had worked out. When she was younger she was a dark skinned, cute and very shapely girl with long curly hair. She had, over the years put on a lot of weight and was kind of heavy now. But, no matter what, she was still one of the 'Sisters' and we all loved her very much. I opened the door for her and I stepped aside as she came in. All of the girls greeted her with hugs. She could see that we were already having a blast and she seemed a slight bit irritated.

She said in a snippy tone as she turned to me, " I've been calling you guys for almost three hours, wondering where you were."

With no explanation, I said, "Come on in girl and get comfortable."

I locked the door and proceeded to lead the way as we all returned to the family room, to our designated spots and got comfortable.

After about thirty minutes more of chit chat, Morgan came home and into the room where we were to say good night to us. He kissed me on the forehead and disappeared through the doorway in the kitchen and went up to bed. We stayed up for another forty-five minutes or so and decided to try and get some sleep ourselves, because tomorrow would be a pretty long day for all us and as it was, it was already two a.m. All of the girls had been up since early this morning with their last minute work and chores at their jobs and at home, plus packing, and then traveling today, so they were tired. Kelly bid us a good night with the promise to return early the next morning, so that we could all spend the entire day together.

PART III

The sun rose early, but it didn't bother us. We slept 'til about eight thirty and were only awakened by the smell of fresh coffee brewing. Morgan was up as always, bright and early and was preparing for his morning run. I stumbled downstairs with sleep still a huge part of my being and kissed him good morning. He gave me a peck on the forehead and said he'd be back in an hour or so. He usually took a run through the neighborhood and back, especially on weekends, when the weather was good. His ritual only included use of the exercise equipment in the exercise room during the week. Don't ask me why, this was <u>his</u> routine, but he always mentioned something about fresh air whenever possible. One by one, I heard the girls moving about in their rooms. A couple of hours later, we all had a lazy breakfast and got dressed for the day. They were all looking forward to meeting the guests who had confirmed their attendance at the party tonight. Since I moved to Atlanta back in early the 70s, I had met so many people. And, not all of them have been pillars of the community.

The guests tonight were, as we call it, some of the "THE MOVERS AND SHAKERS OF THE CITY." A millionaire friend of mine, his wife and several of their friends were also confirmed. George was from Cincinnati, and his work was paramount in discovering the use of wireless communications and ultimately led the revolution of cordless phones and eventually cell phones. The president of a national Black men's social group and his wife, two Black college presidents, a president of an Atlanta area school board, several city council members and their significant others were all going to be in attendance. In some cases a single person or two and throw in some high ranking managers of local Fortune Five Hundred companies, as well as many of my not so high ranking friends were also confirmed. I always made it my business to surround myself with people who were not caught up on formalities, because if they were hung up on formalities, to me they were snobs and I personally didn't want anything to do with a snob. As a matter of fact, it was always my motto that "the only thing a snob can do for me is show me where a decent human being is."

It was just about ten minutes 'til two o'clock, when I heard Brenda's car pulling in the driveway. She had one of her employees with her to help serve tonight's guests. She came in the door, and headed straight for the telephone.
"Hi Brenda," I said.
She said, "Hey Taylor, I have to make sure that everything is all set for this evening!"
Her first order of business was to check the arrival time of the caterers. When she got off the phone, she and Myra, who worked part-time for Brenda, inspected the stemware, china and silverware for any spots, etc. and made sure everything else was ready. She is such a perfectionist, which is why I have had her in my employ for so many years. She and her employee pressed over their uniforms. Uniforms??? That made me feel kind of odd. A couple of years ago,

16

I started telling Brenda a little about how I came up in the projects and she was absolutely amazed. To have gotten this far, after all that has happened to me, I believe was a blessing from God and God alone. I felt like, if I could make it, anyone could.

The musicians arrived at the house about five thirty and set up their instruments in the staging area of our big recreation room. We had hired a theme company to come in to decorate the room in a night club setting for this occasion. The group rehearsed for about thirty five minutes and by seven o'clock, the music was mellow and the champagne was flowing. The last of the 'Sisters,' Sidney, made her way down the stairs as the first of the guests began to arrive. We were all playing hostess and assisted in responding to the door bell, if Brenda or Myra were tied up with other things. By eight o'clock, the front circular drive of the house was lined with cars reminiscent of a gathering at a royal palace in Europe. Yes, there were some very influential people in attendance. As I walked through the room to say hello and welcome each person individually, there were all sorts of interesting conversations going on in different pockets of the room and even a little dancing. I motioned for the musicians to lower the music as I picked up a fork from one of the tables to tap the stem of my champagne goblet to get everyone's attention. I thanked everyone for coming and took that time to introduce the 'Sisters.' After which, I asked everyone to continue enjoying themselves. Brenda and Myra were really making sure the guests had everything they wanted and kept the guests' hands full with a cocktail or food at all times. At nine thirty a surprise act appeared, my guests were amazed and very pleased! One of his hit songs was being played as he made his entrance into the room. Everyone stood on their feet and applauded as a gesture of welcome. Teabo Cryson entered the room and what a surprise he was to everyone. He performed what seemed to be his best private concert even by his own standards. We enjoyed song after song. "Reaching for the Moon," "I'll be so into You" and many more. When he finished he said to me that he felt it went very well. He had done very few private concerts since his career skyrocketed in the mid-seventies and did this as a special favor to me. We had known each other since my early days in Atlanta, when he was working to get his career started. We met in the early seventies, a few years after I arrived in Atlanta. We became instant friends after being introduced by a mutual acquaintance and we spent a lot of time together in those days. We automatically stayed friends after that time. Since there were only about eighty - five people in attendance, they all got to talk with him one on one afterwards. When he was preparing to go, I thanked him for his performance and when we were alone, paid him for the evening.

Soft music was filling the room and it could even be heard out on the patio, where several couples danced or just sat off to themselves holding hands and talking. A little after midnight the crowd started to thin out a bit and eventually got smaller and smaller. We thanked each of them for coming as they left. They spoke with high praise regarding the evening. All of the guests and the 'Sisters' had a spectacular time and eventually there were only the 'Sisters' and Morgan who remained. Brenda and Myra had been clearing away dishes and glasses all along, so there wasn't a whole lot left for them to do. They finished everything and bid us a fond farewell. As they left, we retired to our rooms to change into our bed clothes with the commitment to get back together to toast the evening. Even Kelly decided to spend the night. We re-assembled in the family room about one thirty to enjoy another glass of wine together, as we did just that, toasted the evening! We sat there talking and talking and really enjoying each others company, like we did when we were kids on the high school steps. I had a big surprise for them near the pool and gazebo area and asked them to walk with me outside and into the night. It was a beautiful evening as we strolled to the back yard. Much to their surprise, I had a mock rendition of the high school steps built just for this occasion. It was covered with a large tarp cloth, and as we

18

approached it Aaron said to me, "What have you done?"

I said, "Everyone take a corner of the tarp so that we can pull it back to see what's here!"

As we did just that, they all were in awe. They couldn't believe how their minds opened up with floodgates of memories. We took our respective seats on the high school steps, just as we did back then.   We all felt right at home. They thanked me for all that I did to make this moment happen for us as we all really settled in. From that moment on, one thing led to another and before we knew it, we were reminiscing about the days when we were kids, how we all came to know each other and all that had happened since then. We started going way, way back, back to the beginning..............

BACK IN THE DAY...

CHAPTER TWO

COMING OF AGE...

As far back as I can remember, it started for me in some small projects called the Barracks in Lincoln Heights, just north of Cincinnati, Ohio. This was one of the many suburbs of Cincinnati. The area was run down at best and my mom and dad were working hard to get us moved out of there and into the Laurel Homes downtown. They felt that we would stand a better chance in life growing up in a better neighborhood. Besides, they knew that the Barracks were going to be torn down in a couple of years, so they were constantly making plans about it all. I heard them discussing it many nights, after my older brother Bobby and I were put to bed.

At the time, we were at the age of kindergarten and elementary school. We attended the little red school house just up the road with other little children from the neighborhood. The other kids were just like us, very unsuspecting and full of promise and hope. We simply did what we were told and went on about our merry way each day. Even back in those days my mom loved to play poker for money. She and my dad put us to bed one night in the early spring. They were headed to a neighbor's apartment to gamble. Bobby and I were just about sleep when they left. A few minutes after they left and when we were just about sleep, we heard a noise. We both woke up somewhat and then started to dose again. The noise stopped and then started up again. It sounded like there was someone trying to get into our apartment through the back bedroom window.

After a few minutes of this, we heard a man's voice practically whispering, "Let me in. All I want is the little girl." Bobby and I froze in our beds. The man then whispered in a stronger voice, "I won't hurt her."

Bobby jumped up from his bed and ran to the doorway of mom and dad's room and said, "Get a way from here."

The man kept fumbling with the lock on the window. Bobby ran to get in bed with me as we sat there hugging trying to console each other. Bobby got a bright idea to climb out of our bedroom window and run up the street to get our dad.

I said, "No Bobby, I'm scared to stay here alone."

Bobby said, "The man will never know you're alone. Just get in the closet and stay quiet. I'll bring dad right back."

He walked me to the closet and told me to get down on my knees behind the clothes and off he went. It seemed as if he were gone for two days. I was getting very hot in that closet especially with the door closed. I kept hearing the man's voice and the fumbling noises too. The sounds were getting louder and louder. The next few minutes, I heard footsteps. They were coming directly for the closet. I was shaking so hard. I was truly afraid and thought that this intruder would take me off to a desolate place and harm me. Tears started streaming from my eyes. The door of the closet opened. All I could see through the clothes were a pair of man's shoes standing directly in front of me. I peeped through the clothes, to see it was my dad, my mom and Bobby! My dad grabbed me in his arms and held me very close to him apologizing to me for allowing this to happen and assuring me that he would protect me always. My mom stroked my hair while kissing me on the cheek telling me that they had been back out to investigate and that they didn't see anyone. But, all I wanted was to stay in my dad's arms. He and Bobby had saved me and I was safe now.

I remembered playing most of the time with the little boy next door named Ronnie. His family was a large one with lots of children, maybe nine or ten kids, mostly boys. They had a much larger family than ours. Their parents, Mr. and Mrs. Islay reminded me of my mom and dad, in as much as they also worked hard for their family and they, like my mom and dad were always trying to catch up it seemed. There were also several other families that lived in the immediate area, as well as the other projects across the street called the Valley Homes. The Valley Homes were supposed to be a little better than the Barracks, but to us they all looked about the same. According to the history of the Barracks, they were some old government buildings that housed some of the soldiers in the Second World War and because the war was over, the government commissioned them to be used for subsidized housing for Negro families. When my mom and dad first got married they lived with my grandparents in downtown Cincinnati on Clark Street. There they lived in very close quarters, my mother's mom and dad, my mom's two younger sisters, three brothers, my mom and dad and Bobby too. All of these people in three rooms was as tight as it could be. So, when I came along it was really the last straw. Not one more person could fit there. My parents were forced to find housing for our family. I have often been told that I was two months old when my grandmother gave me a bath , woke my mom so that she could feed me and went to the store. On her way back from the store, as she walked up the five flights of stairs, to get to the floor where we lived, she had a stroke and died right there on the top landing right outside of our door. That was the last time she held me. As I remember growing up, we were told many true stories like that which happened in the old neighborhood.

My father was a veteran of World War II and was selected through the Veterans Administration to move into a substandard, low-income housing project referred to as the Barracks in Lincoln Heights. He had put in an application for government housing about three years earlier. In the Barracks, Ronnie and I lived right next door to each other. We played as little kids do and we became very close. The other kids were a lot older than we were and didn't want to be bothered with us, so we only had each other. One day before either of us realized it, my family was planning to move downtown and the sadness we shared when we learned of the move was overwhelming for two such young kids. We had become so close. A couple of months later, as our truck pulled away, I could barely see Ronnie in the distance through my tears. We moved away to start a better life. I promised Ronnie that I would never forget him and we vowed that we would stay friends forever.

CHAPTER THREE

YOUNG GIRLS LIVING IN THE *projects...*

Living in the projects was all we knew. I guess we were poor, but we didn't know it. Everyone around us was just like us. Besides the poorly constructed old single family houses and the old houses that had two family apartments in them, there were two major projects, the Laurel Homes and the Lincoln Courts in our neighborhood. The Laurel Homes and the Lincoln Courts were divided by Lincoln Park Drive. All of the Laurel Homes rows of buildings had six entrances in each building with four floors and three apartments on each floor. All of the buildings were accessible through archways, which provided access for foot traffic through these massive buildings. The common areas in these court yards had touches of greenery in each yard that were fenced off to keep the residents from walking on the grass. There were also maintenance men called building supers to keep them repaired and in good condition. In other words, we lived in a semi upscale *projects* if there was such a thing. There seemed to be hundreds of them, much larger than the Barracks. The Lincoln

Courts were basically the same, but there were no archways and there was no grass and trees like there were in the Laurel Homes. This was our new world. I really missed Ronnie, but we had vowed to find each other when we grew up. So, I depended on the new area to keep me busy and provide a starting place to make new friends.

Growing up in the Laurel Homes was interesting to say the least. It seemed like here in our new world, as well as the Barracks, all of the parents took turns keeping an eye on all of the neighborhoods kids, which was a feeling of complete safety. On any given day, any of the parents would look out for us, scold or reprimand us, if it were necessary. I remember once there were five boys about ten years old huddled up together piling up some old papers. Anyone watching could easily tell they were up to no good. I stood in the background just watching as they went about their mischievous way to complete their scheme. Then I saw the matches. About the same time, I also noticed Mrs. Danner, one of the neighbors, looking out of her window directly at them, watching every move they were making. They didn't see her. Just about the time the boys had finished piling up the paper and were just about to strike a match, Mrs. Danner disappeared from her window and ...well, came flying out into the courtyard screaming in a high pitched voice with her arms flying up and down, which took the boys attention away from their mischieviousness.
"What in the world are you boys doing?" she bellowed.
"I am going to take all of you home and let your parents know what you are up to and then you'll get it!" she said.

As she was running toward them speaking in her high pitched voice, they looked around in her direction and immediately began to disburse. They ran every which way, like little rabbits. Everyone got away from her except Tony, the ring leader. She grabbed him by the ear and started marching him toward his apartment. As she walked him there, he wiggled feverishly trying to break free of her hold. When they reached his apartment, she knocked on the door. When his mother answered, Mrs. Danner handed him over to her, as his mother took a break from cooking dinner. Tony was still wiggling as Mrs. Danner let go of his ear. He screamed and made a motion toward Mrs. Danner as he said, "She was pinching the shit out of my ear!"

Tony's mom gave him a back hand lick, and said to him, "Watch your little nasty mouth," while keeping her eyes on Mrs. Danner and continuing their conversation.

"What in the world was he doing now?" his mother asked with a look of disappointment on her face.

"He and several of the boys in the neighborhood were piling up paper in the courtyard and were about to strike a match to burn it," explained Mrs. Danner.

"It was a good thing I was looking out of my window and saw them. There were at least a dozen cardboard boxes that were near them, which someone put out for the garbage man. They could have caught fire too....so this could have ended up a disaster."

"It could have all gotten out of hand!" Mrs. Danner said with excitement.

Tony's mother and Mrs. Danner talked things through in detail! Mrs. Spaulding, Tony's mother, thanked Mrs. Danner and promised that his dad would deal with him when he came in from work. Needless to say, later that evening, Tony got his butt whipped, after his father explained to him why what he did was dangerous. I wasn't aware of him trying to do that again. Incidents like that kept us from doing too many bad things, because even if your own mom or dad wasn't around, we realized none of the adults in the neighborhood would turn their heads and act as if they didn't see us doing inappropriate things. We often thought how horrible it was that everyone meddled in everyone else's business! Bobby was mischievious, but not in the same way as Tony. I wondered if my new little brother Curtis would be like Tony? Since he was still just a little baby, I would have to wait and see.

PART II

The only activities in the old neighborhood were church every Sunday, which all of the parents, without fail, made sure we all attended and the movies now and then plus playing in the yard with the other kids. As Negroes, we had two choices for entertainment, either the State Theater or the Regal Theater. The State Theater was where most of the kids in the Laurel Homes frequented some Saturdays for movies and the Regal Theater was mostly for the kids in the Lincoln Courts. Sometimes, for special big events, when there were performances by major Negro Entertainers scheduled for Cincinnati, the shows were held at the Regal Theater because of the large seating capacity. So, anyone that could afford tickets would go to the Regal Theater for these shows. The older kids were the ones that went all the time. We could only stand outside of the Theater just to see what we could see. It was a great time to be growing up. It seemed like there was always something good to see or to do.

In the late 50's, I was in my last two years of elementary school, where I first started to realize what people and life were all about and some of the pitfalls that could plague my life. I met a girl named Juanita Mathis when I was in the fifth grade. She was as mean as a snake and all the other kids thought so too. She had several older brothers, who were also very mean tough guys. Juanita roughed me and several other kids up every day by pushing, shoving and she even took our lunch money for months. I was really afraid of her. It was so bad sometimes, that I didn't even want to go to school. My Dad always made me go anyway though, but I was shaking in my boots all the way there and back everyday.

"Hey rotten teeth," she said as she shoved me, "where is my lunch money?"

You see, I had two big cavities in my two front teeth. I would simply go in my pocket and hand it over. Then when lunch time came, I had nothing. Many days I was starving by the time I got home from school. This went on, off and on, for almost an entire school year. Many times I tried to hide from her and sometimes I actually got away with it. On other days by the time she got to me I had already bought my lunch and eaten it, so she was too late. But, more often than not, she'd take it away from me.

One day she came up to me to get my lunch money and I said, "no". The words were barely audible.

She said "What?"

"I'm hungry and I'm not giving you my money no more," I said more defiantly. "You do whatever you want to do to me , but I won't give it to you no more."

She said, "I'll see you after school you little bitch, I'm gonna kick your little ass!" I had a big lump in my throat for the rest of the day just thinking about getting my butt kicked. It was scary to say the least and my first encounter with this type of thing! Besides that, I'd never been around any kids who used those kinds of words. I'd heard grown people say things like that though. Well, I thought, this day had to come eventually and whatever I have to do, I want to make sure I won't go hungry no more! All the kids at the school heard that she had threatened me and they were excited and planned to gather around to see what would happen after school. They hated her like I did. So, it was the big thing that was happening for the week. We were going to meet and settle it once and for all.

At three o'clock, about sixty-five kids gathered in the middle of Armory Street between Lynn and John Streets, which was about a half block from the school and in the direct path that I took everyday to get back to our apartment. Juanita was standing in front of all these kids waiting for me, cursing and looking like a little hard black man. She was mad as hell. There was nothing feminine about her at all. As a matter of fact she could use some Royal Crown and a hot comb right now. She was short with real dark skin and real short kinky hair. She had muscles in her arms and legs which made her look real tough. Before I even got there, I heard her loud talking to me in the distance.
"C'mon, little bitch! This will be the first time you get your little silly ass kicked , huh?"
She loved this kind of stuff and was ranting and raving about kicking my butt.

As I approached the area, I was as scared as I could be. When I got fairly close to where they were all standing, the crowd got louder and louder. I started walking slower and slower. When I was almost there, Juanita ran toward me, lunged at me and pushed me so hard in the chest that I fell back on some of the waiting kids. As I got my balance back, I seemed to get a little nerve in my belly and ran back into her to push her back. I had to do something. We began to tussle and fell to the ground. I was pulling her hair as short as it was, as she punched me over and over, much harder than I could ever imagine. She was beating me to within an inch of my life! After about two minutes of this with the kids yelling in voices that appeared like they were two blocks away, I heard one of the big boys yell, "Here comes Mr. Bannion ."

Obviously, Mr. Bannion saw the crowd gathered and ran to get into the middle of it. He was determined to break it up. I was never so glad about anything in my life! He stood there with his arms stretched out trying to keep us apart. He really didn't have to worry about me, I didn't want anymore of that. There I was thinking that he could rest the arm he held out for me, because all I wanted to use him for was as a shield from her.

"Girls, girls, break it up and back to the school you go!"

He walked us back to the school, with one of arms in each of his hands. When we got to the principal's office, my clothes were torn and my nose was bloody and it looked like she didn't have a scratch on her. Her hair was in disarray, but it was barely different than what it was normally. The principal talked to both of us as he expressed great disappointment. He told us that we were expected to live together in peace and finally we were dismissed after getting a punishment of two weeks of detention.

I thought about all of it as I walked home and no doubt about it, I got whipped pretty badly, but I no longer had to give up my lunch money. The other kids at school really respected me and from that point on, no one bothered me again, even Juanita! This was the beginning of my self-reliance and understanding that I had to speak up and stand up for myself. I started realizing that I had it in me to take care of myself and the fact that Bobby couldn't always be around to take up for me. When I got home my Dad was really upset! He drilled me about what had happened and promised to get to the bottom of it. I begged him to leave it alone, but he was very insistent and protective as always.

I saw Juanita just about everyday from that point on. She was continually harassing the other kids and taking their lunch money. She left me alone after that so, I guess the butt whipping I got was worth it. I spent the remainder of the school year mostly observing Juanita's actions because, all I wanted was to stay away from her. It was pitiful the way she carried on.

PART III

The next year, I graduated from elementary school to Bloom Junior High School. It was very different from Washburn Elementary School. The main difference, at that time, was I was in school with kids a lot older than I was. My altercation with Juanita was really of great benefit to me because it helped my self confidence. I began to have an understanding of how this all worked. I was grateful that I was no longer afraid of the bully that taunted me in grade school, even though she was also starting at the same school at the same time. I felt that I would be fine after all. Juanita and I had reached an unspoken agreement and she knew, as far as I was concerned, I was no longer on her list of kids that were to be treated like she still treated so many other kids. I wouldn't allow her to continue to kick me around or treat me like her personal banker and slave. In a way, I was grateful to her. She was someone who had forced me to become tougher.

Bloom Junior High School was twelve long blocks from our apartment, which we walked each day. These walks were long, but with other kids coming and going the same way everyday, it didn't take too long to get to school in the morning or to get home in the evening. In Ohio, the winters were very cold with heavy snows from time to time. When the weather was like that, these walks to school were horrible. By the time we got to school or back home, we were frozen solid. We learned to wear layers and layers of clothes to survive the weather. We got used to it as the days, weeks and months went by.

Just before it got really cold during my seventh grade year, I met Sidney one day when we were walking from school. I had also met several other new kids when I first started too, but there was something different about Sidney. We were all on the threshold of becoming young adults, which created a certain curiosity about everything and everyone. I had become very selective about each step that I took and was careful to carry myself in a positive light. Bobby had protected me so much that his actions had instilled in me a certain cautiousness about myself. We were all excited about this new phase in our lives and it showed. Sidney appeared to be very studious, smart even. That day she was walking just ahead of me.

I yelled, "Hey, wait for me!"

She turned around, "Me?"

"Yeah" I said.

"Okay," she said. She stopped altogether, turned completely around and watched me as I approached her.

"I figured, since we were practically going the same way, we could walk together, okay?" I asked.

"Okay," she said in a very quiet, soft voice. As I approached her,

I said, "My name is Taylor and I live on John Street."

"I've seen you several times in the neighborhood and walking home from school," I continued.

She said, "Oh, I've seen you too, and you're right we are going the same way."

We both smiled. We walked along for awhile in total silence.

After a couple of minutes I said, "Would you like to come outside after we both finish our homework and chores? Maybe we could jump rope or play hop scotch or just talk?"

Sidney said, "My mother doesn't let me come out everyday, but we will see."

"Okay, we will meet at five o'clock under the first archway on the John Street side, all right?"

She said, "Okay."

At that stage of my life, everyday was pretty much a ritual for me. Mom and Dad had recently had another baby and now I had a cute little baby brother. Everyday, I'd come in from school, change my clothes, play with little Curtis and begin my chores, then homework. My older brother, Bobby was as crazy as they come. It appeared that the sweet young boy that I once knew had developed a chip on his shoulder for some reason. His head was too big for his body and he was constantly being called jug head by his counter parts at school and he stayed in one fight or another. He was also really pissed off at life because we were poor. He seemed to be the only person that I knew that realized that we couldn't afford the normal things in life. Of course, I really didn't understand because I seemed to have fun everyday, somehow and that was all I needed. When Curtis, my little brother, grew up I wanted to be able to tell him what to do. Bobby would boss me around and I would boss Curtis around. Life would be good!

My dad was always at home after school everyday. He was laid off from his job at the blue print company, so he would have dinner just about ready when we got in. My mom was always asleep, because she typically stayed out all night every night gambling, trying to make us some money. She usually got home about five to six o'clock in the morning from the night before or sometimes after we had already gone to school, so my dad was keeping Curtis and watching me and Bobby as well as doing the cooking.

During the day we would always have to move around the apartment very quietly. My dad always made sure of that, so we wouldn't wake her. So, everyday after our routines, we got to go outside to play with the other kids in the yard, to ensure the apartment stayed quiet. We were never supposed to go very far. Those were the rules and we knew to keep them because my dad was really, really strict. He had a torturous way of giving us whippings and we didn't want any of that at anytime. Dad always kept a close watch on Curtis and me, but not Bobby. My big brother was almost never there. He didn't follow the house rules too closely. I wondered how he was able to get away with it. We didn't even know where he was most of the time.

I went outside about ten minutes to five that day and waited for Sidney. I waited for almost two hours, she never came, so I started playing a game of ledge ball with some other kids. We teamed up into four teams. We played eight games. I was becoming a master at ledge ball because I played so much. After the games were over, we went into Mrs. Lewis' apartment for awhile. That's where all of the kids went some afternoons when there was nothing to do. In her apartment, I could still hear my dad if he was looking for us. Mrs. Lewis was Kendra's mom. She was at home everyday and liked having us around. She made a big pot of dynamite corn based vegetable soup several times a year for us and boy was it good. We all wanted it whenever she made it and couldn't wait for it, especially when it was really cold outside. She knew that we would all eat it, so whenever she made it, she made a lot of it. She would make sure there was enough so we could all have some. It was just about time for it and we all knew it. After we had our bowl of the soup, we thanked Mrs. Lewis and little by little we went back outside to play.

A few minutes later, the same crowd of older boys ran through the courtyard as they often did making rough neck remarks and horsing around. It had come to be expected but, they never bothered us. Some of the boys were from those two family houses just across the street from the high school. Just as fast as they ran through there, they left. I stayed outside just hanging around until I heard my dad's whistle. Over the years he had set a standard for us and when he whistled, that was our signal . This meant that I had thirty minutes before I had to be in. Just before I started up the steps, my mom came out , as she normally did, headed for Mrs. Silva's apartment just across the way. They gambled there sometimes, playing poker. It was either Mrs. Silva's or someone else's apartment or house in the city. My mom was a card dealer and was well known all over the city for being the best dealer in town.

"Hi mom," I said. "You really look pretty!"

"Thank you darling. Did you finish your homework?" she asked.

"Yes ma'am, just about, I only have about ten minutes of it left."

"Well, leave it on the cocktail table in the living room and I will check it when I come in tonight. And by the way, your dad tells me that you left home this morning looking a little ashy. You must always remember to oil your legs and arms with the vaseline because little girls shouldn't go out looking ashy."

She leaned over to kiss me on the forehead. She smiled, turned and walked toward her destination.

"I love you," she told me.

I love you too mom, see you in the morning," I told her.

I always liked for her to kiss me because she smelled so good and she left her lipstick print on me. Later, I would, as I did whenever she'd kiss me, remember to wash around that area where her lipstick was, when I took my bath because I didn't want to wash her lipstick off. I thought somehow that would help me to be pretty too, like she was, when I grew up. I stood there for a few more minutes to watch as she went in. I saw several other regulars go into Mrs. Silva's too.

Everyone thought my mother was beautiful. She really was to me too. She was about five foot five with a golden brown complexion and long thick naturally curly hair. She had big legs and a tiny waistline, which afforded her a gorgeous figure. She had learned to hustle for a living a few years ago, back when my dad was laid-off. All of her female friends also knew how to make money playing cards, but her friends also made money by shoplifting clothes and things too. They were altogether a lot at the poker games. So, every day my mom would wake up, take a bath, put on her make-up flawlessly and get dressed in some of the most beautiful clothes that any of us had ever seen and go to her job, the poker game. She was a real sweet and generous person and exceptionally strong-willed. But, if you crossed her, she'd let you know about it in a heartbeat! About ten minutes later, I walked up to the fourth floor to our apartment. I finished my homework and prepared for tomorrow. It would probably be the same as today.

CHAPTER FOUR

NEW FRIENDS...

A couple of days went by and I ran into Sidney again at school. All her classes were different from mine, because she was a grade ahead of me, so I didn't get to see her that much. We walked home from school together again that day. While we were walking, I asked her what happened to her the other day? I wanted to know why she never came outside to meet me. She started to come out of her shell a little by telling me a little about herself. She said her mom was insistent that she stay in the house.

"But, maybe sometime soon I can come out," she declared.

She pledged, " I'm really working on it, but it has been rough. My mom is always in such a foul mood. It doesn't appear that anytime is a good time to ask her."

Day by day, Sidney asked and her mother always said no. Ultimately, she wore her mother down. Sidney and I met at the archway as often as we could, that is, whenever her mother would allow her to come out. One day several months later, we were playing hopscotch out in the courtyard. We took turns winning. We were having so much fun together. Some of the other girls in the neighborhood came to play with us too. We made an afternoon of it. Toward the end of the last game Sidney leaned over to whisper to me,

"I am really glad to have you to meet after school I've been really lonely and have always wanted someone special in my life. Taylor, I really want to do this as often as we can, don't you?"

Bobby passed by us headed only God knows where and said, "Hey little girls...stay in the yard and behave, you hear?"

I ignored him as Sidney and I went on talking.

I said, "Yeah, it's fun and we can, if your mom will allow you to come outside." She asked me with a questioning look on her face, "How do you manage to get out everyday and why are your parents letting you do it?"

I told her that my dad was laid off from his job at the blue print company and my mom stayed out all night playing poker to make us money. She was awe struck! I guess, little by little, we were both opening up to each other. We started to become best friends each time we were together. She told me that her mother almost seemed mad at her about something and she had no real idea why and that sometimes living with her mother was awful. From what she could remember, she hadn't done anything to cause this. Besides, what could a young girl have done to make her mom so angry? The little information that she could get from hearing her mother talk to her aunts and other grownups was that it had something to do with her father, who Sidney knew very little about. She said that her dad was someone famous and she never understood what exactly happened between him and her mom. Of course, I didn't believe her. Famous? Why does she live here then, in the *projects*? Sidney never said exactly who he was and I never pressed her about it. I was just happy to have a real friend and not just any old kid who happened to be playing in the yard. Now I have someone special, just like Ronnie used to be to me. Most of the kids I played with were fun, but Sidney was someone that I could really talk to about everything and someone I could say was a very special friend now and forever. This was something that neither of us had , except maybe for my relationship with Ronnie when I was little, but that was different.

Following several more months of seeing each other in school and meeting outside we became very, very close. We saw each other almost everyday at school. Her mother still didn't want her outside that much, but Sidney was determined to finish her homework and chores early and beg to go out so that we could be together. It worked sometimes and of course sometimes it didn't. We were working on becoming inseparable in spite of her mother. She and I were persistent about our relationship and decided that since I had two brothers and no sisters and she had no brothers or sisters, we were settled on the fact that we would become each others 'sister'. We talked about becoming blood sisters so that there was no doubt about it, but we were both too chicken to cut our fingers and go through with it.

We agreed that we didn't really have to cut our fingers to become sisters We should just make a pledge that from this point on, no one could ever take us away from each other! We held up our baby fingers and crooked them together and made the pledge to each other! We made-up an oath and repeated it to each other in a chant. It said: FROM THIS DAY FORTH WE ARE 'SISTERS' AND THERE IS NO FORCE ON THE EARTH THAT CAN EVER SEPARATE US FROM EACH OTHER. It was the beginning of a true adventure for us!

One afternoon in late March, after I finished with my chores, I waited for Sidney to come out. She was nowhere to be found so I went around to her apartment to see why she hadn't met me. This was the first time that I actually met her mother. She was a dark skinned woman about five foot- one with thin shoulder length hair, who was very average looking. I was used to other mothers looking as pretty as my mom and was shocked because she was definitely nothing like my mother. She was very stern and not particularly friendly when she opened the door.

She said, "Hello," kind of dry.

I said, "Hi, my name is Taylor, is Sidney at home?"

She said "I have heard a lot about you. She's in the kitchen, come on in."

She stepped to the side as she motioned for me to come in.

"You're the kid who has been playing with Sidney everyday after school and the reason that she begs to go outside all the time."

All in the same breath she said, " No child should be outside everyday."

She closed the door behind me as I started down the hallway toward the kitchen.

I could navigate my way to their kitchen, because most of the apartments in the Laurel Homes were the same with the exception that they either had two or three bedrooms. As we moved down the hallway, I turned to her and asked, "Why?"

"Because you should be studying or helping out in the house. Afterwards you can play in your room," she explained.

"I don't have a my own room," I said, "I share a room with my brothers."

"Your brothers?" she said with an air of confusion.

"Yes ma'am, they have one bed and I have the other, what's wrong with that?"

She didn't say anything else, she just stared at me with the strangest look on her face, which I found very hard to understand.

Sidney heard us talking and made her way down the hallway toward us. From that point, we went into Sidney's bedroom as her mother walked into the living room, then we closed the door. It was odd for me to see a bedroom that had all little girls stuff in it but she had her Royal Crown hair dressing and the trusty vaseline on her dresser just as I did. Seemed as if they had a little more stuff than we did. I wondered why, but I didn't dwell on it. We just messed around for the next hour or so. I was trying on some of her clothes, we were polishing our nails and we were telling each other secrets 'til it was time for me to go home. She told me more about her famous dad. In addition to all the things that she had already told me about her and her mother, she said that her dad was a singer and that he spent a lot of time on the road in every big city in the country performing in concerts. I still didn't know who he was, but again, I didn't pressure her, but, boy oh boy was I becoming curious!

The next few weeks, while we were in school, everyone started to notice that we were hanging out together a lot. We walked to school together and back home again everyday. In between classes, we met and giggled, while whispering about everything from how fat someone was to what kind of get-ups people had on. Several people mentioned to me that they thought it was strange for us to be so close, because we were so different. I was a very out going girl and she was introverted and definitely kept to herself, before we met. But, we didn't care what they thought. As a matter of fact, the more people spoke about it, the closer we became.

We found satisfaction in being the topic of conversation for so many people. We were together as often as time would permit. Even though there were lots of other people that we knew and liked, we seemed to prefer each others company more than the others. We had a special bond, which is why we had become such good friends. We actually fed off of each other. She was easy to talk to and I tried to be that ear for her when she needed it. For weeks and months we talked about our hopes and dreams for the future and how we planned to get there. We had dreams about being in charge of our own destiny someday, and for us, that would be like reaching for the stars and grabbing them.

CHAPTER FIVE

GETTING OUT INTO THE WORLD...

Sidney was a member of the track team and track season was approaching. At first, she had to stay after school for practice three days a week. Then, a month before the actual meet, she had practice every day after school. The first track meet was three weeks away. There they were after school, stretching, sprinting, galloping like horses, running short runs on the prepared courses and all the antics necessary to become the best at what they were about to undertake. Bloom Junior High School would face off with Porter Junior High School in the spring. Porter was the Junior High School where all of the kids from the Lincoln Courts attended. These two schools were arch rivals and competed in everything from baseball to marching bands. Starting that next Monday, the track team would have two practices, one in the morning and one after school every evening It was clear to me that I wouldn't see Sidney for a while. During that time, we mostly saw each other in passing in between classes.

Almost a month passed by and it was just about time for the track meet. Finally, the date was set. All of the students at Bloom wanted the Porter kids' blood. All of the kids and the coaches took this very seriously. Everyone would be there! Sidney wanted me to be there to cheer her on. I asked my dad if I could go and he said I could, as long as I was at home before dark. He also added that as long as I was with some of the other kids from the neighborhood, both going to the track meet and coming back home. I assured him that many of the kids from Bloom would be there.

I got dressed that day in a red full skirt with two petticoats and a red and white pullover sweater and some red pointed toe flats that were pinching my toes. But, I wanted my feet to look smaller than they were, so I would have to endure the pain. I was growing up so fast that not many of my clothes fit me for very long. My parents didn't have enough money to keep buying me clothes as quickly as I needed them, so I did the best that I could and I made it alright. I caught up and walked along with several of the kids who were headed that way.

When we got there, I saw Sidney and the other girls and boys stretching and sprinting their short runs. Boy, Sidney was fast!! I had no idea that she was that fast! In the track stands there were people cheering and jeering at each other in seats on both sides of the track field. This was really cool! I was excited to be out. I was also surprised that my dad said yes. This was my first time attending anything like this. Sidney told me where I should sit, while we were making plans, so I followed her instructions to the letter. We also made plans to walk home together afterwards.

The group that I walked with arrived a little early, but it was thrilling watching the whole event from practice to the very end. About fifty five minutes later, the stands started filling up with parents, teachers and students from both schools. Finally, the first race was about to start! We could see all of the participants doing their warm-up activities. The field was full of officials, coaches and track participants. The coaches had all of their runners in huddles giving them pep talks and pumping them up with last minute instructions. After about twenty minutes of that, they all went to take their seats or went off to the side to continue their preparation. The first race was about to be run. First, some of the girls lined up for the starting race. It was happening! Then the boys. One race after the other. They took turns. One by one the races were run. A couple of them were very close, but the Porter team was beating the Bloom team in most of the races. As a matter of fact, Porter won six out of the eight races that had been run. Sidney's race was coming up next. All six girls in Sidney's race were heading to the line at the starting point.

The official said through his megaphone, "On your mark, get set" and the gun went off! The pack stayed together into the first curve. Then Sidney and a very long legged girl pulled away from the others. Little by little, the two of them were really running away from everyone else. They were neck and neck. They went into the second curve still together. They came into the third curve still neck and neck moving just as fast, leaving all of the other girls in their dust. They were in the final stretch with the finish line right there in their reach, closer and closer to the finish line and finally, it was Sidney at the finish by an eyelash! I had been screaming to the top of my lungs cheering for her, so much so that I nearly lost my voice. There were two more races to be run. While the last of the races were in progress, I was on my way down to the track to congratulate Sidney!

On my way there, I saw a boy who I thought was really cute. He was tall, about six foot-one with curly hair and a very fair complexion. He had a very nice body and was slightly bowlegged. He reminded me of Smokey Robinson of the Miracles. I asked Lana, since she was also on her way down to the track too, who he was. She said his name was Phillip and that he was a student at DePorres Junior High School. It was an all boys school about two blocks from Porter. She told me that the boys who attended DePorres thought they were God's gift to girls. He and I gave each other mutual glances as I tried to maintain my composure and continued on to my destination. I kept a look see in his direction, by giving him quick glances. He met up with some other boys and they went off in their own direction as I made my way down to Sidney. When I got there we hugged and hugged.

"Girl, I had no idea that you were that fast. You always told me that if you concentrated real hard, you could do anything that you wanted to do and now I see what you mean."

While I was completing my sentence, I noticed out of the corner of my eyes that the long legged girl, who ran neck and neck with Sidney, was standing to the side and was obviously very upset about losing the race. She and a friend of hers were talking loud and making idle threats, but to no one specific. Sidney glanced in her direction and the two of them began to shooting daggers at each other with their eyes. This went on for several minutes. Everyone could see that there was obviously no love lost between the two of them. Sidney and I hugged again and continued rejoicing in her victory! After the coach congratulated everyone and gave them their last instructions, we left the track field to start on our walk back to the Laurel Homes.

On the way home, we decided that we would stop by the "Sweet Shoppe" to get ice cream cones as a way of congratulating Sidney on her victory and to celebrate. The "Sweet Shoppe" was where most of the kids from both High

Schools hung out after school and on Saturdays. We were a little young for the crowd, but we hadn't expected to stay too long, only enough time to get the ice cream. When we got there, I saw my older brother Bobby. He was sitting on one of the lunch counter stools in between two other boys. He was actually having a good time, which was one of the only times I have seen him laugh so deeply. His great mood was spoiled for him when he saw me come in. He was really furious to see me in there. He leaped from his seat at the counter and shuffled toward me and Sidney.

"What the hell you doing here Tay?" he said.

"I am here with Sidney, to get some ice cream. She won her race today," I said with a big proud smile. My smile wasn't too pretty, because of the two big cavities in my front teeth.

He said, "I don't give a shit about any damn race, take your little ass home , now! You can wait for the ice cream man to come and get your ice cream from him while you are close to the house."

I told Bobby, "You have no right to tell me where I can or can't be. You're not my father!"

Sidney didn't say a word, she turned around and walked toward the door. As she reached out for the door knob, she noticed the long legged girl out of the corner of her eyes coming toward her.

"You thought your ass was so cute today when you won my ribbon, didn't you?"

"What do you mean, just because you lost? I won my ribbon fair and square and I am not sorry about it either," she said in a soft, but stern voice.

"Well, I better not catch you out of the Laurel Homes or your ass will be mine!"

"Well, we will just have to see about that!" Sidney said.

"Besides, what's wrong with now?" she asked the long legged girl.

The long legged girl had no response. Sidney opened the door and proceeded through it without so much as a slight turn of her head to see what, if anything, the long legged girl would do. The long legged girl lunged toward us! Several people standing nearby jumped in between us before anything could get started, as I backed totally out of the way. Bobby grabbed both of us and pulled us out of the store.

He said, "I can't believe it! You bring your little asses in the store and all hell breaks out." He lectured us for about ten minutes, as we walked back in the direction of the Laurel Homes.

When we got back near where we lived, he pushed both of us in the back and said, "Keep your little asses near home before you get hurt." Bobby turned around and headed back to the "Sweet Shoppe." Sidney and I continued walking and finally made it to the steps of the high school, where we usually sat and waited for the ice cream man to come by. As we waited, she marveled about her ribbon and eventually started telling me more about her father. She said that her mother really hated him and she was warned to never try to get to know him, even if the chance presented itself. Finally the ice cream man came. There were so many children, both young and old waiting to get ice cream. Once we had ours, we returned to the high school steps and ate our ice cream, while just watching all of the activity in the projects. People were going on about their business, as if they didn't have a care in the world. There was talk of Stevie Wonder performing at the Regal Theater sometime soon. Maybe we could sneak down there and just watch all the people coming and going when he came. We agreed and decided it had been a long enough day and we both went home.

CHAPTER SIX

ALONE AGAIN...

A year went by and Sidney was in the latter part of her ninth grade year. She was about to graduate. She had run for the track team in the ninth grade as well, but she told me that she didn't see the long legged girl at all. We wondered where she was? Sidney won more ribbons and finished junior high school with honors.

By the time school was coming to an end, it hit me hard that Sidney would be going to Taft High School and leaving me at Bloom for one more year. I had become so used to being with her that I knew it would be very lonely for me once she left. I started looking for other ways of keeping myself occupied during my last year of junior high. As I investigated the possibilities, I encountered several alternatives. Three other ninth grade girls were interested in forming a female singing group for a talent show that was coming up in the fall at the junior high school. I had met them but we hadn't really spent any time together. They knew that I was real popular and felt it would be a positive move if I was a part of the group. So, they asked me to tryout. I did and I was accepted even though my mother always said I couldn't carry a tune in a bucket. We really sounded pretty good together.

We had visions of becoming the next great singing group like the Supremes. We practiced after school two nights a week. We were all really enjoying it! The fall talent show was upon us and was scheduled for the coming weekend. The show had fifteen acts that were to appear. The first act was a comedian, Avery Cummings. He was a real clown in school and took his talent onto the stage. He talked about people in the audience, about his friends' mothers and even about himself. He had everybody in stitches. We were all cackling so much that many of us were in tears! The next act was a male singing group. They did three numbers. And, one by one, all the acts went on to perform. When it was over, my group, "The Girls of Your Dreams," won second place.

Over the next six months, our singing group was singing all over the area, in local talent shows. On a Saturday night several months later, we were booked to perform at another talent show. It was in Covington, Kentucky at the Elks Grand Lodge. They had a dance scheduled there and we sang as part of the entertainment. My Dad said that I could do it, but would never have agreed to let me go alone, so he and Bobby went with us. The other girls didn't have to have their dad or older brother tagging along after them, but I did. I though to myself, what a joke! It was mostly a crowd of white people with a few Negroes sprinkled about. "What an interesting audience," I thought as we entered the building. Actually, I was not used to being around so many white people because our neighborhood and school was ninety-nine percent Negroes. But, they seemed to be just kids, like we were. We were shown to the area where we were to change clothes and prepare to do our act.

Act after act the performers went on. There were only two Negro acts in the fourteen acts that was to perform. When we came out, the crowd became sort of somber and quite. They didn't know what to expect from us nor did we from them. We agreed to do our best and let the chips fall where they may. We performed our first number which was "Stop in the Name of Love" and got a huge round of applause because all the kids had heard the Supremes and all of their hits. We sang the second and the third numbers and became a very big smash with the audience.

We received a standing ovation from the vastly white audience, which came as a shock to us. Of course, we didn't win the show, but we did come in third place, which wasn't bad considering the audience. We left the Elks Lodge feeling very good about ourselves and our abilities. My dad, Bobby and I saw the other girls home and we made our way back to our safe haven, the apartment on the fourth floor at 1321 John Street.

After that night, I noticed that many of the people in the neighborhood were forming singing groups. Sometimes after school, while walking home, we would pass a group of boys on the corner singing those do-wop songs. Some of them sounded good too, but some of them were awful! I used to hear Smokey Robinson and the Miracles and Martha and the Van Dellas, Mary Wells and others songs being belted out all the time by these corner crooners. "Tracks of my Tears".... "Momma Said There'd be Days Like This"..."Well, I've Got Two Lovers and I'm Not Ashamed"... It became as much a part of our neighborhood as everything else.

Sidney and I realized that we could be best friends and also have a lot of other things going on as well. In the weeks that followed, I encountered countless new activities. In my drama class in school, I met another girl that lived nearby the school, as a matter of fact, just two blocks away. Her name was Kelly and she seemed to be pretty nice. We began talking and got along well too. In due time, we spent some time together in and after school. She stopped by the auditorium often to listen to the group, as we practiced song after song. She was a fairly tall, pretty dark skin girl with long curly hair. She was in the eighth grade.

I was a popular girl now and in my new leadership role, I was becoming the big girl on campus for a high ranking ninth grader. I really was enjoying my life and was beginning to believe that I could take this leadership role with me to high school. I was definitely looking forward to becoming a sophomore and I wanted the ninth grade to whiz by so that my high school days could begin and I could be with Sidney again all the time. Sidney was lonely without me too. We did get to spend most Saturdays together but, she and I had to get involved in all kinds of things to keep ourselves really busy to make sure the year went by fast! I had to make sure that I did all of the things I wanted to do every day though, before I got back to the neighborhood, because of the watchful eyes of the other parents and especially because I was so closely scrutinized by my dad and Bobby.

Kelly and I were together often in between the times that I spent with Sidney. A month later, I introduced Kelly to Sidney . Sidney was a difficult person to get to know as I had witnessed when we first met and she often held back until she felt comfortable with someone new. Sidney was in a so-so mood when I introduced the two of them and she acted as if she could take Kelly or leave her. So, Sidney was indifferent at first and wasn't about to take up a lot of time with Kelly.

PART I

It was the early sixties and we were becoming young women. Before she knew it, Sidney was starting her sophomore year at Taft. We were sure that new worlds would be opening up for her. As for me, I was looking forward to breezing through and finishing my freshman year at Bloom and moving on to Taft in the year to come. I had become an upperclassman to those kids coming over to Bloom from Washburn Elementary. I truly knew how they felt, because a couple of years prior that was me.

All of our families were still virtually poor and the financial constraints that we suffered had us in a dilemma wondering how we would keep up with the other kids in high school and the way they dressed. Even though Sidney and her mother had a little more than we did, she was still having a bit of a challenge dressing the part too, particularly that of a high school girl. With a new school year we all got a few new clothes, but we never had enough, so Sidney and I often shared our things. Most of the things that my mother's friends were shoplifting had to be sold to keep their households going. Every now and then, I would get a few pieces from them, which I was glad to get.

Since Sidney had started attending a new school, it would be a little easier for us to borrow each others things without our schoolmates realizing that some of the clothes on our backs were not our own. Sometimes at six a.m. in the morning, I heard Sidney outside my window, calling my name, "Taylor, Taylor...I need the green or I need the blue, or I need the red." Or, I would be outside her window doing the same thing. We spoke in code just in case someone else was listening to us. We didn't want everyone catching on to what we were doing. Whoever had what the other needed, we would simply roll up the articles and throw them out of the window to the other one. Then we would go on our merry way, back to our apartments to get dressed for the day. We had great fun swapping out clothes. Besides, it was a phenomenon that we were about the same size and could even fit each other things.

I hadn't been on the high school steps in weeks. I decided that as soon as I got home and finished with the things that I had to take care of, I 'd see who was out there on the steps. Sidney was sitting there alone when I arrived. It was five weeks after the start of the new school year. Sidney told me that she had been seeing the long legged girl in school. They were in some of the same classes. She said that the girl obviously still remembered her well and was still angry about the race that Sidney won and losing to Sidney what the long legged girl called "her ribbon." But, at least she wasn't still trying to fight about it.

Sidney had been at Taft for about two months and she had gotten to know several new people in school. It was going very well for her. She was invited to a party being given by one of the junior classmen Charlie Boore. His parents lived in one of the two family houses that surrounded both the Laurel Homes and the

Lincoln Courts projects. The parties that we always heard about were normally at someone's house or at Saint Joseph's Catholic School on Lincoln Park Drive. The auditorium of the school was used for social activities for the "Over the Rhine" children. We often wondered where the area got the name "Over the Rhine?" Of course, we were never allowed to actually go to any of the parties, because we were so young. Now that Sidney was a sophomore, maybe, just maybe she'll get to go. We wondered if Sidney's mother would say yes. It was Saturday night and Indian summer in Cincinnati, perfect for a party. The evening was very mild and clear. You could hear children's laughter while they played in the distance and the sound of automobiles humming along up and down the streets. It was as if everyone was trying to enjoy the last bit of nice weather before the winter came. Sidney talked to my dad that day to try talking him in to letting me go, but he was as strict on me as ever and

I had to stay at home. He said emphatically to her that high school was early enough for young girls to start running around. Seems that if it wasn't Bobby "cramping my style" as usual, it was my dad.

"One day," I mumbled under my breath as Sidney left, "I will get out of here and live my own life."

My dad heard me and said it would be a long time so I'd have to wait.

I was only 15 years old, but I thought...that was old enough to go to a doggone party.

Mrs. Celeste, Sidney's mom, said yes! The party was on Clark Street at Charlie Boore's house. Clark Street was on the Lincoln Courts side of Lincoln Park Drive. We couldn't believe that Sidney's mother said yes, but she did. She was permitted to go to the party with the promise of being back home by eleven p.m. We thought that was great! I sat there watching her lay out her clothes. She took her time getting dressed. She wanted to make sure she looked perfect. She looked really cute. She had on a full red plaid skirt and a pale yellow pull over with a red neckerchief and penny loafers with pale yellow socks. She looked so pretty! Some of the girls in her home room class stopped by to get her so they could all go to the party together. I walked out of her apartment with them and through the archways back to John Street. She hugged me as I said, "Have a good time for me too!" I stood there watching them until they turned the corner at Clark Street. I went to the high school steps just to sit there alone for a few minutes and then went upstairs to our apartment.

As the girls approached the party they could hear the sounds of Little Anthony and the Imperials, blasting "You Don't Remember Me, but I Remember You." There were twelve to fifteen people standing outside of the house in little groups, just talking. There were also two couples kissing and grinding each other, out in the open. That was Sidney's first time seeing people displaying affection like that out in the open.
Since she had been kept, for the most part, in the house after school, she was quite shocked. But, she didn't let on to the other girls because it would have been embarrassing for her to appear to be so jive. When she and the other girls walked into the party, the first person that she saw was Phillip, the boy that I thought was so cute. The second person was the long legged girl. Sidney and her friends began to enjoy the music and was asked to dance a few times. As the evening went on, she and the long legged girl actually started talking. Her name was Aaron and she was from a big family on Clark Street. She later found out that Aaron's family had lost their father when she was merely a very young kid and that her mother did the best she could raising all of the kids on her own. She said that her family had fallen into a lot of bad breaks and the older members of Aaron's family had resorted to drinking alcohol too much. She told Sidney that there were thirteen children in their family, all with a single mother and they all lived in that little apartment. Talk about poor. No wonder that ribbon meant so

much to her. Sidney's heart reached out to her as they stood in a corner of the party continuing their conversation. In between their conversation and the boys asking each of them to dance, they were having a good time. From that night on, they chatted in the classes they had together and sometimes after school too. She and Sidney started slowly becoming pals over the next few months. Before long Aaron was coming over to Laurel Homes everyday after school to hang around with Sidney on the high school steps.

I had been in another tussle with a girl at Bloom, because she made some off the wall comments about my teeth in front of a group of people, so I slapped her. She told me that she was going to kick my ass and dared me to wait for her after school. I told her that she wouldn't get a second chance to threaten me and to let me know when and where and I would be there. I was determined that since my incident in grade school with Juanita, I'd never let another situation get out of hand again.

At three o'clock, when school was out there was a big crowd gathered at the corner of Freeman and Baymiller Streets, just out of sight of the principal's ever roaming eye. That is where I waited for her. I was really known now for being able to look out for myself, especially after the Juanita Mathis encounter at Washburn. Besides, everyone knew that I had a crazy brother and most people didn't care to get involved with me, because of him. Helen was always shooting off her mouth and I meant to put a stop to it. We waited for over an hour and she didn't bother to show up. So there I was the victor and never had to throw a punch! So, needless to say, she pissed me off by wasting my time. Thank God that I was no longer insecure about taking up for myself. That evening when I got to the high school steps, there they were, the long legged girl and Sidney sitting there chatting. I couldn't believe my eyes! It was her! My mood became even more foul. This new person sitting there with my best friend looking like chums. I walked up to them and didn't part my lips. Sidney looked at me and smiled. She greeted me, "Hi Taylor."

When I was introduced to Aaron I was quite short in my response. I was in no mood to make new friends at the time. It appeared that Aaron wasn't going to like me very much either, but what did I care? I must admit that I did have a smart mouth, when I wanted to. Besides, she was Sidney's new friend, not mine. We stayed there for a while with them doing most of the talking about this and that. I interrupted abruptly and insisted that we walk up to the football field to watch the band practice. They said okay, so we did. We stayed there for over an hour. Thirty minutes later the band was really stepping high and sounding good. We also watched the majorettes and the cheerleaders as they practiced in a little area closer to the school building. Both Sidney and Aaron decided that they would try out for cheerleading spots. The band was finished with their practice for the day as they marched off the field. Aaron made the suggestion that we go back to the high school steps. It looked like everything on the field was over, so we all agreed. As we started walking away from the football field, we heard voices chanting and the sound of a lot of heavy footsteps running, much like that of a heard of people. We turned back toward the field only to see the football team running onto the field to practice. There were really some good looking guys on the team, running in their green and gold uniforms with shoulder pads, cleats and all, with most of them carrying their helmets. So, we decided to stay for a while longer to watch them. I began to daydream about next year and the fact that I would be attending this school with these tall, strong, good looking guys. Maybe, one of them would be mine. We stayed there for another thirty-five minutes. I heard my Dad's whistle, which let me know that I had thirty minutes before I had to be at home. A little while later, we all walked back in the direction of the high school steps and went our separate ways. We knew we would see each other at the same place soon.

PART II

The four of us were together just about every evening for a long time. Sidney was talking about her famous dad again. This time she told us his name. He was Jay Ballard of Jay Ballard and the Midnighters. We were in awe, because this guy was really, really famous. There was a hit song out on the charts called "The Twist" and he was the singer. WOW!! Everywhere we went we heard that song playing and lately there was even a dance that everyone was doing when the song was played! We talked about that for almost two hours, asking Sidney what it was like to know someone that was real famous and especially since he was her dad. She told us all she knew about it. That day came and went and it was time to go home, so that we could prepare for tomorrow.

Kelly and I left school on Wednesday afternoon and headed for the West End youth center called the Neighborhood House after talking with Beverly one of the girls that I used to sing with. She was used to going to the Neighborhood House to just mess around and asked us if we would be interested in going with her. Kelly said yes before I could get a word in edgewise, so we went. When we got there, I saw the boy Phillip again from the track meet. He was about to play basketball with some other boys and he looked as cute as ever to me. Just seeing him made butterflies appear in my stomach. I could have stayed there just staring at him, but when Kelly noticed what I was doing, she elbowed me in the side and said, "Stop staring, that's rude!"

"We need to go to see what else is going on today," she snapped.

She pulled me by the arm as I reluctantly left the doorway to the basketball court. We proceeded into another part of the Neighborhood House. Joel Sharp, a local photographer, was in the lobby looking at the activity board. He was the owner of a magazine called "THE SHARPEST in Town" and it was fairly popular in the city and especially in our neighborhood . It featured all kinds of information about Negro people in the neighborhood. We were checking into the other activities on the Neighborhood House calendar of events, when we were approached by Mr. Sharp. He told us that we were some pretty young things and asked us if we wanted him to take a couple of snap shots of us to see how they turned out.

"He never travels without his camera," Beverly said.

We saw nothing wrong with it, so we said yes.

We posed for him for a few minutes. He must have taken eight shots and then we went on with what we were doing. After reading the full calendar of events for the day, we found out about several items of interest. We knew we could really lose ourselves in these activities. We could either take craft, cooking or sewing as well as other things. So, we signed up for sewing because we felt that it, of all the things being offered, would come in handy.

A week later, we ran into Mr. Sharp again. He wanted us to see the photographs. They turned out beautifully. From that point on, Mr. Sharp was after us to sit for him all the time. It was fun and quite a change of pace for us.

We acted silly while working with him and just plain acted period. We posed like we were Hollywood starlets or world famous models. We didn't go to the high school steps regularly for the next few weeks, because we were so in to modeling for Mr. Sharp and we actually looked forward to it. It was giving us the change of pace that we were looking for and it allowed us to meet a lot more people that lived in the area near the Neighborhood House.

PART III

One of Sidney's Aunts was a little younger in age and younger acting than our parents and whenever we were around her we could more or less really be ourselves. We talked to Miss Louise about trying to make some money for more clothes and other things that we needed. She suggested that we have some socials and invite some of the young people in the neighborhood. We talked about it and planned it over the next few weeks on the high school steps and decided that it just might work. We worked out all the details and asked Miss Louise if we could borrow the "get started" money from her. She gave it to us with the promise that we would pay her back out of the first monies that were made. We decided that the method we'd use for people to get into the social, would be to charge each individual by measuring their waist sizes and they'd have to pay a penny an inch. The night of the first social was a huge success. It was a lot better than we ever thought it would be. We had over a hundred people there the very first time. The word had gotten out fast. We sold shots of liquor like VSQ, Brandy and VAT 69 to name a few, and beer to the older kids. We also sold fish and chicken dinners. Miss Louise cooked all of the food for us. We held the socials at her apartment. There were so many people there the third and fourth time we had to hold some of them outside until some left and then we could let some new people in. A lot of the boys in the neighborhood couldn't wait for our socials because it was their time to try and get next to the young girls who attended. The music always played loud above the noise of the crowd. People had a good time eating and drinking and dancing. It was the place to be on Saturday nights. If you looked off to any corner of the crowded room, there were couples dancing and grinding like they were in bed with each other. There were a few boys who even tied small mirrors to their shoes in order to put there feet under the girls dresses, so they could try to see their panties. They even intentionally brushed up against some of the girls to feel their butts or breasts. What dirty little minds the boys had. Sex was all they ever seemed to think about even at such a tender age.

The first two times we had our socials, we sold out of everything. We made what we considered a ton of money and split it up between us after paying Miss Louise back. We felt that it was a lot of work trying to do this on an ongoing basis. Miss Louise thought it was too hard on her, so after a half dozen times we stopped.

We were able to make a little money from the socials. We went on a shopping spree of sorts. Then, it was back to our usual activities. Back to the High School steps.

Finally, the weather was getting too cold to be on the school steps even though we sat there anyway sometimes. If we were not there, we would either meet at my house or Sidney's or go to the Neighborhood House. Kelly's house was too far away and there were too many people at Aaron's. So, we spent most of our time in my apartment or on the steps. My dad taught us how to cook some of the dishes that he knew how to make so well. He took a lot of time with us. One of his favorite dishes was candied yams. They were lip smacking good with his greens and corn bread. Sometimes, we would just sit around watching television. We were one of the first families in the projects to have a television. We couldn't wait everyday for the Mickey Mouse Club, the Honeymooners or I Love Lucy and sometimes even Tarzan.

Things were kind of hum-drum and we were really bored, as we often became when the weather was getting cold outside. There we were bundled up and sitting there on the high school steps, teasing each other about getting the piles from sitting on the cold concrete, when Aaron got a bright idea that at the end of a school week she wanted us to come and spend the night on the upcoming Friday. I was apprehensive, but of course Sidney talked me into it. My dad even said okay. This was a first! I had never been able to stay over at anyone's house, except one time at Sidney's. So I did it! I was glad not to have to be at home with Bobby's and my little brother Curtis getting in the way, besides, I found it very interesting to meet all of Aaron's family members. Aaron's older brother was blind. I'd never been around anyone who was blind. He almost seemed as old as her mother. I didn't quite understand that. There was so much going on in that little apartment, so we sat on the floor just observing mostly, 'til it was time to go to bed. We all laid side by side in a set of bunk beds and off to sleep we went. It wasn't long before I was awakened by something biting the shit out of me!

I sat straight up in the bed and then JUMPED UP, "What the hell?" seemed to fly out of my mouth.

Everyone woke up when they heard me.

"What is it Taylor?"

Something's biting the shit out of me, that's what it is!"

"Oh, those are the chinches that's all," said Aaron, so matter of factly.

"CHINCHES?" I said.

Aaron said, "Yes!"

"What the hell are chinches?" I asked bewilderedly.

She said, "Bed bugs."

"BED BUGS? You sound like you're used to them! I am outta here!!"

At two thirty-five in the morning, I marched my blotched legs down John Street to my apartment. As I walked home I thought how surprised I was that Sidney stayed. I was scared as hell to be outside at that time of night, but I wasn't sleeping with no damned CHINCHES! It took me about six minutes to get to our apartment. I knocked on the door to my apartment, no answer. I knocked again, a little harder this time and that's when my dad made his way to answer, looking extra sleepy, he was shocked (which seemed to have awakened him completely) and pissed to see me standing there in the middle of the night.

"What are you doing out alone at this hour?" he said.

I said "Dad look at my legs, they have CHINCH bites on them."

As I stepped inside, he closed the door and slowly walked into the bathroom shaking his head in disgust and returned the next instant with some salve which he gave me to put on my legs directly on the irritated spots. As soon as I applied it, the salve actually soothed the irritations. I kissed him on the cheek and went into our bedroom to try and get some sleep. I had to wake Curtis, who had taken over my bed, since I wasn't there. Then, I could get into my own bed and he could get in his bed with Bobby. We didn't have a lot, but what we had was clean and comfortable. Finally, I could go to sleep, chinch free. I laid there for a short while and I eventually dozed off to sleep, but it was a long night.

PART IV

We all knew that Taft High School was the School in the city known for having the best dressed students, but when we started going there we really got to see it first hand. This created pressure on the students who were less fortunate to be creative about clothes in order to keep up. Now Aaron was in on our clothes swapping. Unfortunately she didn't have a lot to offer us but, never the less we shared what we had with her. Sometimes, we even found ourselves making outfits on the spot for special occasions. Those sewing lessons at the Neighborhood House really came in handy. But, we wondered how could we get away with clothes swapping in high school? Everyone knew that we were all good friends, so wouldn't they recognize Sidney's clothes on me and mine on Aaron's? These kids all tried to out dress each other and the ones with a lot of clothes could also afford to get their hair done every two weeks. I had a natural knack for doing hair so all of the girls came to me every two weeks to get their hair curled. The kids that were lucky enough to have all of this going for themselves, actually acted like a bunch of snobs. Especially some of those seniors. They wore cummerbund wasted flared skirts, matching sweaters and neck scarves, British brevet shoes (really expensive ones) and the real saddle oxford shoes, the ones that were black and white lace ups with the red soles. They wore different outfits for every day of the week. We didn't actually see them in the same outfits for several weeks at a time. We thought, it must have been nice! Only some of the juniors and most seniors were especially well dressed. They were known in the city as the pretty people. Some of these girls were cheerleaders and majorettes and their boyfriends were the football, baseball and basketball players. They acted like they thought they were better than anyone else. They walked through the corridors of the school gazing in the jocks' faces and was oblivious to the rest of us. Everyone knew their names and tried to befriend them at all costs. It seemed like they were living the life.

Both Sidney and Aaron tried out and made the cheerleading reserve squad. I hoped they wouldn't become like those snobs. I didn't think they would, after all I did know them pretty well. They were not the type to become snobs. Besides, Aaron and I were becoming real close now too, so I felt I knew her pretty well too. She still had to overcome sleeping with Chinches in that little apartment and all those people. She would, no doubt have a long, long way to go to become one of the pretty people. But, no one other than the 'Sisters' knew about the Chinches and her family, so as far as they knew, she was eligible to become part of the pretty people too. We'd have to wait and see what would happen.

PART V

John Morrison of Morrison's House of Styles was located in the Walnut Hills area of the city. His shop was the barbershop where all of the entertainers went to get their hair processed when they were in the city to perform. His hair stylists were supposed to be among the best in the country. There were both young and old men in and out of there every day except for Mondays when they were closed. He was making money hand over fist. So much so that he opened the John Morrison's Hair Styling School to teach even more people how to give processes, so he could make even more money off of them.

We found out through the high school bulletin board that he needed some models for a new contract he obtained from Capital Cadillac on Gilbert Avenue in Walnut Hills. He wanted young pretty girls that could attract attention to the new Cadillacs coming out in September. He called Joel Sharp, the photographer, to see if he could recommend some girls for the photo shoot. Joel thought that the photos he had taken of us were very good and shared them with Mr. Morrison. Once Mr. Morrison reviewed our photographs, he was convinced that he wanted us. He came to see us at the Neighborhood House to interview us. He selected us on the spot. Kelly and I were excited about it and introduced Mr. Morrison to the other girls.

Our parents were not involved in any of this. As far as my dad knew, I was at Sidney's house, Aaron wasn't missed too much, because there were so many of them and Sidney always lied and said she was at my house. We had the killer cover-up for our parents, so we ran the streets as much as we wanted to as long as it wasn't late into the night. Mr. Morrison had us taking professional pictures and he was making loads of money off our finished products. We were so gullible. He was in fact, taking advantage of us. We didn't know enough about his sort of thing to realize that we could even get paid for this, we were doing it just for the shear enjoyment of it. We were so tied up with this for so long that some of the neighborhood parents noticed that we were not on the school steps for weeks and nowhere to be found that they became worried and alerted Mrs. Celeste. Mrs. Celeste started to ask Sidney questions and low and behold, because Sidney couldn't keep anything from her mother because she was so afraid of her, Mrs. Celeste found out all about it. She hit the ceiling! She called Mr. Morrison and told him off! I begged her not to tell my dad because I would be grounded forever. Eventually, Mrs. Celeste worked it out with Mr. Morrison. He was to send us to finishing school as payment to us for the modeling work we had done for him.

Finishing school was expensive but fun and informative. We thought that only white girls attended finishing school. But we found out when we started there that many Negro families saved to send their daughters. I guess this was another thing that poor people just never even thought about. There was barely enough for our families to pay the rent, buy food and keep clothes on our backs and shoes on our feet. This was a real eye opener for us.

As young ladies, we found out that spending all our time on the high school steps wasn't preparing us for the future. Our parents couldn't afford to send us to finishing school, so this was working out perfectly. The teachers taught us first and foremost that we should always strive to be young ladies. They taught us how to get in and out of a car, to be on time and to keep our word when we gave it to someone or to something. We learned how to walk properly, how to stand and sit correctly. We learned how to apply makeup, how to converse with people, proper etiquette when dining and just a host of very useful tidbits as they saw it for our future. We really had no idea if we would ever have the opportunity to use these things, but it was fun learning them.

After finishing school, we agreed that we would start a sorority called the F.O.X.'s. We knew of two high school sororities, ABX and IEX, but those girls were the snobs and we felt we would never be accepted anyway. We developed our own initiation rights and this strengthened the sisterhood. We had our meetings on the high school steps. We knew that those high school steps were the spot for us because, from there, we could see almost everything and we could certainly be seen.

CHAPTER SEVEN

HIGH SCHOOL DAYS...

In the fall of the next year, I joined the other girls at Taft! It was indeed a different world by anyone's standards. Both Sidney and Aaron were juniors and things were really going well for them. They had made the transition into high school really work for them. They had also become very close. When I came on board they always introduced me as their "kid" sister. I went everywhere with them and was introduced to everyone. They introduced me to several of the teachers, one of which was Mrs. Childron. She was the physical education teacher and in charge of the cheerleaders, majorettes and the lead decision maker for a major production that the school produced each year, the Taft Capades. People from all over the city came to Taft High School each year to see this spectacular event! Tryouts were coming up in a few weeks.

I hadn't been at Taft too long when one of the football players caught my eye. He was a huge guy named Bud Johnson. He was the biggest boy I had ever seen. I heard that he was being looked at by the professional scouts. The rumor was that he dated this girl named Mary Lou Jamison. She was a pretty girl who was a senior. She had big eyes and milk jug shaped legs. It was my understanding that she was kind of nice, but I was sure he would want me and I made myself very noticeable to him whenever he was in the immediate surroundings. Neither of us had any breasts to speak of, but I was much prettier than she was and my face along with my long hair hanging below my shoulders, my brown paper bag skin made a nice silky completion, I just knew I could get his attention.

I experienced a lot of firsts at Taft. I had a class with one of the first white students at the school. He had transferred to Taft from a school out west. He was just about the prettiest boy I had ever seen. Many of the girls were looking at "Robert the white boy." We had never really lived around many white people, up close and personal. By the second week of school, many of the classes were adjusted and Robert ended up in two of my classes. I constantly daydreamed about him, wondering what it would be like to kiss someone with such thin lips. He had curly dark blonde hair and was about six foot-two with a muscular body. He must have really felt comfortable with a school full of Negroes, because we didn't seem to phase him at all. As a matter of fact, he seemed to fit right in. The only difference was that he was rather quiet.

As we got more and more into the school year, Robert and I began to talk. At first it was just chit chat, but eventually it amounted to great topics of conversation. He told me about his family and the school that he went to before coming to Taft. In California he had dated a Negro girl. He said he had deep feelings for her and his parents had gotten used to the idea of him dating her. They were very liberal minded parents and weren't going to use the energy it would take to make him break it off with her. He said that California was open like that. California seemed like it was an eternity away from Cincinnati. While he was talking I daydreamed about going there someday. He continued that he understood all about the civil rights noises happening in the South and he was dead set against it. He said he didn't understand how any human being could hate anyone the way that most white people hated Negroes. He told me that all he wanted in life was to be happy and it didn't matter what color the person that he selected for his future wife was. He only knew that she had to be gentle, loving and loyal. I was not used to such straight talk from boys. Or, was this one of the first meaningful conversations that I had with a member of the opposite sex? He said he was determined not to be like those white people that we could see on any given day on the television news. I thought to myself that was very strong of him because from all of the information that I have been hearing about white people versus Negro people. If the KKK caught a white person fraternizing with a Negro they would also be hanged by the neck until they were dead. So, I had a lot of respect for Robert and the way he looked at life. He really appeared to be a decent person.

After we had shared information during our conversations, we became pretty good friends. Jerry, Duane, Shep and several other Negro boys befriended Robert too and it appeared he was totally accepted by every one of the students in school.

Both of the girls had advanced to the varsity cheering squad and cheered at all of the football and basketball games. I tried out for the majorette squad and made the reserves the first year. The Taft Capades tryouts for singing, dancing and acting in the production that would have Hollywood type sets began early in the year. It would take the entire school year to write the script, name the cast, make costumes, build sets etc., so we had to start early. Mrs. Childron choreographed the production, the English teachers and drama teachers wrote the scripts and Mr. Waterfield, the wood shop teacher had his students make most of the sets for the show. Every year he would start his classes making these sets as part of their curriculum. The theme of the show was obviously determined early in the school year and by show time, everything was all done. These students were really great at what they did under Mr. Waterfield's tutelage. We all tried out for the show. The announcements on the parts were forthcoming in a few weeks. It was an exciting time for us. We were all really involved in our classes and with all of the after school activities as well.

In the weeks that followed, we were expected to really hone in on our classes. As we moved through the halls for class after class, I noticed the boy named Phillip again. He was even more good looking than when I first saw him at the track meet several years ago. I wondered why I hadn't seen him since he was at the Neighborhood House? Maybe it was because until I started at Taft, my dad wouldn't let me out. For all practical purposes, I was in jail! But, I am out now and I planned to make the best of it! That weekend, I went to my first real party at Saint Joseph's Auditorium. There were so many people from the immediate neighborhood and Taft there, but from other areas of the city and other schools as well. It was an Indian summer night again, with a light breeze blowing with the smell of late summer in the air. There were couples strolling in the park across the street from St. Joseph. When we arrived in the auditorium I saw Beverly, one of the girls in my former singing group with Phillip. They were dancing cheek to cheek to Aretha's "Try a Little Tenderness." They danced cheek to cheek record after record. He appeared to really be in to her. I longed for it to be me. I had day dreamed about him so long. I know that he must have noticed me, but I would have to maintain my cool, unphased position at this moment. Soon, hopefully soon, I would have someone. I had hoped it would be him or now maybe big Bud Johnson. I would just have to see how it all turned out.

PART I

All of us were selected to be in the production. I got a small part in the play as one of the chorus line dancers and the girls were in several acts. They both had major lines. I guess this was good for a sophomore and that I should be happy that I was at least selected. The theme was from a Broadway musical called "Porgy & Bess." Phillip was one of the boys selected for one of the major parts. I hadn't realized that he could sing and he played Porgy. During that time, I got to be around him up close. He had a great sense of humor and personality. He had all of the boys and girls laughing all the time and several of the girls looking at him, probably wanting him too. I found out during the rehearsals that he and I were in the same grade, but in no classes together. I was finally introduced to him and I melted inside. He said hello to me in the deepest of voices and gave me a semi smile as he reached out his hand for mine. He acted as if he were pleased to meet me indicating that he had seen me around. He was very cool and fabulous!

I believe that he was indeed my first unofficial love! And I knew that one day he would want me like I wanted him at that moment. Later that day I found out that he was dating Beverly, which is why they were dancing cheek to cheek at St. Joseph. I was devastated. I couldn't believe that he could be serious about her, when he could have me. Even though I was a pretty girl, I still had to deal with getting these six rotten teeth out of my mouth, so that I could be complete. I just knew that that is why he never made a play for me. I was thoroughly upset. After Taft Capades rehearsal, I went home that day to see what could be done. I was so upset. I walked in the door with tears streaming down my face. My dad was there cooking and my mother was still asleep. I cried and cried and just when I thought I was through crying, I started to cry some more. I cried so long and loud that it woke my mom. She held me very close to her . My mom and dad both tried to console me to no avail. They assured me that they would look into getting the situation worked out. An appointment was made for me with a dentist to get an evaluation of the overall situation. They agreed with the dentist and together they decided to put me in the hospital to have the rotten teeth pulled. I told the girls that my problem would soon be taken care of. They were all very happy for me.

A month later, I went in to the hospital to get the six front teeth removed. The problem had gone so long without being looked after that the cavities had gone beyond the two front teeth. After the surgery was over, I had to remain at home for a solid week until my gums healed. I was embarrassed but I returned to school without any teeth in the front. I didn't know if this situation would be worse than having the teeth with cavities. For weeks I had to walk around with no teeth at all in the front. For the most part the kids got used to seeing me that way, but it was still embarrassing. The kids made fun of me but I got used to that too. At least it was better than having the rotten teeth . And besides, I knew that I would have a partial plate put in as soon as my parents could save the money.

CHAPTER EIGHT

One day the next spring, a very pretty, popular senior named Claudia asked Aaron if she wanted to go to a fashion show at the Manse Hotel. The Manse Hotel was in the Walnut Hills area of the city and far away from the "white only" hotels in downtown. In the sixties Negroes didn't have many rights. We were kept as the white people called it, "in our place." This was especially prevalent in the South. Recently, we heard about the killing of Medgar Evers in Mississippi. How could white people be so cruel? We heard stories about all that was going on down there, but for us, just like California, it seemed a long way away. Here we had our own little neighborhood and that was what we were used to and it was all right with us. Negroes couldn't hold any functions or check in to the "white only" hotels in downtown Cincinnati. This created a need for hotels like the Manse where Negroes could stay. There had been all kinds of demonstrations in the South trying to get white people to open up all services, such as hotels, restaurants, theaters and everything else to Negroes. Even though we didn't get too much of the fallout from the demonstrations in the South, we watched on television as Martin Luther King Jr. led the way. But for now, this is the way it was.

Aaron said, "Yeah, why not?"

Aaron was sure that one day she would be able to have any amount of clothes that she wanted, so she thought she might as well get started looking and picking them out now. When they got to the Manse Hotel there were lots of people on their way to the ballroom where the fashion show was being held as well as other guests of the hotel. As Aaron moved through the entrance of the hotel, she happened to pass a man in the lobby that favored Sidney a lot. It looked like this man could be some kin to her. Just at that moment, she heard a porter say "Mr. Ballard, I will bring your bags up right away." Aaron said to herself, "Wonder if that could be Sidney's famous dad?"

She got on the phone and called Sidney.

"Sidney!" she said very excited.

"What?" Sidney spouted.

She said, "You will never guess where I am and who I just saw," she said.

"Right, so tell me," revealed Sidney.

"I am at the Manse Hotel and I just saw Jay Ballard, the singer! Your father is here!" Sidney got real quiet.

"Sidney?" said Aaron in a voice that truly had a question mark.

"Yeah?" she said softly, as if she were in shock.

"Are you coming out here?" Aaron asked.

"No," she said quietly, "I am not sure how my mom would feel about this".

"Your mom? What's she got to do with this? He's your dad! You have a right to get to know him, don't you?"

"Well...I guess, but he doesn't know about me, I don't think. We never spoke too much about it."

"Well, let's tell him!" shrieked Aaron. "You look just like him, hell he'll know right away, believe me! Now is the time!"

After a lot of coaching, Sidney said, " Okay, but I have to call Taylor first to get her to come with me too, for moral support."

When she called me, I dropped what I was doing and said "Hell yeah, I am there!" "I got to see this!"

She came to the apartment thirty minutes later to get me. By that time, I was ready and we headed out there. It was a forty to forty-five minute ride on the bus to the Manse Hotel. The tension was mounting as we rode while bumping along talking about it. Sidney was scared for two reasons. She'll finally get to meet her father and once her mother found out she'd be pissed.

When we got there, Aaron said, "I haven't moved from this lobby! And, he hasn't left yet," she reported.

I said, "Good! Let's crack this nut! Where do we start? Let's make some plans." After sitting there for about forty-five minutes fine tuning our plan , Jay Ballard and a couple of his cronies appeared in the lobby again. According to our plan, we made a noticeable noise in order to draw their attention our way. Our plan was working! Jay turned to us, as did the other two men and his eyes seemed to immediately settle directly on Sidney. He had a strange, perplexed and interesting look on his face! Since they favored so much, he was drawn to Sidney intently. He was drawn to us because of the noise that I made but focused directly one her.

He said to her, "Do we know each other?"

She said "I think so," in a tiny voice, just barely audible.

They began talking.

"What is your name?" he asked.

"Sidney," she answered.

She was noticeably nervous, but began to settle down after a few minutes of conversation. She told him about her mother and the bits and pieces of information that she had received over the years. She explained that she never really had a handle on all that was involved. He recalled her mother and a rumor that there was a baby. But,he remembered that Mrs. Celeste wanted to keep him

81

and his lifestyle away from the child. He had made several attempts to get information, but to no avail.

He and the two cronies motioned for us to go with them as they took us into the restaurant and offered us anything that we wanted. Sidney and her dad talked for a long time. She and Jay sat at one table and the rest of us at another. Mr. Ballard's cronies entertained both me and Aaron by answering all of our juvenile questions about the singing business. We asked what is was like to be famous. While we were talking we continued to keep a close watch on Sidney and her dad. They were getting along nicely. While these conversations were going on, someone at one of the other tables played the juke box and low and behold a Jay Ballard and the Midnighters song was filling the air. Shortly afterwards Sidney and her dad rejoined us. She looked so relieved and happy. The three men paid for our orders and said goodbye to us and left. We sat there for a short while longer as Sidney began to bring us up to date. She said that Jay told her the whole story. Mrs. Celeste was a groupie and had consented to have sex with Jay, when he was playing in Cincinnati years ago. Afterwards, Jay told her it was only sex, she became furious. He said that Mrs. Celeste thought she was in love with him, but he only wanted to sleep with not only her but any of the young girls that hung around. He said he was honest with all of them and told them that he wasn't ready to settle down at the time. Jay vowed to never go a long time without seeing Sidney again and assured her that he really wanted to have a father/daughter relationship with her. He told her all about himself and his family in San Francisco. She now knew that she would have to find a way to let her mother know about this...but she also knew that this wouldn't be easy. She couldn't give up her dad again. Never!

Jay had also given her money for us to take a taxi back to the Laurel Homes. We buzzed about this for the entire ride back. I asked Sidney, "Do you want us to go to your apartment with you while you break the news to your mother?" She said, " I have no idea what I want. All I know is that I'm scared as hell." We all got out of the taxi and walked to the high school steps. We needed to plan the story for Mrs. Celeste. We all decided that it would be best to tell the truth. I asked Sidney again if she thought we should go to her apartment with her while she broke the news.

She said, "No because that would only make it worse."

At that time, we all separated and went our own ways with plans to meet tomorrow.

Sidney opened the door to their apartment. In her mind things were moving in slow motion. She knew all too well how evil her mother could be and wasn't sure at all how Mrs. Celeste was going to take this news. From the moment she walked in she could feel the tension in their apartment. She slipped into her room before she actually saw her mother. Speaking in a strong voice she said, "Hi, mom."

Her mother didn't respond but instead walked down the hall to Sidney's room and flung the door open. As Sidney sat there on the edge of the bed, her mother asked, "Why did you go straight to your room, you never do that?" At that moment, it seemed that her mother was is an extra foul mood. Something must have happened because there was too much tension already in the air. Sidney thought perhaps she should put off telling her this for now. I'll tell her in a few weeks, she thought. Just at that moment, her mother started toward her.

"Where have you been?"

"Oh, the girls and I went to a fashion show at the Manse Hotel."

"The Manse Hotel? That's way out on the Hill," she said with a degree of interrogation.

She replied, "What possessed you all to go way out there?"

" Well, Aaron called me to tell me about it, then I called Taylor and we joined her," Sidney explained.

"And what else is it that you are not telling me?" her mother asked.

"What do you mean?" Sidney asked.

"There is something else, I can just feel it," Mrs. Celeste said, "and you had better tell me and tell me now," she yelled. Her eyes became as red as fire!

"I met my father!" she said in her smallest voice.

"YOU WHAT?" shouted Mrs. Celeste. Her eyes turned even darker! Her disposition erupted into that of a soul possessed. This sent her mother into a tailspin!

"You went behind my back in spite of all the warnings that I have given you about him!" She started flailing her arms in the air, hitting Sidney anywhere she could with her fists. Sidney caught a right fist in the left eye and fell to the floor. Mrs. Celeste began to kick Sidney, as the wounded girl tried to crawl to safety. This was much worse than Sidney thought it would be! The madness stopped only after her mother got so tired that she couldn't lift her arms anymore. Sidney was glad that it was over for now, as she laid there abused to the nth degree. As she continued to lay there hurting and bruised she thought, this was now the last straw. She would start working on her plan to leave home as soon as she was out of school.

PART II

From that moment on things moved at a very, very fast pace. We started hanging out with the likes of Jackie Wilson, Gary "US" Bonds, Chuck Jackson and James Brown , to name a few. Here we were 16 and 17 years old living the high life, like adults in many ways. Sidney, at this point, didn't care what her mother thought because she hated her. Sidney wasn't letting her know a great deal about her meetings with her father or all of the things we were doing. We dreamed up a plan to go to all of the concerts that came to the Cincinnati area. We would be each of the stars official fan club. We figured that it would be worth it to get in to the concerts and to get to meet the singers. It worked every time.

My dad was still so strict, I had to tell lies most of the time in order to get out of the house. I had to say that I was spending the night with one of the girls. I realized that if he had just started letting me go to parties, I knew he wouldn't have let me go out to nightclubs with entertainers but I had to be involved, I just had to. My dad did, however, ask me periodically if Aaron's house still had chinches. I would lie and say no, but they did!

Several months later, Jay was back in town for a performance at the Cotton Club. We decided to keep Sidney protected at all costs, so her mother was never told about anything else that had to do with her dad. That evening after my mom had already gotten dressed to go to her regular poker game, the three of us dreamed up a scheme. My dad was at my uncle's house for the evening and wouldn't be back for hours. He also thought I was staying at Sidney's that night.

All three of us left Sidney's apartment and went around to our apartment to start our deceit. We went into my mother's closet and borrowed three of her evening gowns, earrings, cocktail gloves, red fox stockings and shoes to dress like we were grown women. I wore my mom's blue and gold balloon evening dress and her gold sling back high heels. I could barely walk in them, but after practicing a short while, I got the hang of it. Sidney was dressed in my mom's straight gold dress with the back out. It was a tad bit too big, but it still looked good on her. Her feet were a little smaller than my mom's, so she had to find her own shoes. Aaron had on a silver and black a-line cocktail dress with silver gloves and the same for Aaron, I wouldn't let her wear my mom's shoes either, because she had bunions on her feet and that would stretch the shoes out of shape. All I needed was for my mom to know we had used her things and she would have killed me. So, they had to get their own shoes to wear. This was difficult, but they managed. After we were all dressed, we stood together to look in my mom's full length mirror at the three of us. WOW! We really looked the part! We tip-toed out of our apartment and slinked ourselves over to Aaron's apartment where we had told Jay's driver to pick us up. The driver showed up right on time and blew for us. We had drawn a crowd of younger kids and a pair of adults as the driver got out and opened the door for us to get into the long black Cadillac. We were royalty! On the way to get into the car, everyone looked at us. I was scared to death that someone would let my mother know that we were in her clothes, but I'd have to take whatever punishment I had coming, because tonight we were going to have the time of our lives and it would be worth it.

And eventually, there we were, off to the Cotton Club! As we rode along, we freshened our lipstick and made sure our hair was perfect as we went through the antics of being rich and famous. We could feel the excitement as we approached the club. The music was loud, and there were a lot of people there moving about, both young and old. We figured there had to be at least thirty-five hundred to four thousand people in the club that night. We saw several seniors from Taft. There were a lot of the pretty people from the school with their athlete boyfriends and some people from the neighborhood too. I was kind of scared that my mom and dad may even be in the crowd. But, I couldn't worry about that now. This was worth the risk that I was taking. The dance floor was full to capacity, as people were dancing, song after song. They were doing all kinds of dances like the watusy, the uncle willie, the stroll, the mashed potato and the cha cha. As we made our way to the front of the room, Jay noticed that we had arrived. He got up and started to walk toward us holding out his arms for Sidney. As they embraced, he turned toward the table motioning for us to take a seat. We were seated at a table right in front of the dance floor near the stage. We really felt special. We sat there watching Jackie Wilson perform. He was so sexy. After Jackie concluded his performance, Gorgeous George returned to the stage telling his jokes about how pretty he was and then announced James Brown. Toward the middle of the evening, Jay asked us if we wanted to come up on stage for their second set. We, not knowing any better, were thrilled at the suggestion. We were escorted back stage just before they began. When James Brown concluded his performance of "Try Me," his last song, the stagehands started changing the equipment around somewhat. Jay's band's instruments were being placed on the stage again. They also put three chairs out there, based on the instructions of Jay. We marched out on stage before the group came out and we took our seats. Several people had very perplexed looks on their faces when they saw us sitting there. Then the drum roll...and the announcement of Jay Ballard and the Midnighters! All of a sudden the group came on stage and just the mere presence of those six men, got the crowd roaring! The hit song "There's a Thrill up on the Hill" was being performed. The footwork of the group, Jay's voice, the instruments...it was way too cool! By the end of the set and the hit song, "The Twist," we were all partying like animals. Would life ever be this great, this grand, this innocent again? We would remember this night for the rest of our lives! When the show was over and the entertainers left the stage, we got up and marched off, just as we had marched on the stage. Just as we were leaving, we

heard an idiot from the audience yell, "What the hell you all doing on the stage?
Aaron turn to him and said "What 's it to you?" and gave him the finger.
We all laughed heartily and hurriedly went backstage. Sidney was so proud that
Jay was her father and who could blame her?
She looked at us as we stood there watching him conduct his final business.
She said with so much pride, "Just think, that's my dad!"
We were both so happy for her. The sick mess that she had experienced with her
mother was more than any young girl should have to take, but we all thought
maybe this made up for some of it. We were happy that she had found some
satisfaction in her young life with at least one of her parents. We milled around
back stage for thirty minutes more and returned to our table to enjoy the crowd
and the night. The rest of the night was fantastic! We sat at that front table right
at the foot of the dance floor with Jay and his group members. Everyone
continued coming up to them for introductions, conversations and autographs.
They were very gracious and granted everyone the desires of their hearts. We
danced and partied 'til dawn!

A few days later and a little at a time, I slipped my mom's stuff back into
her closet with the exception of the red fox stockings which were basically torn to
shreds. She never really missed any of it, so we were home free.

PART III

Over the next year, Sidney's mom had started to some degree become used to the idea of Jay and Sidney's relationship. Even though she still didn't like it, there was really nothing that she could do about it now, anyway. Sidney was becoming a grown woman and could basically do what ever she wanted, so what was the use? Her mother almost seemed broken in her spirit most of the times. We found out sometime later that her mother was that way because she was always very fearful that Sidney would leave her for her dad, if she ever got to know him.

Jay had started to send his brand new Cadillacs after Sidney on a regular basis. She always asked us to come along. Jay was always glad to see us too. During this last visit, Jay told us that he was disgusted about our names being out on the road with every entertainer that he crossed paths with. He said that they could all describe us perfectly and that we were billing ourselves as their official "Fan Club." We tried to explain to Jay that was only because we used that lie to get in to the concerts. We told him that we posed as school reporters stating that we were going to write a story on them for the school newspaper. They bought it too. Jay said no more.

One day after school, with the convertible top back, Jay and Chuck Jackson drove up to the school right after the last bell and waited for us. When we came out by way of the high school steps where we always gathered, a crowd of a hundred students was formed right at the curb. We made our way there to see what was going on. When we saw it was them, we jumped in and rode off for an afternoon of fun. The other students were so jealous. Aaron had developed a crush for Chuck Jackson and was telling everyone that he was her boyfriend, so this was right on time. Of course, I couldn't be left out of the equation, so I told everyone that Gary "US' Bonds was my boyfriend. We were the talk of the school!

Sidney had become a very active part of Jay's life now and he wanted to introduce her to his family in San Francisco. He invited her to go around to different cities with him when her school schedule permitted. Neither of us had ever traveled, so San Francisco may as well have been in another country. Jay's wife invited Sidney to San Francisco and she took them up on the invitation. Mrs. Celeste really felt low at this point because she was being totally left out of Sidney's life, but her relationship with Sidney was her own fault.

She was feeling really left out of this whole deal. She felt that since Sidney was almost grown and had been raised without any help from Jay, he getting all of her attention. He just walks into her life and gets all of the glory. It just wasn't fair. We began to see why her mother was so pent up inside.

CHAPTER NINE

In between the time that Jay was in Cincinnati we reverted back to our old habits of sitting on the high school steps to relish in the activities that we were so fortunate to be a part of. To some degree, we settled down into the role of everyday students and residents of the Laurel Homes and the Lincoln Courts. The neighborhood was always the same. The same people did the same thing. Over the last few years we had been seeing an older guy that lived in one of those two family houses on Lincoln Park Drive, just across the street from the school, off and on for several years. He was a tall, dark skinned older boy with a huge nose. He seemed to keep himself in and out of many odd situations unlike anyone that we had ever known. He was vastly different! We never quite knew anyone like him. He had a unique way of dressing and was always seen driving several different cars over the years and was always with different women. We were all sort of afraid of him because of his reputation. He often passed by the high school steps to tell us that he was going to take some sex from us one day. We would all laugh at the thought and would reaffirm to him the fact that we would never let him take one of us without the rest of us. He was known to have all of the women that he was seen with all wrapped up in him and all of them fought each other to keep him as their man. We couldn't figure it all out. One day we were sitting on the school steps and Danny drove up in a red convertible wearing a khaki safari pants and jacket outfit with a hard safari hat. He asked us if we wanted to go for a ride. With nothing else to do at the time, we all jumped in the car and left with him. We figured if we were all together he couldn't hurt either of us. He seemed to know everyone. He drove us for over an hour to all kinds of places that we had never seen in the city. We went to Amberly Village, Walnut Hills, Avondale, Evanston and many other places. He stopped six or seven times having brief conversations with people. Two of these were men that we had never seen before. During their conversations they turned to look at us several times as if they were discussing us. We put our heads together to discuss whether we thought they were talking about us and if they were what we would do to get away. We agreed that we would be on our guard, if they tried anything. We rode and rode and then rode some more for what seemed like hours and then as suddenly as he appeared to pick us up, he dropped us off at the high school steps and he was on his way. What a strange person we thought he was.

The Taft Capades production was in a few weeks and we were down to one practice everyday, and I got to see more and more of Phillip along with some new friends, Scoopie a very good friend of mine and a funny little fellow and Raymond who was as ordinary as they come. Then at dress rehearsal it was confirmed that Beverly and Phillip were definitely an item. One of the teachers busted them kissing in back of the stage. The teachers that busted them made an example of them telling us what we couldn't do as "kids," as they put it. They both said they didn't care, that they were in love and were getting married because she was pregnant. Boy was I glad that wasn't me pregnant!

The audience was full for all three nights that the show ran. The community received it well. We got rave reviews and it was even written up in the *Cincinnati Enquirer*! The school made a record amount of money for the production. The teachers got a standing ovation, as well as the cast. The money raised went for new uniforms, books and such. It was a huge success and we were proud to be a part of it!

Two weeks passed and we spent much of our time after school on the high school steps. We talked for a while and decided to go in early. As I climbed up the stairs to the fourth floor, I heard loud voices coming from our apartment. When I opened the door, I saw Bobby sitting on the couch with his head hanging as my mom and dad paced the floor in front of him. They were fussing at him because he had gone and signed up for the army without their permission. Bobby didn't tell them until it was already done. He was dropping out of high school and going into the army. I just couldn't believe it. He never spent much time in class anyway and he felt that because my mom and dad didn't cater to him or couldn't buy him many things to wear like the other boys had, he'd make this call on his own. Even though mom and dad did the best they could and my mom knew some shoplifters, they couldn't find too many things to fit Bobby because he was so tall and skinny. He felt that he was tired of the whole thing and needed to get away. He was always angry about something or the other and being in his senior year with no clothes was unacceptable to him. This was the straw that broke the camel's back as far as he was concerned. He seemed to have caught the short end of the stick, as he saw it, all the way around. He was always mean and we never knew where he was anyway, but I would miss him terribly. He was always around when I needed him and now he would be thousands of miles away. It wouldn't be the same. Bobby was scheduled to be leaving in a few weeks, but he warned me to be extremely careful about boys since he wasn't going to be around to look out for me for a few years.

The weeks went by fast and my sophomore year was about to come to an end, but what a school year it had been! The Jay Ballard episodes, the Taft Capades, the parties, Bobby going to the Army....it was a lot to handle. We heard that Danny, the big nosed boy was opening a record shop in the corner of Lynn and Armory Streets. He was so popular that we knew that it would be a huge success! Later in the summer the shop opened, it was the Fourth of July weekend and Lynn Street was jumping. I hated that Bobby would be leaving soon and wasn't going to be there to have some fun with this, as it became the hottest spot in the West End. Danny had loud speakers installed, so that when he played any of the record cuts, they could be heard for at least a city block. It seemed like all of the West End residents were in the area enjoying this block party. There were even some older men and women grilling ribs and chicken and selling plates with cole slaw and baked beans. There was also pop and beer for sale, it was like a never-ending block party. Just taking a glance around all that was going on, there were small clusters of people eating, drinking or just talking but everyone was having a great time. There were a few people even dancing. Late into the night the festivities continued. From that time on the record shop was the hot spot and the place to be. Danny had many entertainer friends in the shop from time to time. Isaac Hayes, Marvin Gaye, Teddy Pendergras, and others. Each time they were in the shop. Danny blasted their latest album, one song after the other. This would obviously make all of us want to come in to buy the singles or the albums. My older brother Bobby and Danny were friends too and I didn't know how good of friends they were until the shop opened. Bobby was there a lot before he left for the army and that of course made me limit the amount of time that I was in that environment. But, what did I care, I had a lot of things to keep me busy.

We found out in the weeks to come that Danny was not only an odd character but a very sadistic individual as well. Many of the things that happened as far as he was concerned were the talk of the town. He had met a very nice young lady that was from Liberty Hill. Shelly eventually started working for him at the record shop and they began dating after several months. For all practical purposes, he made her feel like she was his number one lady. Little did she know that she was one of many. Shoplifters always brought hot clothes to the shop and he would sell them and split the money. He was involved in all sorts of things like that.

Shelly became known as one of Danny's girlfriends. She worked for him with no pay to speak of because she still lived with her mother on Liberty Hill and he figured he didn't have to pay her. It was my understanding that he gave her some of the hot clothes that he got into the shop. She had become pregnant by one of the college basketball players a couple of years before she met Danny and they had a son together. The basketball player obviously didn't let that stop him, because he never missed a beat with all the college girls. Same old story...project girl gets the shaft.

Even though we knew Danny was sadistic, the entire neighborhood was in shock when we learned that Danny had beaten Shelly to within an inch of her life. He was so cruel to her that he had given her not one but two black eyes and had the audacity to put her in the trunk of his black Cadillac and ride around town. Periodically he would open the trunk and make her sit-up and then invite guys in the neighborhood to look at her. He pulled up to the pool hall on the corner of Lynn and Findlay Streets, where there were at least a dozen guys standing outside the hall singing one of those do-wop songs. With his mere presence, the boys stopped singing, as Danny stepped out of his car, walked around to the trunk, opened it and said, "Look at this ugly bitch!"

They were all drawn to the trunk of his car to look. When they got a look inside they were shocked. They stood there with their months hanging wide open. Just the thought of someone doing something like that was so bizarre to them, even for Danny. I had never heard of anything so damaging, but everyone knew that was how he was. No one could comprehend why any girl would stay with someone like that. It was beyond any of us.

CHAPTER TEN

Bobby left for the army at the end of July 1961. Even though he was a pain in the neck sometime, I knew I'd miss him terribly. We went to the train station with him to see him off. That was the first time I'd ever seen tears form in his eyes. I hugged him so tight, as if I may never see him again. We had all been together for so long and to think he wouldn't be back for a long time was odd to me.

Three weeks after he left, my parents took me to be fitted for my new teeth. The word got out to the boys in the neighborhood that Bobby was gone and it became open season on me. I was considered a pretty girl with golden skin and long black silky hair as well as a beautiful figure, big legs and now a beautiful smile so, the boys were coming out of the woodwork after me. But, by that time, Bobby had protected me for so long and I had been around all of the entertainers, I was very picky about young men. I wanted someone very worldly, sophisticated and hopefully with some cash to boot. I was determined to hold out until the right person came along. Maybe an athlete, singer or actor. That's what I wanted.

Kelly came from Bloom Junior High to Taft as a sophomore. As I was when I came, she was excited. While we went on about our daily routine, we met another girl named Trevor. She was a transferee from one of the schools out on the "Hill." Her mom had just passed away and she was left only with two older brothers. Her brothers lived in the West End and she had to move in with them. Mrs. Childron wanted her to become part of our circle, so we welcomed her with opened arms. She was in my same grade level and we ended up with many of the same classes. She was really light skinned with long hair, a soft spoken girl that appeared to be real smart. Now there were five of us. After week of getting to know her and her joining us on the high school steps sometime had passed. We were having one of our marathon talking sessions, it came to our attention that Trevor was a member of ABX, the sorority that we had always been interested in rushing for. We talked to her about the possibilities of our rushing. We learned that Trevor was to be the incoming President, what timing! Weeks later, we were invited to rush ABX and we were all accepted to rush. During the initiation process, we boarded a bus with the preferred dress of long johns and night caps and our hair in pig tails. We carried buckets which contained worms that we were made to dig up ourselves. We were driven to a grave yard late the night of the initiation and ordered to walk through there alone, one by one, about five minutes apart. When it was my turn, I could barely see the girl that walked five minutes in front of me. As I walked through, there appeared to be motion on the ground near the grave markers. I was literally shaking. The instructions were that we had to walk at a steady pace counting, one-two-three in between each step. The moonlight was bright enough to shed some light on the area, but not enough for me to see anyone in the area. I was grateful that it wasn't pitch black. That was real scary, but it was worth it to be in a real sorority. Sidney and I were accepted. Aaron and Kelly were not. We were disappointed about Aaron and

Kelly, but we had no control over that. After we all got together to discuss it, both the other girls insisted that we stay in the sorority and convinced us that they would be all right about it. We were all determined that even a sorority wouldn't keep us from each other. Kelly went on weeks later and rushed for IEX. She was accepted.

Much of the same school activities happened in the 1961-62 school year. More parties and shows at the Cotton Club, classes, and Taft Capades. I also became a Varsity Majorette and marched at all of the football games. Personally, I was starting to perfect the art of being a high school student and enjoyed the ride as a junior and now as a sorority sister!

CHAPTER ELEVEN

Making the Transition to Womanhood...

Sidney and Aaron went to their high school prom with some less than notable boys. They had been seen around town with all of the entertainers over the past couple of years so the boys who really thought they had it all happening for themselves wouldn't even look their way. Here they were the hottest girls in the twelfth grade, or so everyone thought, and going to the prom with a couple of geeks. It just didn't seem fair. They both graduated from high school in June of 1962. It seemed that we were all off in different directions and didn't spend all our time together as we had in the past. One afternoon in late July, Aaron and Sidney were in Avondale with Jay. They had spent a great deal of time with him and Aaron had to get back downtown. Jay offered to drive her, but she didn't want him to, because his time with Sidney would have been cut short. Besides, she wasn't in any real hurry to get where she was going because she was leaving in plenty time. She told them that she could catch the bus, so they could stay put to continue enjoying each other. They all agreed and Aaron was on her merry way. It was a beautiful day. As she walked the block and a half down Reading Road to the bus stop, she pondered the events of the day and had an internal smile happening inside her. She knew that the future was going to be very bright for all of us and that made her very happy. As she walked and daydreamed she did not notice the car that was approaching. The driver didn't notice her either, he was busy shuffling some papers on the passenger seat of his car. He had to have his mind on something other than driving because it was evident that he wasn't paying attention to what was going on around him. As Aaron walked down the sidewalk, she crossed over a driveway area in which the driver was turning. As he turned into the driveway he almost ran over her! They were both jolted into reality at the near mishap as she began shaking all over. He moved swiftly out of his car, leaving it only partially in the driveway. He ran around the car to her to make sure she was all right. One of the young men who was in the house, which was where the boy was headed, heard the screech of the tires and ran out to see if he could help. They cradled her elbows in their hands and carefully walked Aaron into the house , sat her down in a chair as the driver ran to the kitchen to get her a glass of water. The boy that was driving the car disappeared again into one of the rooms at the back of the house, but was back shortly to continue looking after her. As she started to regain her composure, she began to take in the surroundings of the house that she was in. She noticed there were all sorts of literature laying around like Billboard magazines, music industry news papers and several wall plaques, which were gold and platinum records.

She thought to herself, " What is this place?"

She started to stand to excuse herself, so she could continue her journey.

He said to her, "Are you all right? I am so sorry about what almost happened."

She looked up at him, as he stood there about six foot-four, just a shade darker than paper bag brown with the most handsome face she'd ever seen.

She said, "That's all right, I will be fine, thank you for your kindness."

He looked at her real close saying, "You look like you could sit here for a few more minutes, what do you think?"

She said, "Okay, but I am actually doing okay now."

He motioned to her to keep her seat, as he moved toward the door, he was going out to bring his car into the driveway. He joked that it was still hanging partially in the street and that it had to take a back seat to her. He wanted her to know that she was more important than it was. When he returned a couple of minutes later she was still sitting there. He asked her once again if she was all right and she shook her head yes. They began to talk. They exchanged names and other pleasantries as they began to really hit it off well. She found out that this house was a business of which he was a partner. They ran a small operation in the record distribution business. What a coincidence! All this business with Sidney and her dad Jay and now a young man in the record business too. They talked for at least the next forty-five minutes. Then she stood up and made her way to the door.

"I really have to be going now," she added.

"Are you sure you're all right?"

"Yes, I'm positive," she answered.

"Can I see you again?" he asked.

"Well, I don't even know your name," she quipped.

"In all the confusion I totally forgot to introduce myself. I'm Evan. And what's your name?"

"My name is Aaron. It would be nice to see you again," she said blushing.

He offered to take her where she was going, but she had second thoughts about this, so she said she preferred to continue on with her plans to catch the bus. He walked her out of the house to the street, as they exchanged phone numbers. The bus stop was less than a half a block, so she insisted on walking there to wait for the bus. She said goodbye and turned to walk away. As she continued down the street, she could feel his eyes on her, but she wouldn't turn around to see for sure. The bus came about seven minutes after she got there. When she boarded it, she took a quick glance in his direction but didn't see him. She climbed aboard and smiled to herself as she walked down the aisle to the half way point on the bus, she took a seat near the rear. She exclusively thought of him as the bus shook along, all the way downtown. Her heart was light happy about their near mishap. She was so glad to have met him. As the bus was stopping to let passengers off and others on, she daydreamed about him. I wonder if he's married? Wonder if he really was attracted to me? Wonder if he will really call me. He was so cute and sophisticated. She got off the bus near their apartment. Her mood changed dramatically. She was back in the projects, took a deep breath and went into the apartment.

Three days and no call. She was sure that she'd never see him again. A boy like that would never be interested in her, she thought. But later on the afternoon of the fourth day, he called her. She was so nervous when she heard his voice on the other end of the phone...

"Hi" he said.

"Hi," she whispered.

"Are you all right after that scare I gave you?"

"Yes, I am perfectly fine. Thank you for asking", she responded.

"I wouldn't want anything to happen to such a pretty girl," he said so smoothly.

"What are you doing Friday night?" he asked.

"No plans at the moment. My friends and I usually just hang out," she explained.

"Do you think your friends would mind me stealing you away for one evening?" he responded.

She melted, but kept her composure.

"I don't think so," she said quietly. "We haven't really made any plans at this point."

"Would you like to grab a bite to eat and take in a movie downtown?"

"Yes, that would be fine," she replied.

"Where do you live? I'll come by and pick you up about five o'clock."

"I live on Clark Street, 502."

"Okay, I'll see you then."

She hung up the phone feeling great! She wondered what she should wear. Did she have anything good enough. Maybe she could borrow something from one of the 'Sisters.' Or, this may call for one of those quick outfits that we were so accustomed to making. She hurried out of the apartment to the fabric store. She already had some material, but not enough. When she got downtown, she remembered that she looked good in red, so that's what she'd do, get red material and one of those quick patterns. She picked up everything and headed back to the Lincoln Courts. It would take her about three hours to do. She made the cutest red flared skirt with a matching neck tie. She was going to wear a starched white blouse with it and her red flat shoes that her mom bought her at the end of her senior year at Big Ben's Department Store. It was all working out.

When she heard a horn blowing, she knew it was him. She had gotten dressed very carefully. She looked very pretty. Her hair was in a really neat French roll with ringlets curled right at her ears and makeup was put on to perfection. As she walked hurriedly down the steps anxious to see him again, she developed a big lump in her throat. This could be it! He could be the one! He was a tall and extra good looking boy who came from a good family out on the "Hill." It looked like her future was already being set. She hoped it went well!

PART II

I was going into my senior year and stayed extra busy with all the activities at the school. I had even become Head Majorette and was the main happening at the school. Kelly and Trevor were very involved in activities too and we were together just about all the time.

While moving in circles with Jay, Sidney met other entertainers and music personalities. This was opening up all kinds of opportunities for her. She started her first year at the University of Cincinnati. She was determined to get a college degree. She found college to be an extension of high school, only a lot tougher. But with college, the instructors were not in a "watch over you" mode, which is what we were used to. All the teachers at Taft certainly did make you do what you were supposed to do, or else. College gave her more responsibility because it was up to each student whether they attended classes and even got their assignments right and turned in on time. This meant that during the week, and even sometimes on the weekend, the students really had to buckle down and study hard everyday to keep up. So, whenever she did get to go out, she made up for lost time. The strictness of the college atmosphere and her mother's negative attitude, kept Sidney on edge which was a lot to contend with. But for the sake of her future, she'd have to endure it.

PART III

Aaron and Evan announced that they were getting married. Later she told us that she was a couple of months pregnant. The marriage was to take place in forty-five days. We all helped to make the arrangements around our schedules. Aaron was glowing! She looked so beautiful and the ceremony was spectacular! One of us was getting married and going to be a mom, one was in college and the other, me, still in high school. Wow! Things were changing.

Aaron got married and was happier than she had ever been in her life. She was going back and forth to the doctor making sure that everything was okay with the baby. We quizzed her about having a husband and being pregnant. She was getting as big as a house. She looked down at her stomach and said, "This is some weird shit, there is really a person in here! All that shit about the birds and the bees that we learned in school, ain't helping my ass now."

But, Evan was very attentive to her and Aaron loved every moment of it. She was really into her new life. We were all so very happy for her. One Saturday afternoon we were all together and just hanging out which had become very rare for us. We were all going in different directions and needed to be together. We chatted about any and everything that came up. We even talked about our younger years and the plans that we all had for the immediate future. I told them that my immediate plans were to get out of high school and hopefully go to college. Sidney still wanted to get away from her mother. Aaron mentioned her plans about her baby and husband and the fact that she would never have a million children like her mother did. She wanted to only have two, a boy and a girl, and make sure they had everything that she didn't as a youngster. She was determined not to have a lot of drinking and stuff going on around her family.

One evening several months later, while at a party, Sidney met a Disc Jockey for WCIN, a Cincinnati radio station. He called himself "Don Juan the Ladies Man!" He was the hottest jock in Cincinnati! We all listened to him everyday. He was older than she was, but that was part of the fascination. WCIN played all of the current hits and its' jocks also made public appearances and performed as masters of ceremony at all of the Negro shows in the city. We went to the Regal Theater time after time to see shows and there he was, on stage. Stevie Wonder was to perform at the Regal Theater and the hit song "Fingertips" was on the airwaves. We were all worked up about seeing this concert. What a magnetic presence he had! After the show, we were introduced to the master of ceremonies, the disc jockey Don Juan. He was glued to Sidney, he watched every move she made while we were back stage. It felt kind of eerie and weird to me, especially since he had just met her. This may prove to be trouble for her later on. After that he would somehow just show up at places that we went to and he would manage to end up where we were every time and in the middle of our conversation. It appeared that he was on a mission. Eventually, she began to see him socially. He was married, but that didn't stop them. They had a whirlwind

107

relationship over the next few months! They were together all the time. He took her to fancy restaurants and on one special night they went to one with white glove service and soft music playing low. He ordered champagne and told her, "Order whatever you like!" After dinner, they talked what seemed like forever. They danced cheek to cheek as he whispered sweet nothings in her ear. She never dreamed life and love could be so beautiful. He held her hands as they gazed into each other's eyes over the candle lit table. This was for Sidney like a romantic dream come true. Periodically, we would all hang out, but mostly, it was just the two of them. They were falling in love!

In early 1963, Don got offered a job at a station in Philadelphia. It was a larger radio market for him and paid a lot more money. Sidney was certainly a consideration, but how could he turn this down? After thinking it over for a few weeks, he called the radio station in Philadelphia to say yes, he would take the job. In the spring of 1963, he left for Philadelphia. Sidney was so attached, she was heart broken, but she felt that this would be her ticket to both get away from her mother and have someone in another city to look out for her. She vowed that if he asked her , she would go, but not to live with him but to be close to him. Her father had known for several years that she wanted to leave Cincinnati. He knew about the strained relationship between she and her mother and had always told her, "If you do leave Cincinnati, please don't go to New York because that is no place for a young girl alone." She felt that Philadelphia would be a good choice. Don, of course couldn't wait to call her to ask her to come. The call came about five weeks later, after he had gotten settled. Sidney was more than delighted. She very boldly and defiantly told her mother of her decision. Mrs. Celeste was devastated. In March, a few weeks later, Sidney, my best friend, moved everything that she owned to Philadelphia.

When she got there, she stayed at a small hotel to get her bearings together. She was overwhelmed at finally being away from her mother and on her own. It was both joyful and frightening at the same time. So much so that she stayed in her room for three weeks without going out for anything. She slept hour after hour, watched television and ordered room service, basically withdrawing from life. She knew that she didn't want to shack with him, she felt this wouldn't be right. She finally left the confines of her room and began to find her way around the downtown area. She called Don to let him know that she was in Philadelphia to stay. He was truly excited and told her that he had been trying to reach her at her mother's place. He explained that her mother was very vague about where she was and almost spoke as if she were in a trance each time he called. He thought to himself that Sidney's move to Philadelphia explained everything. He tried to get her to come be with him, but she wanted to make him understand that was not what she wanted. She told him she was trying to find a job first and get settled on her own. She convinced him that they could continue to see each other exclusively and socially, because she knew in her heart that she really cared for him a great deal, but she wanted more. Sidney decided that because he was still legally married, even though he and his wife were not together, she wasn't for shacking up with anyone. She concluded that if she ever lived with a man, any man, she would be wedded to him. She shared her feelings about the subject, of course he was against the idea. In fact he was incensed about it, but what could he do? He kept his cool but tried everything he could to get her to move in with him over the next few months. They went out for evenings where he continued to wine and dine her which led to them going back to his place where they made mad passionate love each time. Always on the next day she would gather her things and go back to her place to get ready for her day. He had a small place in South Philadelphia that was half pre furnished and half his own stuff. It was on the second floor of a Brownstone. The neighborhood was a little beneath middle class and was also home to some with shady type individuals who just hung around on certain stoops on both sides of the street. She never really felt safe in the area. The apartment was neat and clean though, so Sidney didn't mind spending time there, but she wasn't about to move in with him. She was cautious never to leave any of her belongings there either. She felt that if she did, he'd start getting the wrong message and come to expect a lot more than she was willing to commit to.

PART IV

The year went by fast. All of the activities at school kept me busy. I was named Head Majorette and was by everyone's standards "HOT STUFF!" On the last Friday of football season, I marched my best march! Our team was in second place in the standings and this game could boost Taft to number one. We were hoping to make all city champions! We were playing Woodward High School, which was a white team from Bond Hill. They were a tough team who had beat up on most of the teams they had played and currently held first place. There was so much noise in the stadium you couldn't hear yourself think. The rivalry was staggering and the air was filled with electricity. It was the bottom of the second quarter and Taft was leading by a touchdown. Since Kelly and I were both majorettes, we constantly kept our heads together just watching all of the good looking boys as well as the game. Some of the older kids that had already graduated from Taft were back for these games and we loved it 'cause we could flirt with all of them. The time clock ticked down to the final seconds before half-time. I lead the majorettes and band to our side of the field and the other band marched to the opposite side of the field. Since we were the home team, the visiting band was to perform first. We were prepared for them to try and out do us, but we knew we would have it all. We planned well and practiced hard for this finale! They came out with some music that we didn't even recognize and they were very stiff and proper as they marched, the fans on their side of the stadium went crazy in their own way...just what we wanted. It was a good show, but nothing compared to what we had in store for them and the audience. Mrs. Childron had prepared us well. She allowed us to do some of the steps that we wanted to add, so with our steps and hers we were ready. I signaled the band with three blasts of my whistle. Chirp! Chirp! Chirp! Everyone knew that this meant to get in line and get ready to rock. Then they were to get their instruments ready and then I whistled three more times as I stood there facing them, my baton in the air. As I lifted, then lowered my baton three times, up-down, up-down, up-down. Then I gave one long whistle blast, CCCHHHIIIRRRPPP! The drums led off while the majorettes danced a number to the horn section's soft rendition of "Tuxedo Junction." Our footwork was awesome. Everyone one of us was in perfect step with each other. At the end of that routine, we all faced the band and came out marching with our knees literally up to our chins with each step and our white boots with the huge green and gold tassels flipping in the wind to, "LUIE, LUIE! ....OH SAY NOW WE GONNA GO...OH OHOOH, SAY NOW WE GONNA GO......The crowd went crazy! It was all perfect from that moment on. There was so much noise even some members of Woodward's student body and some of their football team were in the archways near their locker rooms trying to see what was going on. WE WENT OUT WITH A BANG! This gave our team the boost they needed to kick Woodward's natural butts! We partied and partied on the field and in the stands after the last touchdown.

I was so excited that I didn't even ride back to the school on the band bus. I caught a ride with Scoopie and a couple of other kids. He and Raymond, one of his friends that I wasn't familiar with, drove to the game. Scoopie jumped out of the car to let me in and I slid in between them in the front seat. I was supposed to meet the other majorettes at the school to change clothes, so we could go out dancing. Raymond dropped everyone off first, except me and another kid. I was anxious to get back and thought we'd be at the school in another fifteen minutes or so. I was surprised to find out that this was not the plan. Raymond and Scoopie had decided that they were going to take me to Mt. Airy Park and make me have sex with them or threaten to leave me out there, so I would have to walk home. I was shocked when Raymond dropped Donnie, the last kid in the car off in the West End and turned his car in the wrong direction, starting to head away from the city.

I said, "Where are we going?"

He said, "We have a surprise for you."

I said, "What?"

Raymond kept driving and Scoopie tried to keep me occupied so they could get me to their destination without a lot of hassle. Ten minutes later we were on Winton Road and still riding.

I became very pointed and demanded to know where we were going. A few minutes later, I saw the signs that read, "Mt. Airy Park." At the entrance of the park, I really got spooked. I became very restless and told them they needed to take me home. As a matter of fact, I demanded that they take me home. One after the other, they both tried to soothe my nerves by saying they had to take care of some business and then they would take me home in a few minutes. They drove me to the deepest, darkest part of the park and immediately turned on me. It was as if their entire demeanor changed in an instant. They told me that if I didn't "do it "with them, they would put me out of the car, leave me here in the woods and the dark all alone.

I said, "*NO*! There is no way I will do this, no way at all!"

Raymond climbed into the back seat and taunted me to climb back there too. He reached up front to try pulling me back there as Scoopie started pushing me in that direction. We began to tussle. I kicked and screamed continuously. I realized that if they were successful in that back seat, it would all be over in a fraction of a second. It seemed to me that I got more strength and energy from somewhere as we all engaged in this frantic battle. I began to get even stronger as the seconds turned into minutes. Before I knew it Raymond was back in the front seat again. One of them held me down while the other pushed his hand under my uniform and into my panties. He started feeling around my vagina area. I felt his finger go inside me as I went into a fit of rage. Raymond then brought his finger out and smelled it.

He said, "Man this smells sweet, " as he offered a whiff to Scoopie.

Scoopie said with excitement, "**I knew it would, you could tell it would**."

I went wild! I started kicking and screaming to the top of my lungs. I got hold of Raymond's arm and bit him tearing his flesh. He screamed in agony from the bite. Their plan wasn't working. They thought I would just give it up. I fought them as hard as I knew how until my refusal to submit, along with scratches, bites and screams, made them feel like the struggle was too much to pay so, they pushed me out of the car and drove off. I laid there in the dark as I watched the car tail lights disappear into the darkness. I got up and turned first one way and then another not knowing which way to go. I wandered around in the dark for what seemed like hours, scared to death. Finally, I came upon two young couples in a parked car. All of them were necking. I hated to bother them, but I knew this was my only way out so, I tapped on the window, which understandably startled them. I apologized to them, while telling them what had happened to me. They were very understanding and offered to drive me to my apartment without hesitation.

On our way there, I thanked them over and over again. When we all got to my house, there was no need for me to even think I was going to go any where else that night, especially after both couples spilled the beans to my dad. Those so called friends of mine had ruined my night. As both couples told my father what they had encountered, he became more and more angry. My dad thanked them for rescuing me and saw them to the door. Upon their departure he called the police to file an incident report and pledged to be a the school on Monday morning to see to it that the boys were thrown out of school and hopefully in jail. He wouldn't rest until they were punished for what they did. My weekend was ruined.

On Saturday morning, I called Kelly to let her know what had taken place. She was shocked that Scoopie would take part in such a thing. My dad followed through with his plan and the boys were given six months in jail for attempted rape and detaining an unwilling participant. The word got all around the school. Everyone thought that Scoopie and I had been really good friends, which I also thought. We all wondered how he could take part in such a thing. This time I was lucky.

PART V

The end of my senior year was approaching and Trevor, Kelly and I were really together a lot. We talked more about our futures and promised each other that no matter what happened, we would never lose touch with each other.

The three of us went shopping to pick out our white dresses that we were to wear under our white cap and gowns. Kelly was so jealous that she still had one more year, but Trevor and I just savored the moment. I was sad about graduating. I knew that high school was the best time of my life and hated to leave. We had so many good friends in school and had so much fun. We learned so much and really got into the environment. It was both a joyous and sad occasion for us. Now I knew what Sidney and Aaron were talking about when they said the same thing during their graduation. We were safe during these times and the future was undetermined. But, we knew there was no going back now only forward.

Graduation was very somber. It marked the beginning of everything new for all of us. College or a job? What was next? My parents didn't have a lot of money for higher education but, I had put in for some grants. I was hopeful that they would come through. The weekend after graduation was upon us. I was sitting in the living room of our apartment thinking...no more school. We were all making plans to go to a big dance at the Armory Hall in July. It was the biggest dance of the season "The Annual Summer Dance."

Fresh out of high school, and what would I do now? It would take something mighty spectacular to top the days of Jay Ballard and the Midnighters, Chuck Jackson and all of them. Now it was time for me to think of my future. My family had moved to the Sadie Coons Apartments out in Walnut Hills. This was supposed to be a step up from the Laurel Homes which was a very small apartment complex. I knew I had to stay busy so, while I waited to hear from the grant committee, I looked for a job. Two weeks later, I got a job in a dry cleaners right up the street on Gilbert Avenue. Mr. McAdams was the owner. He liked young girls and gave me the job, so that he could look at me mostly. I surely didn't care as long as I was making some money and he didn't put his filthy hands on me. He had a reputation in the area that he was a weird-o and everyone in the neighborhood teased him because he had a jerk in his neck. It was said that his neck was like that because he had a wig in his throat. What the hell did that mean?

My plans were to start college in the fall and all I needed was some chump change between now and then. I worked at the cleaners for six weeks before finding out that he needed another cashier. I told him about Kelly. He interviewed her and she got the job. She started working there after school and on the weekends. After several weeks working together we became bored. We got to thinking of how we could get over on Mr. McAdams. Together, we devised a clever scheme to steal money from him. We decided that if an order was really large, we would get the money for the clothes and tear up the ticket put the shredded tickets in our pockets and discard them after we got off. How could he ever find out? And, if he did, by that time we would be gone. We always put the cash for the small orders in the cash register. This was perfect. This went on for almost two months. Mr. McAdams realized that something wasn't right so he started spending more time at the cleaners. We got scared and stopped what we were doing.

In the middle of July, Kelly and I went to the big summer dance at the Armory Hall. They had been advertising it on the radio for four weeks now. We were sure it would be a big one and that everyone would be there. We took some of the money that we had stolen from the cleaners and bought us some sharp outfits. We were ready for a fabulous evening! When we got there, it looked like we were right in the middle of one of the best dances we had ever been to. There were so many cars parked all up and down the streets. We could see the people streaming into the vast building from all directions. It looked like the whole city was there. As we were getting closer and closer, I noticed a good looking, older guy standing next to a white Chrysler 300 convertible. I had seen him somewhere before, but I couldn't remember where. He started flirting with me and of course I flirted back. We walked on into the party and walked through all of the people to find a suitable table. As soon as we did, I had several guys asking me to dance. I took one of them up on his offer. It was a semi fast dance and we got out on the floor doing the Uncle Willie. Another dance that was out at the time was the Monkey. On my way back to my table, I saw the same guy who was standing outside by the car again. He was sitting at the table with Kelly leaning over close to her and talking. I approached the table and he said, "I've been looking for you all my life!"
I said, "What?" But in the back of my mind, I thought that was really smooth!
He said, "Do you want to dance?"

I said, "Yes, we can do that."

It was a slow record and one of my favorites, James Brown's "Try Me." He was really light on his feet. He introduced himself as Jeff and started telling me about himself as if he were bragging.

He said "I was with Mr. Waterfield one day a few months ago at Taft and you passed by us."

He told me that he was formerly one of Mr. Waterfield's students at Taft.

He said, "I told Mr. Waterfield that I thought you were real pretty."

He said that Mr. Waterfield responded, "Ahhh, that's Miss Taylor and she is real pretty. They both laughed wickedly.

Brandon told me he had, from that time on been determined to have me.

We finished the dance and he walked me back to our table. When we got there, he stayed around with us talking for a few more minutes and decided to walk around to see who else was there. Before he left, he asked me if he could see me again. I said that I didn't think so, because we really didn't know each other that well.

"Maybe in time," I said.

He accepted my response and said he hoped we had a good time. While I was boy crazy, I was in no real hurry to do anything, so I decided to coast for now.

PART VI

Sidney found a job key punching for a Philadelphia dairy and for the time being moved into the YWCA. Don began to give shows and even though Sidney had gotten a job at the dairy, he hired her to collect money at each show. It was exciting at first. She got to meet all kinds of artists, some of which she already knew through her association with her father. She had the best of both worlds again not having to be bothered with her strange mother, living on her own and being wined and dined by this soon to be wealthy promoter. After more than 50 shows, Don made lots of money and he had gotten so greedy, he didn't want to pay the artists. One night, Johnny Paylor, a well-known rhythm and blues singer, came in to be paid after his performance. Don instructed Sidney to tell Johnny that he was losing money and he couldn't get paid now. Johnny Paylor told Sidney, "I will cut that Nigger from head to toe!" The same thing was done to Terry Butler, even though he was real cool about it he also meant business. Sidney was tired of being the scapegoat for Don and decided to pay Terry Butler. When Don found out he was furious!! He slapped her several times, blacking her eyes and said "BITCH, I can't believe you gave him my money!" After that episode, he constantly slapped her around all the time.

He had called her several days later to let her know he'd be picking her up for dinner and dancing. She was in the lobby waiting for him. She saw his car and tip-toed out to the car being careful to dodge the standing slush left by the snow.

When she got into the car, he said, "You look good."

She said, "Thanks!"

They rode along in silence for a while then he pulled to the curb of the restaurant where he had made reservations. A doorman opened her door to help her from the car.

"Good evening ma'am," he said.

"Good evening," replied Sidney.

She and Don proceeded to the restaurant. While they were being seated, Don said, "I have to make a phone call, go on to the table, I will join you in a minute or so."

"Okay," Sidney responded. His mood was very somber when he returned to their table. Conversation was at a minimum.

"Are you okay?"asked Sidney.

"Those sons of bitches have fucked with my money for the last time."

"Who?" she asked.

He turned to her and said in a very rough voice, "None of your fuckin' business." He threw a menu to her. "Just order your fuckin' food!"

She thought to herself, "Why am I here with this idiot?" She started making plans in her mind to limit the amount of time she would spend with this guy in the future.

The relationship got even worse. If they were just riding along in the car, he would slap her for no reason. After a few months of this, she decided enough was enough. She tried to get rid of him, but he wasn't hearing her. She told him that she was obviously not making him happy so why didn't they just part ways. He told her that the only way they would ever part was in death. He started following her wherever she went. He waited for her to leave work and would chase her until she found refuge wherever she could. He even called her boss at the dairy to tell him she was a whore and that he should fire her. Her boss called her in to his office the next day to tell her that she should get her personal affairs in order and have whoever that was to stop calling her job. Two weeks later, she came out of the YWCA to go out for the evening to a club with a girlfriend. Don followed them. There was a short line at the front door of the club and by the time they got in Sidney and her friend got settled at a table and ordered drinks, then they were ready to party. One of the guys in the club came to the table to inquire if either of them wanted to dance. Clare jumped at the opportunity. Sidney was relaxing at their table enjoying the music and the surroundings. Don made his way into the club. He, of course, broke the long line that was forming outside and announced to the doorman that he was the popular jock at WXPH radio station . The doorman let him in free of charge and ahead of the others. He stood in the rear of the club for a while watching Sidney. He was in a seriously dark mood and it was obvious to several of the people passing by. After about thirty minutes waiting and watching the girls having fun, Don saw that Sidney had just been walked back to her table by someone that she had been dancing with. Her friend Clare was still on the dance floor.

Don eased up to her table and said to her, "You are going with me, do not open your mouth or I will kill you right here."

He told her that his car was outside just around the corner from the club.

She turned to him and said, " I am not going anywhere with you."

Just as she turned to him, she noticed that he had something shiny in his hand, which flickered in the overhead light of the revolving dance ball. Then she knew this guy wasn't kidding. She calmly picked up her things as he walked her to the waiting car. He shoved her into the passenger side of the front seat, while hitting her across the head with the instrument that he was holding in his hand, then he slammed and locked the door. He hustled around the car in a very clumsy manner getting in on the driver's side and then drove off. She was shaking she was so afraid. After a couple of moments into the ride, she said in a very fearful voice "Where are we going?" She tried to get her composure back.

He said, as his demeanor became more irate and uncontrollable "To dump your body."

Terror took over but in order to gain control of the situation, she knew that she had to try to remain calm.

As they drove, she was so scared that all sorts of things were running though her mind...should I have stayed home with my abusive mother?...what am I going to do?....how can I get out of this?...will he really kill me?...She decided to use her inner ability and cleverness to get out of this volatile situation. She would ease her hand to the door handle and when the time was right, she would pull the handle to open the door and jump out of the moving car. They rode along in silence for several minutes. The silence was interrupted by him asking her what made her think she could dismiss their relationship just like that. She tried to explain that she had to because of his abusiveness. He started to cry, begging for another chance. She told him that she felt it was best that they see other people. He became furious. His eyes became dark and wicked looking. She thought to herself, "That was a stupid thing to say!" Silence once again filled the air. She was just about to release the handle when he glanced in her direction and noticed what she was up to. He reached for her with one hand while trying to keep control of the car with the other hand. The car started swerving with them wrestling about. She managed to pull the handle anyway and jerked away from his grasp. Seconds later, she hurled herself out of the moving car tumbling to the ground into the snow, rolling over again and again. She consciously tried to stop herself from tumbling but the ravine was much too steep. At this point, she didn't care what happened to her. All she knew was that she had to get away from him. He managed to stop the car about thirty five yards from where she had jumped. He hurriedly put the car in reverse, flooring the gas pedal to get back near to the place she had jumped. He jumped out of the car running toward the area stumbling as he moved forward. He slid down the ravine throwing caution to the wind. All that mattered to him was catching her. "She couldn't get away," he thought. She was his and his alone. If he couldn't have her, then no one could. Eventually he caught up with her. They fought furiously, both of them slipping and sliding in the snow and slush. They rolled down further into the ravine. As they fell further, he totally lost his balance. At that moment she got away from his grasp again, although she continued slipping and sliding in the snow too. On all fours, she begin to climb back to freedom. It was very difficult for her to walk in these conditions, especially in high heels. Struggling to increase the distance between them, she finally made it back to the street. As she reached the pavement, she looked back to see where he was. Unfortunately, he had already gotten back to his feet and was starting his climb up the slope as well. In her panic, she ran out into the middle of the street to seek help. Traffic was moving steadily through the area, but she knew that she had to take a chance with the traffic because she couldn't afford to let him catch her again. As soon as she stepped out into the street she was hit by a car that was coming too fast to avoid her. She fell to her hands and knees again rolling over and over four times from the blow. She was lucky that the other cars passing her , didn't hit her as well. One of the cars approaching had seen most of what was happening. The older couple slowly driving that car stopped completely to see what they could do. She cried and passionately pleaded with them to just take her home. They invited her to the back seat of their car asking if she was sure that she wanted to go home and not to the hospital. She assured them that she was fine, explaining that the car that hit her only brushed her. As they pulled away from the area, she was grateful to get away. She glanced out of the back window of the car at Don as he made his way back to street level. Their eyes met. His eyes were admitting defeat and hers were saying goodbye. He looked totally defeated, but she was happy to be alive. She turned from the window as she laid back on the car seat and exhaled a sigh of relief. For now, this was over.

The couple drove her back to the city. They were very inquisitive much like she would have hoped for if she had known her Grandparents. They wanted to know if she was okay and what was going on. She told them basically what had happened because she felt she needed to talk about it. Her heart was still racing, but she was calming down more and more as she talked about it. She had skinned elbows and knees and knew she would be sore for days, but she knew she was lucky because that was the extent of her injuries. The older couple pulled up to the front doors of the YWCA asking if there was anything else they could do for her. She thanked them profusely and then disappeared through the doorway of the Y. When Sidney was finally safe in her YWCA room, she was very fearful that this was only the beginning. She knew that no one would ever believe her story because of his status in the city, so she didn't go to the police. Instead, she would have to devise a plan to get rid of Don permanently. Between now and that time she would have to be very, very careful. Don could no longer be trusted and he obviously wasn't going to take no for an answer.

In the weeks that followed, she moved cautiously about her daily routine keeping an eye out for Don. He turned up out of the blue periodically just waiting for the chance to grab her again. Sidney always traveled with someone whether she was going out for lunch or to or from work. She knew how dangerous this guy was and she couldn't take anymore chances. Several weeks later one of her friends at work invited her to a gathering . She was reluctant to go but had been basically hemmed up in her room since the incident, so she decided to take Carolyn up on the invitation. Carolyn, her friend knew several policemen and she knew that many of them would attend the function. Carolyn knew all about Sidney's troubles with Don and hoped that Sidney would be able to remedy her problems by getting assistance from some of her cop friends. When Carolyn and Sidney arrived at the cookout, Sidney was reserved and stand offish. She had just been through hell with Don and wasn't at all interested in another man at this point. Carolyn had other ideas though. She wanted to find a way to get Sidney involved with one of the guys as a protective measure for Sidney. As the evening progressed Sidney began talking to one of the guys. After a couple of dances and some casual conversation she found Byron very grounded. She opened up a little and found herself at ease with him. That's when she, all by herself, came up with the brilliant idea that if she started to date this cop, she could use him to get rid of Don once and for all. Carolyn's game was working. Although Byron seemed to be a really nice guy, Sidney wasn't ready to see anyone steady but she would talk to him at least until her problems were over. As a matter of fact, only until she was rid of Don. Then she would little by little stop seeing him.

Don was up to his old tricks. While Sidney and Byron were on a couple of dates, Sidney saw Don watching them twice. She started to feed Byron information a little at a time about Don, giving him only information that was necessary because she didn't want to scare him off. Byron had to get physical on two occasions with Don to let him know that Sidney was his woman now and he had better back off. Byron gave three of his cop buddies Don's description and tag number so that they could harass him into leaving her alone too. Several of

Byron's fellow cops were around many times when he and Sidney were together. They had all been hoping to get a chance to meet Jay, her father, when he was in town. Sidney saw Don a few times and he didn't look well at all. As a matter of fact, he looked awful. Finally, after almost a year, Don did finally leave her alone. And, in late 1965, she heard that Don was found dead in a hotel room. It was all over the news, on television and in the newspapers. They said his death was from an overdose of pills and alcohol. How sad. He really used to be a decent person. She called Cincinnati to let the 'Sisters' know what had happened. We were all sad about the whole thing, but our main concern was Sidney. She said she was fine.

CHAPTER TWELVE

Sidney attended Temple University for two years while still working at the dairy. She wanted to become a programmer and took up electronics and data processing programming. She was doing really well in college and got high marks, as she did in high school . She decided to go to the college administrative office one day to get a copy of her transcripts in order to send them to several agencies for future job possibilities. She didn't want to key punch for the rest of her life. Hopefully, these employment agencies could help get her started in a junior position in programming at a large corporation. Her dream was to land a job in a company where she could grow with the organization. She sent out copies of the transcripts to about twenty agencies. After reviewing Sidney's college transcripts, one of the agencies called her to let her know that World Airlines was hiring programmers. They set up an appointment to meet to discuss the paperwork she had sent to him. "In reviewing your transcripts, it appears that you are doing quite well in school," he said.

"Well, I have worked hard at it," Sidney responded.

There were no Negro employees in the employ of this major airline, except in janitorial positions. The NAACP had threatened to go out to the tarmac to stop the planes from taking off, if they didn't hire some Negroes. Her friend's contact that had given her the job lead told her that this would be a good time for her to have her application in with the airline because the NAACP was determined to make something happen for Negroes. During this same time Martin Luther King, Jr. was marching in Alabama protesting the treatment of Negroes. They had water hoses, with water on full blast, sprayed on them. The Negroes' skin was literally being torn away from their bodies. They also had attack dogs going after some of them. Things were heating up all over the country, but mostly in the South. The residual affects were felt across the country.

In her first job interview, she was sharp. The interviewer was a third level manager, which really amounted to his being a mere gopher. She summed him up after about two minutes. He was white and seemed like a nerd. His posture was that of an antagonistic individual as he leaned forward toward her with his arms rested at the center of his desk. He asked her,

"Why would World Air Lines hire you over all of the other applicants?"

She said, "Because I have a lot more to prove than your average applicant, wouldn't you agree? Not only for myself, but as a representative for all Negro people."

"Most Negroes are very determined to be the best that they can be, because we have not had many opportunities to prove ourselves. I feel that World Air Lines wants the best people for any job that can assist them in helping to further their position in the industry. And, I know that I am one of the those people, because I'm hard working and dedicated to whatever I have committed myself to."

The interviewer listened very intently as he began to relax and lean back in his chair. He seemed to become very comfortable with her and looked as if he was genuinely interested in what she had to say. He almost seemed surprised that a Negro would be able to converse so astutely. In their communication exchange during the interview, her responses became more and more impressive and understandable to him. At the end of what seemed to be an hour or so, he began to wrap up his questioning. He had taken very careful notes as the interview went along. He stood up and moved around his desk to shake her hand.

He said, "I am going to recommend you highly for the position, but you will have two more interviews to go through."

He continued that she shouldn't be too alarmed or concerned about the following interviews because as he put it, "If you handle the last two as you did this interview, you are as good as hired."

He also said, "You are a credit to your people."

As she left the room, she was very disturbed about his last statement, but wasn't sure that he was aware of the way it came across to her. She knew that most of the white people that she had met were oblivious to the plight of Negroes. The times that we were living in clearly revealed to all of us that white people were not even sure we were really human, much less had the ability to work along side of them in decent paying positions. The NAACP, Martin Luther King, Jr. and others were involved in the civil rights movement at this very time and had begun to make small strides for equality. So, white people were being forced to recognize the injustices that were being dealt to Negroes. She knew that the interviewer wouldn't have made a statement like that if she were a white woman. She felt that she was treading on uncharted territory. She left really expecting never to hear from them again.

Several weeks went by as she went about her everyday activities. She was busy working, going to church, parties, clubs and other social gatherings and getting her life back in order after the terrible mess with Don. She was really shaken after their whirlwind romance, the odd relationship and finally the circumstances surrounding his strange death and wondered why he had turned into such a possessive, sick individual. She reviewed her relationship with Don from the very beginning and suspected that her relationship with her mother was the underlying reason that had ultimately pushed her to seek refuge in this man. The fact that he wasn't doing too bad for himself during the early days was also a factor. She wondered now if it were worth it, but she couldn't afford to let herself get bogged down with these negative thoughts now.

The second interview was scheduled exactly four and a half weeks later. She had written off her chances that she would seriously be a candidate from the moment she left the first interview and especially now since it had been so long. When she got there, she was seated in the very large waiting room, which must have been some big wheels outer office. She had to wait for maybe fifteen minutes. A very pasty faced, middle aged white woman with very little make-up on approached her. She was dressed in a dark suit, basic pumps and her hair was pulled back in a bun.
"Are you Ms. Crane?"
"Yes, I am."
"Please follow me."
The lady showed her through a set of big mahogany double doors, where a well dressed white man was turning the corner of his desk and was headed toward her. "Good morning, Ms. Crane, please have a seat." He motioned to a chair in front of his huge desk.

He introduced himself as Maury Slokum, Sr. Vice President of Human Resources for the airline. As he took his seat, he picked up what looked to be six or seven sheets of paper, while simultaneously putting on a pair of glasses. The glasses were on the tip of his nose, as he looked at her over them with his piercing blue eyes. He said,

131

"I see here that you met with Jonathan Long several weeks ago and according to his notes, he was quite impressed with you. Tell me a little about yourself.

She asked him a question to his question, "Well, what part about me would you like to know about?"

"Oh, you can start anywhere," he said.

"Well, I'm from Cincinnati, Ohio and I have been living here in Philadelphia for a couple of years. Currently, I have a key punch position at a local dairy. I attend Temple University and formerly attended the University of Cincinnati before moving here."

He interrupted her, "And what is your interest in World Airlines?"

"I am interested in becoming a programmer with the airline. The classes that I have been taking for the past two years have to do with electronics and programming, and that is the field that I plan to pursue."

For every other question she was asked, she gave the perfect answer. Sidney knew that he was trying to catch her not knowing what to say or in a negative situation a couple of times, but this cat and mouse game, she was determined to win. They went on and on and finally the second interview came to an end. He thanked her for coming in and told her that they would be in touch with her soon.

The third interview came a week and a half later and by this time Sidney had completed some research as to her possibilities with the company and was not actually too pleased with or interested in the jobs that the airline had available. She was more interested in programming which is what the employment agent told her was open. She believed they would come back to her after all her time invested in the interviews and offer her a job as a ticket agent. She felt that she had been to college to get a better job than that, even though she didn't have a degree yet. She went to the third interview just to say she completed the process. When it was all said and done, she found out that was what they were definitely going to offer her. She was very professionally sarcastic, not nasty, but professionally sarcastic at the last interview and really didn't care if she got the job or not. When she left the interview, she felt a weight had been lifted. She would never get the job now she was sure, as she exhaled.

The Fourth of July was coming up. Donna from Sidney's office had some friends that were having a barbecue party on the holiday. Donna asked Sidney what she was doing over the long weekend.
"Nothing special," remarked Sidney.
"Well, why don't you come along to the barbecue that I am going to?"
"Who's giving it?" she asked.
"Some friends of mine involved in entertainment," Donna replied.
"Are you sure it will be okay for me to come along with you?" asked Sidney.
"Oh yeah," said Donna, "these are real good friends of mine, but if you would feel better about it, I will call to ask first."
"I would feel much better asking, before I just show up, you know what I mean?" Donna called immediately. When she spoke to her friend, they were on the phone for about ten to twelve minutes. Their supervisor was down the hall and headed their way, so Sidney gave Donna a nudge suggesting that she get of the phone before the "old hag" got to them. Donna concluded her long-winded conversation and hung up just in the nick of time. The "old hag" was just passing through and leaned in the door to see if things were going all right. Both the girls smiled and kept on key punching, as if there was never a pause in their work. When the "old hag" closed the door, they both giggled, as if they had just gotten away with something big. Donna told Sidney that the hostess of the party would be thrilled to have her join them.

The three days passed by quickly as they completed a full weeks work. They walked out of work together and Donna pledged to pick Sidney up at two o'clock the next day, so they could get there an hour or so after the festivities had begun and by that time it was sure to be hopping. Donna was on time! Sidney hadn't ever actually seen her car, and as she came out of the door, just seeing her sit there in the 1959 blue Thunderbird convertible reminded her of home. As she climbed in the car, she said, "Taylor, one of my 'Sisters' had a red car just like this a couple of years ago. It reminds me of her." Donna said, "I'll have to meet your 'Sisters' when they come to visit." Sidney smiled and wondered how that would work, because of the distinct personality differences between the two women.

When they got to the barbecue, there were about twenty five people already there. The food was smelling good and we walked in to "The Duke of Earl" playing on the record player. As she was being introduced around, they came to a guy named David. He was very good looking and very popular with all the guests. She wondered if he would be attracted to her and he was wondering the same thing too. But, she thought he was just nice. They talked in groups and in one on one conversations. She found out he was a model and had high hopes for the future. About forty-five more people came in within the next hour and a half. They had games all setup and several card tables too. This was really a big occasion. No wonder the hostess didn't mind her coming. One more person couldn't have made a huge difference. Sidney and David spent a lot of time together after that. They went to fashion shows of which he was the main attraction. Sidney was seated in the VIP section each time. This was right up her alley. He was very talented and knew just about every one in the city and Sidney figured it was just a matter of time before he struck it rich, and she wanted to be there for the ride.

Sidney got the phone call from World Airlines. She got the job as a ticket agent! She couldn't believe it! Even though the position wasn't what she wanted, she took it with the hope that she could work her way into programming. Her future looked promising. After the rough start, she was involved with a decent guy and was starting on a new job that had tons of potential. She couldn't wait to see what was next!

CHAPTER THIRTEEN

Aaron's marriage to Evan was heart warming. They enjoyed each others company tremendously. Evan was part owner of a record company, so that had him in the "fast lane." He was in and out of town and traveled all over the place. He met a lot of people in the business. There were a ton of record companies popping up all over the place. So his business started to dwindle somewhat. Too much in fact. He now had a family to support and he found himself moving into other lines of business. Just eleven months after the baby's birth, he got caught in some unlawful activities and was put in jail. Aaron went to get him out on bond. She had to borrow the money because she wasn't working. She scraped it up and got him out. He knew that it would be difficult for him to get other things going in Cincinnati, so he told Aaron that they were moving to Detroit. He said he knew several people there and they could make a clean start. He skipped out on his bond. He went ahead of Aaron and the baby telling her that he would send for them as soon as he got settled. Week after week she waited. Finally he called to let her know that he was sending her two bus tickets and she was to catch a bus the next night. She was relieved to have heard from him. She wanted to know if he was okay.

He said, "I'm doing okay, I got us a room and we can build from there," he said.

"I can't wait to see you," she whispered.

"Me too," he responded.

"I hate to tell you like this, but we haven't seen each other in so many weeks."

Then there was a long pause.

He waited for a few moments and asked, "Well, what is it?"

"I wasn't really sure when you left, but I found out I'm pregnant again."

"That's wonderful, baby! I'm looking forward to seeing you all."

The next afternoon, she was all packed and ready to go. Her sister took her to the bus station with her two tattered bags. We all rode with them to see her off. She was sad in a way, but happy about being with Evan again and finally starting their family. Cincinnati was all she had ever known and now she was off to a strange city with no friends or family and wasn't sure about the whole thing. We consoled her and said that she would be with the man that she loved and everything would work out. She found out two months ago that she was pregnant again and hadn't told anyone. She wanted it to be a surprise to him when they reunited. He had always wanted a boy and she hoped this time that's what they would have.

When she got there, he was standing at the area where the buses unloaded with a big smile on his face. It was like one of those scenes from a romantic movie, they ran to each other and hugged tightly as they kissed a long wet kiss. He took the baby from her arms and tossed her in the air and the baby smiled and began to spit up on him. He didn't like that because he was clean as the board of health and now his expensive shirt smelled of sour milk and would probably stain. He immediately shoved the baby back into Aaron's arms and ushered them to a waiting beat up car outside the building. As they rode along he told her all about the neighborhood where they would be living and he appeared to be quite excited that she and the baby were there. When they pulled up to the rooming house that he had for them, she thought to herself, "What a dump," but she didn't say a word. She collected the baby and followed him up the short flight of stairs and into this "room." She was disappointed but thought with them working together they could overcome this situation.

As the days passed, she met a lot of flaky-looking people that also lived in the building. They were always whispering and saying things that were over her head. The other tenants in the building were in and out of their rooms all throughout the day and night. She wondered what the hell was going on but she knew she had better mind her own business.

After she had been there for just over a month, the baby was taking a nap and she was about to do the same when she felt the urge to pee. Evan had just left and said after he used the bathroom he'd be out for a couple of hours. The new baby she was carrying was in an awkward position and probably laying on her bladder. She slipped back into her slacks and threw on a blouse to run down the hall to the bathroom. When she flung open the door to the shared bathroom, the first thing she noticed was a needle along with some rubber tubing laying on the back toilet. She hoped that this wasn't Evan's, since he just left the bathroom, but there were at least seven other possibilities in this rooming house. So, she used the toilet and scurried back down the hall to her waiting , sleeping baby.

Before she had taken the bus ride from Cincinnati to Detroit, Evan had gotten a job with a record distributor, which was an affiliate of MOTOWN. Surely things would look up now. As time went by, he spent less and less time with Aaron and the baby. But she thought he was working and that was okay. She dreamed of having a healthy baby boy and hoped that six or seven months after the new baby was born, she could get a job and help out too. After being gone for two days this time, he showed up looking whipped. He said he was going to take a shower and get a few hours of sleep before he had to go back to work. He came back looking somewhat refreshed and had a can of pop that he polished off in what seemed like one gulp and headed off to sleep. He got up about three a. m. and began to get dressed in the dark. He was trying to move around quietly, so he wouldn't wake them. He didn't want to have to explain his leaving in the middle of the night even though she knew he would be leaving early. But, he had to go now .

Aaron, still half asleep whispered, "Where are you going?"

He said, "A big shipment of records is coming in at six a.m. and I have to be there to take inventory of them."

She said, " Okay, I love you," as she turned over and went back to sleep.

Evan was gone for two and a half days this time. Things were really looking more and more odd to Aaron. Where was he spending so much time? Why was it necessary for him to work so many hours. And, the fact that there was no real money to speak of, was very perplexing to her! When he was home, he was easily irritated and short tempered. When they talked, at times, he would nod off like he was so tired that he couldn't keep his eyes open. He also tossed and turned and scratched a lot, while he slept. He had never done these things before they moved to Detroit. It was all very strange to her. Seemed like the very moment he hit the chair or the couch, he was out. She paced the floor wringing her hands and wondering how all of this could have happened and wondered what was it was that was really happening.

This time four days had passed. He came back and it was apparent that

139

something was very wrong. He had a far away look in his eyes. He blew up at
her for the slightest mention of his whereabouts or anything else. She didn't
know which way to turn. She asked again if she could help. He turned to her and
looked at her as if he despised her and stormed out of the room. How long would
he be gone this time? She paced the floor some more and as she continued to
pace she would periodically look out of the window as if that would make him
come back sooner. She finally became too tired to continue pacing and laid down
to try and sleep. She laid their crying streams of tears. She was worried and
extremely uncomfortable with the new baby kicking and turning flips in her belly.
The noises from the other rooms in the rooming house were loud and even strange
at times. What on earth were these people doing? She had never heard these
types of noises before, because most of the time when the three of them were
there the noises were drowned out. More and more, especially when the baby was
sleeping, the house noises disturbed her. They were so happy at first, when they
were in Cincinnati. She started to look back over the past weeks since she got to
Detroit. She remembered that he was always nodding off and scratching but, she
chalked it up to his being tired from running around all day and into the night.

He returned three days later and had nothing much to say for himself. She
quizzed him and asked if she could help him in any way. He nearly bit her head
off. She became very quiet and withdrawn. At this point, she decided that she
wasn't going to have much to say to him from that moment on.

The next few weeks were the same. He was in and out. She stayed in the
room and took care of the baby, half scared to leave because of the neighborhood
and those flaky people living in the rooming house with them. Besides that, she
had no money and really no where to go. What on earth was she going to do?
He came and went as he saw fit. He came back again after being gone almost

four days this time.

She asked, "Where have you been and what am I supposed to do about food?"

He threw a few dollars her way and shouted, "I have been at work and this is all I have!!" he shouted.

She told him "Well, I have to go to the store, so you will have to watch the baby while I 'm gone!"

He said, "Okay." He seemed to calm down a bit. "But you have to hurry back because I won't be here too long."

She threw on some clothes presentable enough for the street and hurried out the door. She hadn't been out for two weeks. She noticed several dirty looking men sitting on the stoop as she walked past. They made some snide remarks under their breaths and all started laughing out loud. She tried not to pay any attention, but it was hard not to. These were some of the same people that had to know that she was in that room alone most of the time. She didn't want to give them any reason to bother her while Evan wasn't at home. This really made her even more nervous about this rooming house. But she could only handle one thing at a time. She gathered a few things at the market and scurried back down the street to that dingy place where she lived. She hated to go back but she had no other choice.

When she returned, he was busy putting together his ensemble for the evening. He gathered some clean underwear, his tooth brush and tooth paste along with a wash cloth and towel, as he headed for the bathroom down the hall. He took a quick shower and came back to the room to get dressed. She just sat there watching him.

He finished dressing and turned to her and said, "I will see you later."

She responded with her head hanging down, "Okay."

She was really becoming depressed. She whipped up some tuna for a sandwich and put away the rest of the food and then slumped into bed.

That night, he came back early. She and the baby were already asleep, but he slid in the bed beside her, hugged and cuddled her and went to sleep.
The next morning, they had breakfast together like a normal family. She was getting very big again and was concerned about the baby, because she hadn't seen an obstetrician since she moved to Detroit. He promised her that he would take her to see a doctor in the next few weeks.
"I will be getting paid for all the overtime that I have been working and we can go to a private doctor then."
He said, "I have to go out again this morning, but be assured that I will not be gone too long." After breakfast, he excused himself and went to the bathroom again before leaving.
She said, "Okay, but please remember you promised not to be gone too long."
He said with a bright smile on his face, "I know, I promise!"
She thought to herself, there's the man I married. He looked like the Evan of old.

Because she was getting so big, she was very uncomfortable. The baby must be laying on her bladder again and she had an uncontrollable urge to pee. She had to hurry, because the urge came on so suddenly. She waddled down the hallway about ten minutes after he had left or so she thought. She flung the door open, only to find Evan sitting on the toilet with some kind of tubing tied around his arm and shooting something into what seemed to be his veins. It looked like he had just finished and the intrusion startled him.

"What in the hell are you doing?!"
"Shhhhh," he said, "Do you want everyone to hear you?"
"What the hell are you doing?" she said lowering her voice.
"What does it look like?" he said, as his eyes began to droop. He was feeling the effects of the drugs that he had just shot into his arm.

"You brought me and your baby up here to do drugs?!" she screamed.
"Damn you, damn you!" She ran down the hall towards the room forgetting
that she had to pee.

He got up from the toilet seat gathering his paraphernalia quickly all in the same
motion. He hurried down the hallway, went into their room and grabbed
something from one of his "cheesy" drawers in the dresser and headed out the
door without so much as a word to her.

"Where are you going now?" she asked bewilderedly.

"I'll be back later," he said curtly as he rushed out the door.

She was devastated!

How could he? Was she ever going to get past this moment?

They continued on over the next four weeks the same way. She tried to talk to
him.

"Evan, are you a drug addict?"

"When did you start all this?"

"Is this why you are never at home?"

"What does this mean to our marriage?"

"You ask too many damn questions. I'm still keeping a roof over your head
aren't I?" "What more do you want?"

"I want a husband and a family, that's what I want," she screamed through a river
of tears.

"No more questions, I gotta go," he told her.

Easter was coming up and she had asked him to give her money to buy the
baby something pretty to wear. He thought by doing this, it would make up for
what he had been doing all these months. He gave her some money and she went

shopping at the neighborhood five and dime store. There was nothing in this neighborhood like Big Ben's in Cincinnati, but she would make it do. She found a pretty pink lacy dress and some black patent leather shoes and laced socks. On Easter Sunday, they both went to church which was about five blocks away. When they got dressed and walked toward the church, she saw mostly women about her own age with their children too. There were very few men accompanying the other women. When she arrived at the church, Aaron prayed that things would get better between she and Evan and asked God to help her husband with his huge problem that he obviously had.

After the service, she and the baby strolled back toward the rooming house really trying to enjoy their walk. The day was sunny, but still a little crisp. But, since it wasn't cold, which was usually the case in Detroit during this time of the year, she wanted to make the most of it. She got back to the room and started to prepare some lunch. They had their late lunch and got undressed and decided to take a nap. Little did she know when she went to sleep, things were about to get even worse. The baby had looked so cute walking like little babies do. They had both been in the Easter parade, enjoyed church and had lunch. They laid down and before she knew it, they were in slumber land. When they woke up, she noticed that the baby's clothes were gone. She panicked again. She knew where she put them! She hoped she was mistaken.
"Maybe I put them in a drawer or in the closet," she said out loud.
She searched frantically! They were not to be found! She sat on the side of the bed in a complete stupor!
"What is going on here?" she said to herself.
It must be Evan, but I can't believe that he has become that desperate!
She found out later that Evan had sneaked into the room and took the new clothes down the street to sell them. She knew that the situation was bad, but never

dreamed it could ever be this horrible. Aaron knew that it was just about all she could take.

To top off everything, the landlord came by early in the morning two days later to collect the rent. She was still asleep that morning and was awakened by the loud thuds on the door! Whoever it was, continued beating on the door even though she was screaming, "Who is it, who is it?"

She got up and put on a pitiful excuse for a robe that was much too small to cover her big stomach. When there was a break in the lumbering on the door, she called out, "Who is it?"

"The owner of the building," he said in a deep voice with authority.

"What do you want?" she asked in a very weak voice.

"I want the rent to be paid, that's what I want," he shouted loud enough for the entire building to hear.

"It hasn't been paid in forty-five days and it is supposed to be paid by the week. Now I have given your husband more time because I like him, but I need my money!"

Just then she opened the door thinking that if he were to see that she was pregnant, he wouldn't be so strict and give them a little more time.

To add insult to injury the landlord became even more obtrusive, "I can't believe that he is laying up with you fucking and not working. You tell him that if I don't have my money, and all of it by Friday, you'll have to get out by the end of the week," he declared.

Aaron said, "By the end of the week? Well today is Thursday and the end of the week is tomorrow."

"You think I don't know what day it is missy? Pay and pay by tomorrow or you are out on the street!"

Now she was profoundly tense, almost neurotic. She hadn't seen Evan in two days and obviously didn't have the money to pay the rent. She had been in Detroit and the rooming house all this time and Evan had paid the rent directly to the landlord or so she thought, because she had never seen this guy before now. But this month, here he was. She didn't know what to tell him.

She said to him, "My husband isn't at home, but I'll tell him when he comes back that he needs to pay."

He turned and stomped down the hallway.

The night came and went with no Evan, no more money or food either. The landlord was mad as hell. He told her that if the rent wasn't paid in twenty-four hours, she and the baby would have to get out. What if Evan doesn't come back before then? What would she do? She paced and paced. She decided to pack as much as she could in the two raggedy suit cases that she came to Detroit with. She had to stop periodically to rest, because her back was giving her the blues.

"What in the world have I done, I left the Lincoln Courts, where I was at least safe and comfortable," she mumbled to herself.

"Even if it was the projects, it was home and I didn't have to worry about being put out on the streets."

She did as much as she could and had to lay down because her back couldn't stand anymore pressure. While laying there she fell asleep and before she knew it, it was morning. She finished gathering the remaining things that she would take with her, if she was put in the situation of leaving. She and the baby had a snack for breakfast and sat together looking out the window hoping that Evan would return.

The landlord came about three o'clock the next day and insisted that they leave the premises. As a matter of fact, he had someone else with him that would be taking over the room that she occupied and he had paid the landlord for two months in advance. The landlord actually took her suit cases and put them out on the steps in front of the building. He actually put them out! He had no heart at all! All she and the baby had was what was on their backs and in their suit cases. Luckily, a little boy from the neighborhood was passing by the area where she was sitting, felt sorry for them and helped them to the bus stop. She would take the city bus to the Greyhound bus station. The bus finally came along and she and the baby climbed aboard. The few passengers on the bus looked at her with pity. As she rode bouncing along on the bus, tears streamed down her face. She had no idea what she would do. All she had was eight dollars and some change, a toddler and a new baby on the way. The bus stopped at least twenty-five times taking in new passengers and letting others off. Aaron was in no real hurry to get anywhere because she didn't even know where she was headed. When the bus got downtown , she solicited some help getting off the city bus and into the Greyhound bus station. She made her way to the ladies room right off the terminal. While sitting on a stool in the ladies room she tried to think things through. What a fool she had been. After all these months sitting there waiting for Evan night after night. She was too embarrassed to call home to ask for any help. When she packed, she remembered to pack some of the food that they had left in the room. She brought along the peanut butter and jelly, some bread and cracker with sardines and some graham crackers for the baby. They had mainly lived on this type of food over the past few months anyway. She had to make sure the baby had something substantial. She remembered noticing a small store a couple of blocks from the bus station, which she had seen on the city bus ride downtown. Later that evening she and the baby walked there, after hiding their suite cases in the broken stall area in the ladies room Aaron had to get the baby some milk to make sure she was fed and many times thought to herself that she herself could wait to eat. Surely something will come along to help her out of this mess. They stayed in the bus station for three days, sleeping on the floor of the ladies room. She used some of her clothes to make a pallet for the baby and herself and never went to sleep before late hours, because there was much too much traffic in and

147

out of there during the day and early evening. On the fourth night, Aaron was awaken in the middle of the night, remembering that there was a girl who used to live in Cincinnati that moved to Detroit two years before. Her named was Thelma Hanks. She got up from the floor and waddled to the pay phone near the ladies room in the lobby. She looked up her number in the phone book and called her. There were three Hanks' in the phone book and she didn't want to waste even a dime calling the wrong person. But, what choice did she have? On the second number, Thelma answered the phone. Aaron could hear the sleep in her voice dripping off the phone line.

"Hello, Thelma?" Aaron said timidly.

"Yes?" she questioned.

"This is Aaron Ray from Cincinnati, remember me?"

"Who?" Thelma began to wakeup somewhat.

"Aaron Ray from the old neighborhood in Cincinnati," she explained.

"Aaron?" more awake now. "Where are you and why are you calling me at this unGodly hour?"

"I am at the Greyhound bus station in downtown Detroit. Can you please come to get me? It's a long story that I will explain when you get here. I am in trouble, bad trouble and I just remembered you lived here."

"Yes, my husband and I can come right away!"

Thelma and her husband Tom, got up and got dressed and headed for the bus station. While they were getting dressed, Thelma told Tom a little about the girl on the other end of the telephone. About forty-five minutes later they were pulling up to the side of the bus station. When they went in, they looked around the lobby of the bus station but didn't see anyone that she could recall knowing. Aaron wasn't anywhere in sight. She had gone back inside the ladies room to pack her things and in about 45 seconds later came waddling out. Aaron recognized Thelma right away. When Thelma and Tom saw her, they were shocked. Here was a woman with a small kid right at one year old in one arm, eight or nine months pregnant dragging two loaded down suit cases. This had to be very difficult and it was obvious that she was in dire straits and had been sleeping in the bus station.

"Aaron, what on earth is going on here?" Thelma shouted.

Aaron began to explain, while holding her head down as if she was way too embarrassed to look Thelma in the eyes. As she talked, Tom picked up the suit cases and Thelma helped her and the little one to the car and got both she and the baby safely inside. At that very moment, Aaron had a sharp pain in her lower stomach and she let out a yell that startled both Thelma and Tom. She was beginning to have labor pains and instead of taking Aaron and the child to their apartment as they and planned, they took her directly to the emergency room at the county hospital. Aaron sighed and moaned with pain a couple of times as they rode. It appeared that she was in the early stages of delivery.

They finally reached the hospital and had an orderly bring out a wheel chair to help Aaron into the hospital's admitting area. They waited in the waiting area for over an hour. Aaron's name was called and she was wheeled back into an examining room. Once she had been seen by the doctor, they acknowledged that she was only hours away from the birth of her new baby. They took her to the maternity ward for the remainder of her labor time. Thelma and Tom stayed with her for several hours pacing the floor and discussing this situation, being careful to keep their voices down so that the baby who was curled up on top of a blanket in one of the waiting area chairs wouldn't hear them. They were eventually approached by a doctor and told that she had anywhere from six to eight more hours of labor left. The doctor told them that they should go home and get some rest and perhaps come back later since there was so much time left. So, they decided that might be a good idea since she wasn't due to deliver for several hours. They would take the baby back to their apartment to clean her up and themselves also. Both Thelma and Tom were appalled at the situation and what

Evan had done to both Aaron and her baby. They discussed how they could help her and agreed that they certainly wanted to do all they could. When they returned to their apartment, they began to clear a space for Aaron and the baby. They wanted to make her as comfortable as they could. They also wanted to be there for her to offer any assistance that she felt she would need. About four hours later, they returned to the hospital. As it turned out they were just in time for the delivery. Not thirty five minutes after they got back, she was ready to deliver!

Aaron was the brand new mother of an eight pound - two ounce bouncing baby boy! But, as she laid there, sadness took her over again. She wondered what had happened to Evan. Had he returned back to the room only to see that they had been put out? What would he do then? She had two kids now and she couldn't worry about him. He would have to take care of himself. She loved him, but he didn't trust her enough to ask for her help in solving his problem. She would have to think more about that another day.

CHAPTER FOURTEEN

TAYLOR

I was now headed for my senior prom. I was a tad bit luckier than Sidney and Aaron were. I had a hot date with one of the football stars of the high school. Brad had transferred from a high school in Knoxville. His parents had been killed in a car accident and he moved to Cincinnati to live with his grandparents who also resided in the Laurel Homes. Mrs. Puckett, his grandmother, lived in my building and we almost instantaneously became good friends. I got lucky and was able to go to what amounts to a girl's most important introduction into society with a gorgeous boy. Kelly didn't do too bad either. She was only a junior and had a date for our Senior Prom with a boy who lived very close to the Neighborhood House. He had been highly sought after during our senior year too. As for Trevor she went to the prom with the boy she was to marry right after graduation. It was a great night and one that we would remember for the rest of our lives. The days of football games , marching in front of the band, French class, and the Taft Capades were at an end. What was I going to do with my life from this point on? I was looking for a response from the government regarding the Grant that I had applied for so I could start at the University of Cincinnati in September. Not a word yet.

I was still involved with Brandon. He was treating me real nice and we had fun when we were together. I met a couple of his friends, Ned and Richard. All three of them were together most of the time, even when I was the only girl around. They were older, just like Brandon and had graduated five or six years before I did, from one of the high schools on the "Hill." Brandon had attended some years of college and gotten a good job with Proctor & Gamble. He made a pretty decent living for himself, which is why he had a brand new car. His white convertible Chrysler 300 was really classy and every time I was in it, I felt like I definitely belonged in this kind of car or maybe even better.

I was still living with my parents, and I really had to be careful how late I was staying out with Brandon. My dad was as strict as ever and still from the "old school." He felt like, as long as I was under his roof, I had to keep his rules. So, I was very careful to be back in the house before eleven o'clock, whenever we did go out. One night I threw caution to the wind and stayed out very late. After all, it was the weekend and I felt that it wouldn't be a crime. When I finally got back home, it was almost two a. m. My dad was sitting there waiting for me and he hit the ceiling! We really had a big blow out. He yelled and told me that I would have to leave his house if I ever tried that again. The next morning I called my Granddad to ask him if I could stay there with him for a while until I sorted things out. He told me I could move in on the third floor of his house, but I would have to pay him every time I got paid. I was shocked! My own family charging me to live with him. How absurd!
He said, "Taylors," he always put an "s" on everybody's name, "you have to learn how to pay your way in this world."

He also said, "Nothings free! And it is my job, since your mother and father haven't, to teach you this lesson."

I couldn't believe what I was hearing. He was making me pay. My own granddad! We agreed that it would only cost me five dollars a week, because I wasn't making that much, so I said all right. What else could I do? I moved in a week later and was finally out on my own, sort of.

Brandon and I became very close and were together more and more. Kelly met the guys and hung out with us some times too. The more we were together the more she and Richard ended up off to themselves. She and Richard started to like each other, so that was kind of nice. Ned was the only one that didn't have anyone and he used to always have something smart to say when we were out. He was a short fellow, kind of skinny and wore glasses. He wasn't ugly, but he wasn't cute either. We all acted like we were pals so Ned wouldn't feel like a third wheel.

It was in the dead of winter one Saturday evening, Brandon came by to pick me up at my Granddad's house. He and Ned sat outside and just blew the horn for me. My Granddad was also a man from the "old school" and had his carved in stone ideas on how courting or dating should go. He was really upset that Brandon didn't come to the front door, knock and ask for me in person. When he heard the horn, he hollered up the steps, "Taylors, who is that out there making all that doggone racket?"

I skipped down the steps and met him on the landing, "Oh Granddad, that's my date."

He said, "Tell that boy to come in here, you ain't going nowhere until he acts properly."

My eyes rolled back in my head, and I mumbled under my breath, "Man, these parents and grandparents get on my nerves."

I didn't realize how good the old guy could hear because he said to me, "No matter, he still has to come in here, so that you can receive him proper."

I went to the door and motioned for Brandon to come in. He motioned like he didn't want to. It was taking longer than my Granddad though it should so, he came to the door and stood beside me. When Brandon saw him standing there, he immediately got out of the car and started walking toward us.

"Good evening sir," Brandon said while extending his hand.

"Good evening," my Granddad said, while extending his hand and stepping aside in order for Brandon to step inside.

Brandon looked perplexed. When we were all inside, Brandon was standing there looking nervous. Granddad motioned for Brandon to take a seat.

Granddad said in a calm and gentle, yet serious tone, "These are the rules, whenever you come to my house to pickup Taylors for a date, you do not blow you horn for her! You get out of your car, step to the door, knock and ask for her like a gentleman, do we understand each other?"

Brandon's eyes were wide open, he looked as if he was just not sure how to take all of this, but he said, "Yes sir."

My Granddad said, "The men in this world have to learn to treat lady folk with respect and dignity."

Just at that moment, I stood up to put on my coat and Brandon rushed to my aid, in order to impress my Granddad by helping me with my coat.

Granddad said, as we were leaving out the door,

"Have a good time Taylors, and you sir, take care of my little girl!"

Brandon turned to him, looking like a little scared rabbit, and said, "I sure will, sir."

Finally, we were on our way. We pulled down to the end of the street and Brandon stopped the car momentarily and leaned over to ask me,

"What was that all about?" He kissed me on the cheek. It was almost as if he was trying desperately to get his cool back. But, I wasn't impressed.

We went to pick up the rest of the gang and proceeded to a party in Avondale. It was a very elegant affair, there was champagne being passed around along with a variation of finger foods. The music was mostly jazz which added a touch of elegance to the affair. While I was used to hearing some Aretha, James Brown or Chuck Jackson being played loudly, this was a nice change. It was held in a big house owned by someone that Brandon had known for awhile. At all the parties that I had been to, which wasn't that many, there was either very little or no food at all. There certainly wasn't this high class stuff. Brandon was introducing me to another side of Cincinnati society. He and I danced a couple of slow dances and after that he was off to the races. He must have hit on every single girl in the place. Initially, I didn't pay too much attention because we were all dancing and having a good time, but after eight or nine songs played, he was still moving around the room. I saw him with a couple of girls whispering to them as they where blushing and giggling. As he moved around the room, several of the single ladies there were flirting with him too and he was not letting the flirts get past him. He was all in their faces, which began to tick me off to no end. I watched him intently for a while. He was actually having the time of his life and hadn't given me a single thought. I took it for a while and then went over to him to interrupt. "I am ready to go," I said sarcastically and with the intention of letting that young lady know that we were together.

He looked at me in a disappointed way and said, "What's your problem?"

I told him, " I don't have a problem, it appears that you do."

He said, "Well, you're certainly being childish!"

I told him, "I'll show you how childish I can be by creating a scene if you don't take me home."

Reluctantly, he excused himself from the girl that had his full attention. He got our coats and said his good-byes to everyone. We proceeded to the car. Of course all of our friends had to leave too, because they were riding with us. I fussed and pouted all the way to the car.

He said , "I can't believe what a baby you are!"

I said, "And I can't believe what an asshole you are. If you wanted to come to the party alone, you should have."

"Well," he said, "Granddaddy's **little girl** can't take it huh?"

When he said that, without thinking, I lunged at him catching him totally off guard. The force of my full body shove knocked him down. That told me that he definitely wasn't expecting that. We started to roll down a slight knoll in the fresh snow. Everyone else was laughing at us. We tussled for a couple of minutes, not actually fighting but more like playing around. Our friends started throwing snow balls at us to demonstrate how silly they thought we were acting. When we realized what they were doing, we got to our feet and did the same thing to them. We ran, while trying to dodge the snow balls coming at us from several directions, and continued to throw at each other. It all turned into a big snow ball fight and became a ton of fun. Brandon and I forgot about how this all started and soon we were huddled together and hugging while riding along the snow covered roads to our next destination. I was falling in love! I could only hope he felt the same way. A few minutes later we were at the Sweete Shoppe near the Laurel Homes. We ran into twenty or so of the people that we knew from the old neighborhood. The juke box was red hot and blasting out the latest tunes. There were people dancing and enjoying their Saturday night. We were no different.

There were many weekends that we were all together. I felt we were getting closer and closer. I tried to call him in between the times we were together on several occasions, but his brother always answered and said he wasn't in. Brandon always called me back a few hours later with one excuse or the about why he wasn't at home. We would stay on the phone just talking for hours at a time. About a month later, he came over on a Friday night. We hadn't planned to see each other, so I wasn't expecting him. I was sitting in my room at my Granddad's house reading a book. I heard a faint noise but decided not to pay it any attention. Then, I heard it again. And again. He was throwing peebles at my bedroom window. He was determined not to let my Granddad know that he was there. When I realized that the noise wasn't going away, I got up to see what it was. I pulled back the curtains and opened the window. He looked like he had been at it for a while, because he was rubbing his hands together indicating that he was cold.

He said in a whisper, "Come down and let me in."

"Okay, give me a second," I whispered.

I tip-toed down the steps and across the living room to open the front door. He eased in and I very quietly closed the door behind him. We both snuck back across the sometimes squeaky floor and went up to my bedroom. We talked and talked keeping our voices to a low pitch. My Granddad and Grandma were on the ground level of the house and we were on the third level, so they didn't hear a thing. After a while, Brandon moved over to the foot of my bed, where I was sitting. He told me that he thought I was so pretty and he took my hand and started to kiss it. I felt uncomfortable because I had never been alone with a boy before. Before I realized it we began to kiss. He was French kissing me and man did it feel good. These kisses were long and deep. I could tell he was experienced at this. This was all brand new to me and so far, I liked it. He grabbed a towel from the folded laundry in the chair, which was at the left of my bed and spread it out on the bed, all in one motion as he continued to kiss me. His hands started to caress my body. I was getting worked up unlike anything I had ever imagined! Would this end up being my first time? Were we too involved to back out now? How I wanted him...oh how I wanted him. He very expertly unbuttoned my blouse and slipped it off, while still kissing me. It was as if his lips were covering a complete half of my face. I felt his penis poking me in the side as we lay there. The next thing I knew we were both almost naked and he was on top of me. I felt his penis enter my private and it hurt like hell! He continued to thrust himself in, deeper and deeper. I muffled a soft cry. How could people enjoy this pain? What could make people want to do this over and over again? All of the hot passion that I felt at first was over the moment he put his penis inside me and began to pump at a feverish pace. I wanted this over! I was disgusted and wanted this over now! About thirty seconds later, he rolled over off of me, gasping for air. He sounded like he had been running a marathon. He was sweating like a pig! I, on the other hand was disgusted and felt wet and dirty. There was all of this stuff coming from my private area, I could feel it oozing out and all I wanted to do was take a long hot bath and pretend that this night never happened. He got up, wiped himself off with a tissue from my vanity and got dressed.

He said, "Are you all right?"

I said, "I don't know," as I covered myself with the towel.

"That wasn't what I expected at all." And, at this time, I was more embarrassed than anything.

He said, "You will enjoyed it more the next time."

I thought to myself, "Like there will be a next time!"

He said, "The first time for girls is always like this. It hurts you because you were a virgin. But, I busted your cherry and now you are a woman." He said that as if with bragging rights. Who the hell does he think he is??

"My cherry, what the hell does that mean?" I asked.

"It sounds like you have done this a lot."

He told me that he had been around, but that he was very selective. After all he was eight years older than I was. When I did get up and go to the bathroom, which was in the main floor of the house, I let him out and went to clean myself up. When I sat on the toilet, I noticed that I was bleeding along with that other stuff. It frightened me, but I remembered what Brandon told me. He said that every girl has a cherry before she has sex. I put two and two together and realized that is what the blood meant. That was my cherry. I wonder why my mom never told me about this stuff? I took a bath and crept back upstairs to crawl into bed. Boy, what a night!

A few weeks passed and I saw him a couple of times. I tried to call him four times and his brother always answered the telephone. This was becoming more and more peculiar to me. Why didn't he ever answer the telephone? Did he really live there? Something was really off, but I couldn't figure it all out. I decided to go over to their apartment and just wait there for awhile just to see what I could see. When I got there I sat down across the street to observe the traffic in and out of the building. People were coming and going as they would normally do and of course, no Brandon. About forty five minutes later, I saw Brandon pull up to the front of the building with a dark skinned sort of average looking lady in the front seat sitting up close to him. She was holding a baby in her arms. Brandon proceeded to get out of the car and seemed to be giving her an explanation of his plans and the lady stayed there to wait. He went inside and came out about ten minutes later. I walked over to the car as he was coming out. Before I could get within twenty feet of him he noticed me crossing the street headed toward him and he jumped in the car and sped off. What in the hell was that all about? Who was that lady with the baby and why wouldn't he acknowledge me? It was all starting to come together now. He didn't live there. He just stopped by there to pick up his messages. That lady must have been his wife! All sort of things started running through my mind. What a fool I have been!

By now, I was getting over the pain of that dreadful night, but I was beginning to feel strange. I was getting sick in the morning with the smell of my grandmother's cooking filling the air every morning. This had never happened before, but I calmly dismissed it and continued on with my daily routine.

It was time for me to start at the University of Cincinnati. My Pell Grant hadn't come through for the first quarter but it arrived the third day of the second quarter, finally I was all set! That was great because I needed to do something to keep my mind off of Brandon and that whole situation. Starting college was very exciting. I was becoming a woman in more than just one way! As I began my classes, I was in for a real shock about college. Things were so very different than they were at Taft. My classes where very difficult. I should have paid more attention to my math, history and English classes in high school. Learning to add, subtract, multiply and divide wasn't all that I needed in college. And, my reading level was far below that of some of the other freshmen. But, I made a pledge to myself that no matter what it took, I was going to graduate college, because I had to do well so I wouldn't have to live in the projects as an adult. I planned to get a good job and have a big house that sat way back on a hill with all the trimmings. This was what it took and I wouldn't settle for less so, even if I had to study everyday and night, I was determined to make it happen!

Forty-five days into college, I realized was pregnant! I missed my period and I just knew that the episodes with the morning sickness while smelling my Grandmother's cooking was the evidence. I was sick! Why did I have to run into someone like Brandon. A liar who was married and already had a baby. I knew I had a couple of choices. I could either quit school now or go for as long as I could and then drop out. I decided to try and make it four more months. This way I could have a half year on the books and once the baby was born, I could go back. My mom and dad would be heart broken . I'm real glad that Bobby wasn't here. He'd kill me for sure.

I got a hold of Brandon through his brother and told him of the news. He was very distant and non committal about the whole thing. We had two or three conversations about it on the telephone over a three week period. During one of the conversations, he had the nerve to ask me if I had been with anyone else. That bastard! He knew that he was my first and that I wasn't that kind of girl. I really resented he accusation! I was obstinate about the whole situation and convinced myself not to fall into a depressed state about it. Somehow I would make it through all of this, I just had to.

Day in and day out, I attended my classes. I threw myself into it too. I wanted to get all I could out of the time I had. Two months of school went by and I started to show just a little bit. Going from an eighteen inch waistline to a twenty four inch waist in a matter of nine and a half weeks was a real downer for me. My mother made sure I had larger clothes to camouflage my condition as much as I could, while I continued in college. It would have been real embarrassing if any of the kids at school knew what was going on with me. There were only a handful of Negro students at the University of Cincinnati, so, any peculiarities about any one of the four of us would be noticed immediately. At the end of the semester, I informed my counselor, who was a young white woman, that I would be leaving the University to attend Ohio State in the spring. She asked me why the sudden desire to change? I made up some idiotic excuses and hoped my words would be enough to convince her. As it turned out, the excuses I gave did convince her, as she tried to talk me out of leaving giving me all kinds of reasons, but the main one being that I would be away from my family. What did she know about Negroes and their families? She was fishing for anything to find out the real reason for my sudden decision and kept trying to keep me there. I made some other lame excuses and couldn't wait to get out of her office. After about ten more minutes of meaningless conversation, she stood up and walked me to the door. Thank God, I was out of there.

I moved back in with my parents, so that my mom and dad could help me through this situation. Mom was upset about the entire thing, but clearly disgusted about Brandon's attitude and wanted to see him face to face to discuss his plans for me and the baby. It took her close to three weeks to even get in touch with him. When she did, she wasn't very pleasant during their conversation. She told him that she wasn't going to accept his nonchalant attitude and that she wanted to meet with him in the next few days to discuss his plans. When she hung up the phone, she was furious!

She said, "I can't wait to see that bastard! He has met his match now!"

A few days later, I responded to a knock on the door. He finally came over to our apartment. I opened the door not knowing it was him and as I opened the door the embarrassment that I felt was indescribable. I stepped aside as he stepped in. We didn't exchange one word. The silence was interrupted by my mother entering the room. She immediately jumped on him to find out what his plans were. He was very noncommittal the same way he was on the telephone and my mother read him the riot act.

She said, "You <u>will</u> take care of this baby!"

He said sarcastically, "If it is mine, I plan to."

I jumped into the conversation, "What do you mean, if it is yours? How could you be so heartless?" By this time I was an emotional wreck.

He said, "How do I know that it's mine?"

My mother interrupted, "You <u>will</u> also take her to the doctor on a timely basis, so that to she can see about herself."

His attention turned from me to her.

He said, "I don't have time now."

She said, "You make time!"

She then said, "I don't want to have to come looking for you. This is the last warning that you'll get. This is as much your responsibility as it is hers and you <u>**will**</u> own up to it!"

He looked real stupid as he just stood there. He looked at me sitting there and turned to walk away. What a real live bastard, I thought. After all the fun, all the time we spent together. All the chasing he did to get my attention. I must have only been a conquest to him. I was hurt, ashamed, embarrassed and now pregnant. My thoughts were to call his wife to let her know, but I felt that in time, he'll get his.

In the weeks that passed I spent a lot of time reading and watching television. I was getting hooked on the daytime soap operas, *Peyton Place* and other television programs at night. *Peyton Place* was a weekly television show that was very popular during the mid-sixties. I was really into it. The Harringtons, the main characters on the show, were rich white people with two very handsome sons one of whom was named Rodney Harrington. He was a nice, respectful, well bred, highly educated young man with a lot of style and class. I thought if I have a boy, I'd name him Rodney. I was at home everyday not working and not going out because I was much too big and miserable.
The next few months were horrible. I was getting so big that I couldn't even wear any of my own shoes. My ankles and feet looked like that of an elephant. Whenever I did go out to the store or to the doctor, I wore my dad's house shoes because they were the only ones that I could comfortably fit. Brandon came around a few times to take me to see the doctor, but most of the time my dad took me. By this time I really despised Brandon and wanted little or no connection with him. I thought he was the lowest of the low. Whenever I was in his presence, I was very quite. As a matter of fact I didn't even want to look at him.

Bobby came home from the army on leave. When he walked in the front door, I was sitting on the couch watching television. He demanded that I get up to hug him. When I stood up, he saw my stomach. He was really ticked to see me in this condition. He ranted and raved for well over an hour. He wanted to go

find Brandon to kick his ass, as he put it. Then he ranted and raved some more. He said, "This would never have happened if I hadn't gone to the service!"
I told him, "Bobby, you can't always be with me."
He hugged me tight and seemed to calm down a bit.

Later, he thought better of it all after he settled down a little more. Thank God he wasn't as wild now as he was when he left to go to the Army. I was so glad that he was back. I hadn't realized how much I would miss him before he left. As much as we had argued when we were younger, we were now getting along so much better.

Bobby and two of his friends, which I had seen him with off and on over the years, came to the apartment one afternoon shortly after he got back home. One of the boys was Roy and the other Randy. Roy was a boy from the Avondale neighborhood. He was real wild, like Bobby which is probably why they got along so well. Roy had a reputation for fighting all the time and had started boxing when he was younger. He had won a Golden Gloves title twice. He was also into playing semi-pro football with a local team. He was real good at it too. Randy and Roy were just a couple of the older boys that I would see from time to time with Bobby in the Laurel Homes. Roy started coming around trying to talk to me even while I was pregnant with Brandon's baby. We would sit and talk and talk and talk. I found out in the next few weeks, several very interesting things about him. He confessed that he had always had feelings for me but because of Bobby, he wasn't permitted to say anything to me. He told me that I was the prettiest girl that he had ever seen and that he would marry me with no thoughts of the baby that I was carrying which was his or not.

Eighteen days later Bobby left to go back to the army. But before he did, he gave me his blessing on Roy. He said that he was comfortable with Roy and the fact that he was positive that Roy would take care of and look out for me. So,

Roy and I became an item. I felt safe with him even though I didn't love him. Roy had a good job at General Electric as a welder on the assembly line. He could provide for me and my baby. We spent a lot of time together doing nothing fancy, just keeping each other company. He was very gentle and considerate. In the weeks that came he took me over to meet his family. His mother, Miss Constance, worked keeping house for some white folks in Amberly Village and his dad was a laborer at a welding plant which made chassis for cars at General Motors. His dad drank a lot of liquor and was very drunk when I first met him. He seemed harmless enough while he continually told me how pretty I was. They accepted me, pregnant and all. After about four months, we were married with little fanfare in his older sister's house. I marched down her long staircase to my waiting groom in front of thirty family members and friends. It was a nice and simple affair .

We moved to an apartment in Avondale which Roy had already gotten ready for us. Shortly afterwards, I went into labor and was rushed to Bethesda Hospital to have my baby. I was in labor for eighteen hours and finally delivered my baby. As it turned out, I had a beautiful baby boy and I did name him Rodney. Of course, Brandon was no where around and didn't do a thing to assist in the support of my son. I heard that he and his wife became even closer than before. They already had a child, Andrea who was 4 years old when Rodney was born. So, I was now a mother and a married woman. Life had a slew of surprises, but these that I was thrust into, where two big surprises that I just wasn't ready for.

CHAPTER FIFTEEN

Bobby went to boot camp at Fort Brag in North Carolina. He and I sat around the apartment during his days at home talking about what it was like. He had turned out to be a young man that I had no idea had so much going on inside of him. I often thought about him while he was away and wondered what he was running from during the years that we were young kids. This talk gave me an opportunity to try and get inside him. I wanted to know more about the young man that watched out for and protected me so closely. Was it that he was really angry or scared? We spoke about his experiences in the service and the fact that he was afraid to go to his next post. He had heard that a lot of young men had been killed in the war that was happening so far away. He knew that when he returned to his unit after his leave, he would be shipped out to some training fields, a short distance from Viet Nam. That is where all of the devastation was and I became fearful for him. I thought that I hadn't had a real chance to get to know him since we never spent any real time together in our earlier years. How could you spend years in a little apartment, even sleeping in the same bedroom with someone and never really get to know them? It was as if we were living on separate planets then. I was grateful for this chance now. He told me some of the stories that gave me a good idea what he had been through since he left Cincinnati. When he first joined the Army he was in the Artillery Division, where he learned to shoot heavy field guns. One morning while they were running through their daily drills to get them prepared for war, an Airborne officer came through the area and offered an opportunity to a few of the soldiers to come with him in order to join the paratrooper unit. Bobby was one of the Negro boys that raised their hands and he along with seven others were whisked off to another section of the army located on the same base. Since the military had been integrated in the early fifties, he was among both Negro and white soldiers to participate in this operation. When he left Cincinnati, everything was still segregated. It wasn't possible for any Negroes to even eat at the same lunch counter as white people, but in the armed services they could fight and even die together. This was fucked up to him. Bobby had no idea what he had committed himself to by raising his hand to join the paratroopers. The next thing he knew he was in an aircraft and they were teaching him to jump. In a few weeks, he had passed all the training and tests and had become a paratrooper.

Less than a month later he and his company were shipped off to Ben Wah in the Ashaw Valley in Viet Nam. Each day their unit penetrated further into that area and crept closer and closer toward the fighting. It took almost two months of advancing to get to the real action. When they arrived in the middle of it all, there were companies on the ground advancing toward the enemy and war planes flying overhead. All were fully engaged in the fighting. The battles were fierce and after days of gun fire and bombs, they were run completely out of there on the morning of the twelfth day. A friend of Bobby's, Curtis Jackson from Indianapolis,

Indiana was blown to bits just 30 yards from him. This shook Bobby up, but all of them had to keep on going or suffer the same fate as Curtis.

As the twelfth day progressed, Bobby got hit by some shrapnel in his tail bone. He was rushed from the battlefront to the field hospital. Little did he know that this shrapnel would lead to almost two years in the hospital. In the hospital, the operation to remove the shrapnel was painful and the wound took a long time to heal. Bobby was bedridden for eight weeks. While he was recuperating from the operation, he had a major attack in his right knee that was unexplainable. His knee became swollen and very tender. The doctors had no medical explanation for what was happening to him. They ran all sort of tests to try and diagnose the situation. They ran even more tests but were unable to come up with a diagnosis. The pain medication that Bobby was given only cut the pain down, it was not strong enough to stop the pain completely. The episode that he experienced eventually went away. Bobby was scheduled to be released fifteen weeks after his surgery. Three days before his release he had another episode of the tenderness, swelling and pain in his left elbow. The doctors were very perplexed. These symptoms were something that they had never seen before and knew absolutely nothing about. They began to research all the medical possibilities. While they researched, Bobby stayed in the hospital. Month after month, they tested him and did research. Eventually, after seven months had come and gone and after many consultations between Bobby's doctors and other medical professionals around the country, reviewing his symptoms, they realized that there were other Negro patients in the country experiencing the same symptoms. These were actually the early stages of a rare blood disease. Bobby had sickle cell anemia.

CHAPTER SIXTEEN

Marriage was hard for us. Roy was still very wild and had a bad habit of drinking much too much. He was a really decent guy though and tried to make me content. He was always right on me, no matter where I turned. I truly believe that he loved me but he was too close sometimes. We were home one evening a couple of months later, enjoying being parents when I first felt another twinge of morning sickness again. A huge wave of nausea came over me, I must have looked green in the face. I wasn't about to let it pass like I did when I was at my Granddad's house. As soon as it passed, I mentioned it to Roy. He said it was probably nothing, maybe something we had for dinner.

He said, "You know how finicky you are about food."

The next day, I didn't have the feeling again, so I went on about my business. My period came on schedule, so I just knew I was home free. Five weeks later, no period. I went to my gynecologist just to be sure. Low and behold, I was pregnant again! This was much too much for me! Even though abortions were illegal, that was the first thing that I thought of. I decided that I was going to get one. I couldn't see having another baby. Me with two kids? Roy and I talked about the abortion, but he was definitely against it. A few days passed and I kept on him about the abortion. He was afraid that something might happen to me. He was so protective of me, sometimes so much that it made me uncomfortable, but I convinced him that it would be all right. I finally talked him into it, or so I thought. Several days later, he took me to a doctor in Lincoln Heights. He had heard, he said, through the grapevine that this doctor had a new method of abortions, one where he gave the women a shot and the shot would automatically dissolve the fetus. When we arrived, we walked into a waiting room full of young and older women. The look on all our faces was basically the same. We had the look of deer caught in the headlights of an automobile. Most of the young women appeared to be about my age and had obviously gotten caught up in the same situation. We sat there with Roy's arm around my shoulders. When my name was called after about an hour, I went into the inner office. Ten minutes later, the doctor came in to see me.

He said, "How are you today?" In the same breath he said, "Are you sure you want to do this?"

I said, "I..."

Before I could answer how I was, he had already asked another question and I whispered, "Yes, I am sure."

He took my arm, held it tight right under my left armpit and shot me in the arm near my shoulder area with a long needle filled with a solution. That shot hurt like hell. But, I thought, it would be worth it. At least now no more babies.

He then stood up quickly and said, "Good luck," as he turned to walk out of the office.

I said to him, "Is that it, is it over?"

He didn't say a word, but hurried out of the door.

Well so much for his bedside manner.

I stood up feeling dazed and confused and made my way out of the examining room. I slowly walked back into the outer office, as Roy stood up to escort me to our car. We walked arm in arm. There wasn't too much said as we rode along. Finally the silence was broken.

"Are you okay?" he asked.

"Sure, I'm okay," I whispered. "I'm a little weak but I'm okay."

When we got home, Roy help me along as he walked with me into our apartment. He helped me to undress as he put me to bed.

He leaned over to kiss me on the cheek and then said, "I love you."

He also said, "I'll be back in a little while honey, get some rest. I'm going to get Rodney."

A couple of seconds later, I heard the door close as I drifted off to sleep. I must have slept for a long time, at least three hours, because it was getting dark when I was awakened by Rodney running to me calling out 'mommy, mommy,' as toddlers do. I scooped him up and squeezed him holding him very close to me. I couldn't help but to wonder, did I do the right thing about the baby that was inside me?

The next day and a half when I felt, according to what the doctor told me, that things should be getting better, I was having sweating spells, one right after the other. I wondered what in the world was going on? This lasted for two weeks off and on, then they went away. Two weeks later, I fully expected to see my period, but never did. This was real strange to me, but I again dismissed it to the effects of the shot. Maybe my body was trying to get back on its regular cycle. Maybe this was appropriate for the type of shot I got. I just didn't know. Surely, that doctor knew what he was doing. At least I wasn't having those God awful sweating spells. Perhaps it would take longer than even the doctor thought. Maybe it was a different amount of time for each of his patients.

My breast became heavy, just like they did when I was pregnant with Rodney. I even started having morning sickness again too. And at last, a little more then seven weeks later, I realized that I was still pregnant. I was heartbroken! What had happened to me? What was the shot that I took? I spoke to several other girls about that doctor and found out that this particular doctor gave women vitamin shots instead of abortions. He was actually making each of our bodies stronger, so that there was no chance of my miscarrying. I was highly pissed. The doctor had deceived me and Roy was obviously in on this deceit. I couldn't prove it, but I know Roy had to be in on it! He was so in love with me and wanted me to have his baby. When I think back to his face when I first mentioned the abortion, he had to have known all along what he wanted to do. He knew about this Doctor. That's what took him so long to take me to a doctor. He wanted to make sure that this pregnancy happened. It was his way of making sure I stayed with him. I stayed angry for quite a while. I calculated the time frame of the pregnancy and it was too late to have the abortion. Then I thought, "What's the use? There's nothing I can do about it now." I finally accepted the fact that I was actually going to have another baby.

The months moved along slowly. Roy was still drinking and laying off from work too. All too often he'd come in from a drinking binge wanting to have sex while trying to get me in the mood by rubbing on me all over. It was sickening. I thought to myself on many occasions that this was the reason that I was in this condition anyway.

I got just as big with this pregnancy as I was with the first one but this time when I was rushed to the hospital, I had to have an emergency c-section. The baby was much too big to pass throughout my pelvic area. The doctors told my parents and Roy that this baby almost paralyzed me. At the end of my second pregnancy, I had two boys. They were both so adorable. We named the new baby after his father Roy. I pleaded with him to stop drinking . He told me that he would and that only lasted for a month or so then he was right back at it again. This went on for months. My life was becoming more and more boring as the days passed. I had nothing to look forward too but changing diapers and fixing formulas. It was clearly up to me to make a change in my drab existence. It was time for me to start thinking about what I wanted to do. I wanted to either go back to school or go to work. Of course, being me, I wanted to do it all, so I tried. My parents helped out as much as possible. I still had my government grant and decided to reapply at the University of Cincinnati. I didn't want to tell Roy until it was all done, so I filed the paperwork and waited. Each day I checked the mailbox for a response. I knew I had to retrieve the paperwork before Roy got home, so every afternoon, I was in the doorway when the mailman walked his route down our street. A few weeks later, there it was, I got the paperwork. I had been accepted! I simply couldn't stop smiling! I cooked a special meal and had it all laid out when Roy came through the door. About forty five minutes after I had finished everything I took a shower and got myself all dolled up and was there waiting for him when he walked in the door. He smiled and told me how pretty I looked and mentioned, "Something sure smells good." I told him to get relaxed and come on to the dinner table. While we were having dinner, I broke the news to Roy. At first he didn't say a word. Then he looked at me and said, "This isn't enough for you is it?"

He was kind of angry that I had kept the whole thing from him. He ranted and raved about me being an ingrate and the little regard I showed. He brought up the fact that he worked to keep a roof over our heads and that what he was doing wasn't enough for me. I tried to explain to him that I needed more and I wanted to help us get to where we were going. I told him that I had never been the type of woman who could just sit at home and have a house full of kids. He got up and stormed out of the house. I was sorry if I had gone about this in a way that was unacceptable to Roy, but I was doing what I had to do for me. Roy came back after midnight as drunk as he could be. Naturally, as he fell into bed he wanted to have sex, but I couldn't stand the smell of the liquor and I fought him off. He was in no condition to fight, so with my last major push he fell off to sleep and I was relieved.

The spring school session was about to begin. I had worked out plans on leaving my boys with mom and dad during the day and some evenings. I needed to take a part time job to help Roy make ends meet. As difficult as it was, I was able to go to school for the next year. It was extremely hard on everybody though. After that amount of time, I was becoming worn down and it had created a strain on my family, my marriage and my health. I eventually had to quit school. In the weeks ahead, I looked for a full time job and finally got one with Cincinnati Bell as an operator. As I got settled into my new job at Cincinnati Bell, I began being a wife and mother.

Things were tight for Roy and I with two kids even though we were both working. I had the entry level job as an operator, but it wasn't paying much money. I knew I could make more as I tried to move along in the levels of the phone company, but that would take time. We had to look for a sitter for the kids while we worked because now we both knew that we had imposed as much as we should on my parents. We muddled through it working together.

It was all working out and before we knew it, we realized that two years had passed. The boys were as cute as little buttons. They were so close together and looked so much like each other that I dressed them like twins. Everywhere we went, everyone made googly eyes at them thinking that they were indeed twins. When Roy and I were alone at home with the kids they wanted to always be around Roy. They really loved their dad. They hung on him every chance they got. As the weeks and months passed by, it was getting to the point that I was beginning to get bored

Roy was working a lot of overtime. He was also still having beers with the guys and shooting pool and hanging out at the gym and I was in the house during most of it. In between working eight hours, running behind the boys, cleaning and so on, I spent a lot of time on the phone talking with my friends. All I heard was every detail about their weekends and about this guy and that guy. They also did this and that. They were partying animals and here I was stuck in the house with my little kings all the time. If it wasn't work, it was being a wife and mother. This was a lot of responsibility for someone so young. Although I loved them, it was difficult being so young and not really having a lot of time to be a young adult and able to go out and party. I moved from my mom and dad's house to my Granddad's house and then to this apartment with my husband with no time for myself and on my own. I felt trapped and smothered, even though I loved my family. It was a feeling that I couldn't explain. I knew that no one would understand anyway, so why should I even bother.

PART II

Kelly was a senior at Taft. It was all the same for her. She was left without any of the 'Sisters' at school so she pal'd around with any and everyone to muddled through. She wasn't seeing anyone special, she was just enjoying herself one day at a time. We still spent as much time together as possible although things were changing for me. Most of the time we had spent together recently was over the telephone. Kelly had been out to our apartment a couple of Saturdays before but she had a lot going on in school and had to stay close by. Her main objective was to do all she could so she could graduate and be out on her own.

Two of my other girlfriends called me on a Thursday night to ask me if I could get a sitter for Friday. It was beautiful outside and I knew Roy wouldn't be at home until late anyway. They invited me to go to a party with them in Avondale. These were two people that I met at the new sitter's house. Their kids were there everyday with mine. I called my mother to see if she could look out for the boys Friday night.

I greeted her in a cheerful manner, "Hi mom."

"Hi baby," she responded.

"Can you watch the kids for me tomorrow night? I want to go out for a while," I half pleaded.

"No problem, I'll be here tomorrow night, but you have to come back for them tomorrow night, because your dad and I have an early engagement on Saturday morning," she replied.

"Okay, I will get them about midnight, if that is okay."

"That'll be okay," she answered.

"I love you mom and tell dad that I love him too, okay?" I uttered.

I didn't mention it to Roy because by the time he came in the rest of us were asleep. When I got up the next day to get ready for work, I dressed the boys and had breakfast. Roy was still sleeping. He smelled like liquor. I guess he stopped off to have a few before he came home last night. I kissed him on the cheek and left to take the boys to the sitter as usual. I scampered down the hill to the bus stop and went off to work. I was glad to be getting out of the apartment for a while, so I jumped at the chance with whatever demands that my mom placed on our agreement. All I was doing lately was working, changing diapers, cooking and having sex three to four times a week, whether I wanted to or not. So to get out would be really, really nice.

Abegayle and Charlene picked me up about six thirty that evening. We drove to my parents apartment and dropped off the boys. We rode along hooping it up as they were bringing me up to date on the night. We were on our way! It was about a twenty minute drive to get to the party. Things had changed drastically from the days when Jay sent his fine, long, sleek Cadillacs for us when we were in the *projects* No longer was there any excitement in the air. I was grasping for a chance to get out and from under this feeling of complete domesticity. Even though the music was playing in the background and we were as chatty as ever, there was definitely something missing. We drove up to the four story apartment building on Reading Road where the party was being held. There were thirty or so people standing outside of the building in small groups talking. We parked the car and started around the corner toward the entrance way. We went in, climbed the stairs to the third floor and knocked on the door. When a young man opened the door, it became obvious that this was where it was happening. The music sounded good. Couples were dancing and the room was filled with good looking men all standing around the perimeter of the room! We got in the groove too and within a couple of minutes, we were having a good time.

I danced four records straight, after which, I went to find a place to cool off. I hadn't danced like that since high school days. Everyone knew I loved to dance. It was really fun to see some of the folks from the old neighborhood and it was such a change from the past year and a half. I sat down out of the way of the main stream of traffic to catch my breath. I had only been sitting there for thirty seconds when I felt the presence of someone else in the immediate area. I turned my head to investigate and as I turned, I looked into the face of the most handsome young man I had ever seen.

He said, "I've been watching you from the moment you and your friends walked in, you are beautiful and you can really dance!"

I turned my body all the way toward him and I said, "Oh really?"

I thought to myself, what a stupid thing to say.

He said as he smiled, "What's you name?"

I responded, while grinning and unaware that I was, "Taylor, what's yours?"

"They call me Slim," he said as he slid down to sit next to me.

He was too close for comfort, after all I didn't even know this guy. He smelled clean and fresh, like he just showered and put on after shave lotion. He started the conversation by asking what part of the city I lived in. And from that point on something about him made me feel really comfortable talking to him. As we listened to the records in the background we sat there mainly chit chatting. We must have talked about twenty minutes, when Abegayle rushed into the area where we were sitting and said,

"Taylor, Roy is outside asking if anyone has seen you and he looks mad as hell!"

I jumped up and made my way to the door and started down the steps.

Slim was right behind me saying, "Who is Roy? Do you want me to handle this?"

"No, stay out of this!" I yelled.

As I pushed through the outer doors I ran to the street. I saw Roy standing there boiling!

"What in the hell you doing here?"

"Get in the car!" he shouted.

Slim came running after me and before I could say a word to him Slim stepped up to Roy and said, "Man, she's with me!"

And what did he say that for! Roy sucker punched him and Slim went to his knees. When Slim caught his breath, he didn't realize that he was bleeding. He started to get up and seconds later made his way to Roy again, Roy brought out a pistol and pointed it at Slim and said,

"Back off, motherfucker, this is my wife!"

I screamed and said, "Roy what in the hell are you doing?

You couldn't possibly understand that there is nothing going on here," I said!

Roy shoved me into the car on the driver side and slid in after me. I fought him to get out. This was crazy, I wasn't doing anything, nothing at all. He pinned me down and put the gun to my head and he said with fear in his voice,

"I love you and you will never leave me, not for no one, do you hear me?

I have big plans for us and our future and we have to stay together!"
I looked up at him and then glanced out the car window. I saw Abegayle and
Charlene right at the door trying to see what was happening. By this time, there
was a crowd of at least a hundred people watching the whole thing. I was
thoroughly embarrassed. Roy started the car, put it in gear and drove off.
Everyone watched as we passed them. Slim was just getting his head clear. I
really hoped he would be okay.

Roy drove like a bat out of hell back to our apartment. Words were at a
minimum. When we got home, I reminded Roy that I promised my mother I
would stop by and pick up the boys. He put his key in the lock to let me in the
apartment, then left to go get them. Roy was all right as long as I was in the
house with the kids. We never discussed the incident again, but I knew that this
would never work From that point on, I was afraid of him and started making
plans to leave. I didn't know when or how but I knew I had to do it.

We ended up staying together two more years. It became harder than I
thought to leave. I didn't want to go back to my mom and dad's and I couldn't
afford to be out on my own with the boys, so I stayed. Following the events of
that night Roy started drinking more and more. The nights when he came home
from work, he reeked of liquor. He would crawl on me to try to have sex and the
smell of his breath would be so foul, it was unbearable and would turn me off. I
still cared a great deal for him, especially the fact that he was so nice to me and
married me with Brandon's baby. But I wondered if that was enough for me to
stay with him?

One Saturday a couple of years later, after playing in one of his semi-pro
football games, Roy came home with his knee hurting, so much so that he could
hardly walk. I put an ice pack on it which he said soothed it enough for the

180

moment. On Monday we made an appointment to see his doctor. We went to the doctor, who was assigned to all of the employees of Fisher Body. We had a long wait. After about two hours we were escorted into the office. Roy hobbled in and fell back on the examining table, letting out a big sigh. The doctor came in a few minutes later. He read Roy's chart and asked him to move his leg back and forth. It was quite painful to Roy. It was discovered that Roy's knee was slipping out of place, which is what was causing the pain. Dr. Raymond was concerned that Roy's knee would have to be operated on sooner or later. The doctor said that as long as Roy was involved in strenuous activities, he would have trouble with this knee. Roy wasn't for having an operation anytime soon, so he put it off.

In a few days Roy was feeling better and could go back to work. For five weeks, he did not play ball or box or anything regarding sports, so he started becoming restless. Eventually he eased back into it and after practicing for a couple of weeks, he was himself again.

Another semi-pro game was coming up and Roy wanted me and the boys to be a part of the audience, so we got dressed and rode with him to the football field. It was rumored that some pro football scouts would be there and could be selecting some of the players for the pros, if they were good enough. This brought many spectators out to see the game. All the players were excited about their possibilities and planned to lay a mean one on the opposing team.

The game got underway and from the first whistle, the hits were hard! They were really playing like there was no tomorrow. Our team was showing their stuff. They looked great. Roy was playing wide receiver and had gotten a touch down. On the first play of the second quarter, Roy took a hit that all of us heard. The officials halted the game and a stretcher was brought out on the field.

Roy was being carried off the field to a waiting ambulance.

I hustled down the steps with the boys to the area where he was.

When I got to him he looked like he was in an incredible amount of pain.

"Don't worry honey," I said, "I will follow the ambulance in the car and meet you at the hospital."

He looked up at me with a very odd look in his eyes, one that I couldn't read.

I became very upset about it but had to shake it off and do what I had to do. We arrived at the hospital and the nurses wheeled him up to the desk. I walked in right behind them and said "I am his wife, I will provide you with the information that you need. Then they put him in an examining room. I gave the desk all of the information about Roy. Because I had the boys with me, I wasn't able to be in the examining room with Roy. But the nurses kept me informed. After several x-rays it was determined that his knee was torn to shreds and they had to rebuild it, so he was admitted. We thought it would be a relatively simple procedure and that we would all be at home in a week or so with Roy resting while his knee was healing. We were relieved.

The operation was a success! But, Roy began to have other unrelated symptoms that the doctors were very perplexed about. After a battery of additional tests, it was determined that Roy had bone cancer. When the knee was cut on to get it back in shape, apparently the air opened up his system and the cancer started to spread rapidly through his body. The doctors could only guarantee us that he had less than two months to live, because it was so advanced. I was in shock, there is no way that Roy was going to die. How could this be? All my thoughts about leaving him left me. He was the person that saved me from being pregnant with Brandon's baby and with no questions asked married me and made a home for me. How could I be so selfish? I felt very bad about it all. But right now wasn't about me, it was about Roy.

Both our parents came to the hospital to be with us. All our family members came too. I was numb, as a matter of fact, I couldn't remember most of what was happening around me. We all got together and made a collective decision that we wouldn't let him know about his condition, so he could live his final days out without this worry. More and more frequently he got the pain shots that would enable him to bare the awful pain he was enduring. The shots had him sleeping and sleeping. He would often wake for only minutes at a time, only to ask me when he was getting out of there and going home.

I would always tell him "Soon, honey, soon."

My heart was breaking. Here he was twenty six years old and I was twenty-three and I was becoming a widow. I wished I had more time with him. I would take all the liquor'd nights now , if I only could. This was a nightmare. But no matter what, I was by his side night and day.

As the days went by he was wasting away to practically nothing. I simply couldn't believe it. Day after day, we all stayed by his side. It was the most difficult thing that I had ever thought about having to do.

Three weeks later, Roy died. I was in shock about all of this. I was being led around in a daze to take care of the details by my family and the 'Sisters' because I couldn't shake all that had happened. I simply couldn't function on my own. I didn't even know how the 'Sisters' found out because I couldn't remember calling them but they were there. I barely remembered getting dressed for the service and getting to the church. That day the church, St. Timothy's on Reading Road, was filled to capacity. There were even people standing on the outside of the church, because they couldn't get inside. He was well liked and respected. I slightly remember walking up to the casket and looking down at him thanking him for loving me. I bent over to give him a kiss goodbye. Then I walked back to the front pew and slumped down as I took my seat. While we were sitting there in front of his casket, Rodney pulled at me while pointing to the casket and asked me, "Mommy, why is Daddy laying in that funny bed?" I broke down. I must have blacked out, because the next thing I knew we were riding along in the limousine, leading a caravan of sixty-five or more cars to the burial site at Spring Grove. After the graveside service, everyone, I mean everyone returned to Roy's sister, Ivene's house to fellowship with the family. She was the only one of her family that had a house big enough to accommodate a group of this magnitude. There was food for days and enough people in and out that you'd want to stop counting after a while.

For weeks, I knew I would never be the same. My family moved my furniture out of our apartment, because I told both our families I knew I couldn't stay there. Roy had left me with financial assistance social security payments for the kids, so I went on a leave from the phone company. I had to take some time to get my self together. I moved back to my mom and dad's until I could figure out what was next.

CHAPTER SEVENTEEN

It took me quite some time to get back to my right mind. I just couldn't believe that Roy was dead. It was too much, really too much to bear. I was living with a black cloud over my head for almost a year. Eventually, I went back to work only to find that everyone walked on egg shells and was almost too nice to me. They were very cautious about every little word they said to me. Believe it or not, this got on my nerves more than if they would have acted normally. After a couple of weeks, Clairice, a girl that I had had lunch with just about everyday before all this happened, told me that everyone was saying that it was as if I had a chip on my shoulder. I didn't realize it, so I thanked her for telling me and tried to be more open and receptive to everyone around me. I made a conscious effort to remember how I treated people. As time passed on I became a little more like my old self, but I wondered if I would ever be the same? Several young men tried to take me out, but I had no interest in that. The last thing that I wanted was another relationship. Somehow, I didn't feel that my relationship with Roy was finished. I had many conversations with Reverend James. He was the pastor of

Mt. Moriah, our family church. He tried, as much as he could, to help me through this period. He had known me since I was born, and I trusted him. My parents knew that I needed counseling and insisted that I continue these sessions. As long as I was living with them, I couldn't say no. And besides, they were probably helping me. Who knows?

Finally I broke away from my parents and the counseling. I moved in with Charlene over by the University. She had a one bedroom apartment and she and her two kids Carolyn and Kevin lived there. We shared the shopping, laundry, cooking and everything. We paid fifty-fifty on the rent, food and the utilities as well as the phone. It was crowded, but she made me welcome and I really appreciated it. I was hoping to get my own apartment in a couple of months, if I could find something decent, clean and affordable.

After three and a half months, I found a little one bedroom apartment just four blocks up Vine Street. I decide to move in, just me and my two boys. I knew it would be tight, but I had no other choice. Charlene and I would be close to each other, but it was time for me to move on. Weeks went by and I was walking in what seemed to be a continual fog. I needed to get out and start to live again but it was very difficult. I needed a distraction. What could it be?

Charlene and I were still very close and when time permitted, we partied together. She was into major league baseball players. I started going to the ball games with her and afterwards, we would go to the spot where all the players hung out. I couldn't believe it, I was actually having fun! I figured that there was no chance that I was going to end up in a relationship with one of these guys, because all they were after was fun. So, I didn't have to chance that. Maybe I was starting to find my way back...back to living. I could only hope.

CHAPTER EIGHTEEN

LIFE GOES ON WHETHER YOU WANT IT TO OR NOT

Aaron was now the mother of two and was determined not to let the hardships that she had experienced take her down. Thelma and Tom had been very supportive to her and had seen her through these last few months, which were the worst of her adult life. She hadn't seen Evan, but heard through some of Tom's contacts that he was knee deep in the drug scene and no one was holding out much hope that he would get better. Aaron knew that she had to go on with her life, especially for her children.

Thelma and Tom were Muslims. Several weeks had passed and they were on their way to the mosque in celebration of one of the Muslim holy days. Aaron was feeling a lot better and wanted to get out of the apartment. She decided to go with them to give her thanks to God for all that had happened and the fact that she made it through.

Things were very formal at the mosque. All the women were dressed in white and the men were dressed in suits, white shirts and bow ties. They all seemed very disciplined, looking and moving with a strong since of purpose. She walked in with Thelma and Tom but according to custom the men and women had to separate. Aaron was urged to walk to the left of the room with Thelma and the other ladies. The service started promptly and since this was all new to Aaron, she was amazed as she watched the activities. The minister spoke of unity and togetherness and a greater sense of community. He referred to the Holy Quran as their Bible and recommended that any member who had questions, use this holy book as a reference.

After the service, Thelma, Tom and Aaron walked outside of the mosque together. Once they were outside of the building, the three of them walked toward the car. As they were making their way, one of the men asked Tom if he could speak with him privately and Tom stepped away from the ladies. This gentleman was a very attractive, light skinned man with a full beard. He stood about six-foot five and he was someone you couldn't help but notice. After a brief moment, Tom rejoin the ladies and they proceed to the car. Tom opened the doors to assist them. Once he was in the car, he started the engine and pulled away from the curb.

The ride back to the apartment was quiet with the three of them reflecting individually on the service. The silence was broken by Aaron asking some questions about the Muslim faith. She asked why the ladies were all dressed in white and why the men all seemed to be dressed the same with the suits and bow ties. Tom explained the general doctrine of the Muslim faith and why they believed in it so strongly. He said that their leader, the Honorable Elijah Mohammed believed in self discipline and felt that if they were neat clean and orderly they would have better control over their destiny. Aaron was impressed and wanted to learn more.

She visited the mosque a few more times and determined that she would be interested in belonging to this faith and eventually with the type of man that she had witnessed these men to be. Tom was certainly a great example of the type of man that wouldn't want to have a family living in a rooming house. The type of man that would protect and care for a wife and their children. The type of man that would have nothing to do with drugs and other sordid activities. She was determined to have a decent life and perhaps this is the structure she needed.

She eventually joined the mosque and became a Muslim. Aaron changed her name to Rashida and was quickly indoctrinated into her new faith. Over the next few months, during her visits to the Temple, she was feeling a lot better about everything. She was living an orderly life and raising her children around very caring and helpful people. The Muslims lived in a community which was like a little world of its own. The Muslims were very self sufficient and everyone had a particular task to complete, which made things run very smoothly.

As she moved deeper and deeper into her new life within the religion she felt a sense of belonging and stability. She also started to frequently see the tall light skinned man that came up to Tom on her first visit to the mosque. Tom approached Rashida several months later to let her know of his friend's interest in meeting her and perhaps courting her. Things were done so formally within the Nation of Islam. She had developed an interest in him as well and Tom went forward with the introductions and finally a date of sorts. They found out that they had mutual interests, in fact they had gone through some similar things in their young lives and came to Islam because they were both looking for refuge.

His name was Wahsef and had been a Muslim for four years. He was really deeply involved in the Muslim movement. But, Rashida could sense something a little off about his involvement. After all of the ups and downs that she had experienced with Evan, she had developed a keen sixth sense about life. He was a little jazzier than the other Muslim brothers. He seemed to have a little more on the ball than even Tom. She couldn't quite put her finger on it, but there was something about him that stood out.

They started to become serious about each other and after only seven months they got engaged. Wahsef was really crazy about Rashida and her two children. Since the new baby was so young, this presented the perfect opportunity for her new son to get to know a decent man as his father image. This could really work out for her. Wahsef explained to Rashida that all of the marriages in the Muslim faith had to be ordained by the head of the organization, so they had to take a trip to Chicago to go before the Honorable Elijah Mohammed for sanctioning. They were planning to take the trip in two weeks. They continued to see each other and she was as happy as she had ever been. She wanted this relationship to last forever.

On their way to Chicago, Thelma and Tom acted as their chaperones, which was a matter of practice in the Muslim faith. It was a little less than a two hour drive from Detroit to Chicago. Here was Aaron, a product of the projects of Cincinnati, who went from living in a rooming house in Detroit to an apartment with friends and now she was pulling up to the tall buildings and the excitement of Chicago. She was on her way to becoming a decent man's wife, if this was approved.

The security in the building was odd to her. She really wondered about why this was necessary, because it was so different than anything that she had ever experienced, but pushed the thought aside because her happiness was just one more step away. There were several layers of guards to get through in order to keep their appointment with their leader. It was as if this man was a god to these people. After the protocol was met and the necessary steps had been followed, they were taken in to meet with the Honorable Elijah Mohammed. He asked them several hard hitting questions and after a forty-five minute session, he finally gave them his blessing. In a matter of five hours they were on their way back to Detroit to prepare for the wedding at the mosque. She called me and Sidney to let us know of the upcoming marriage but didn't ask if we would be there.

I said to her, "Do you want us to come?"

"I always want my 'Sisters' with me, but this religion is so different than your traditional religions and things are done so differently, we couldn't really spend the kind of time together that we would have liked. So, just wish me well and I will call you both." We concurred with her wishes and waited to hear how everything went. Two months later they were married in a simple ceremony and were off to live a happy life, or so she thought.

The next year was great for Aaron. They had come together as a family. Wahsef was a very enterprising young man. He wasn't, however, the religious man that Rashida thought he was. He was indeed a Muslim, but he was connected with some people involved in shoplifting and smuggling electronics and other things. Rashida and Wahsef had a beautiful apartment and he was responsible for getting all of the things in it. The children had for the first time in their lives just about everything that they wanted. Rashida was enjoying living this way and was becoming more and more involved in the activities that Wahsef was entangled in.

Eventually, they and some other people moved around the country stealing loads and loads of clothes, furs, and anything that wasn't nailed down. While they were on the road, they shoplifted during the day and shipped back the goods that they got. They stayed in the fanciest hotels, ate in expensive restaurants and really lived it up. When they returned back to Detroit, they would pick up their shipments and set up a spot to sell their goods. They had a big warehouse type building where they stored all of the goods until it was time to sell them. This was a multi-thousand dollar business. Rashida vowed that she would never be poor or hungry again and that she would do whatever she needed to do to make sure of that.

CHAPTER NINETEEN

Sidney was in love! David wined and dined her all over the New York, Pennsylvania, and New Jersey area. She and David were making plans to be married in the summer. She was finally going to have the perfect man in her life. The cream of the crop of Philadelphia were all invited. She hoped to have all of the sisters in the wedding. She called me to see if I felt up to coming to Philadelphia.

"Taylor, girl, I miss you!"

I said , "I know that's right, and I miss the hell out of you too!!"

We giggled. Oh how I missed her! It was as if years had passed and it had only been ten months since we had been together, if only for a day. With Aaron (now Rashida) in Detroit, Sidney in Philadelphia and me still in Cincinnati, we couldn't spend the time together that we used to. We all missed each other and constantly thought of one another in between the busy moments of our very busy lives.

"David and I are getting married in three months, can you come up to be in the wedding!!?"

"How are the boys?"

"Are you starting to accept Roy's death? Is it getting any easier?" Sidney asked in rapid fire succession.

"Slow down Sidney...you are asking too many questions too fast...I want to answer all of them, but let's take them one at a time, okay?"

"Okay, I'm sorry girl, I guess I'm trying to catch up and I'm running everything together. When I left Cincinnati after the funeral, all I had time for was a quick hug and I had to run to the airport. I knew you were in good hands but now, I want to know how things are coming along? And besides, I have tried to call you so many times and your mom said you didn't want to talk to anyone."

"It took me quite some time to accept all this. I am starting to accept it now but it's still so hard. I'm too young to have gone through this. I'm still not sure what all this means. I'm so confused, but I know that I have to continue to try hard because I have the boys to consider. Besides, I have to see what's next for me. But to get to your question, yes I will be honored to be in your wedding. Maybe that's the type of distraction that I need. Is Aaron, I mean Rashida, going to be there? You know I can't get used to her new name."

"Same here. I have left a few messages for her but the person answering her phone says she is out of town," she told me.

"Well, you know her, she will be there no matter what," I added.

"Let's talk again soon."

"And, Sidney, I'm so happy for you and David. He's a fine guy."

We hung up the phone and I started to think how all of us were changing and moving along in our own lives, but how we were all still very connected.

I would have to start saving for the trip to Philadelphia. Sidney needed me and I could really use her company too.

As it worked out, Rashida and I were in the wedding. It was beautiful. It was held in a huge church. The decorations included hundreds of white roses and candles, five bridesmaids and groomsmen, a best man and me as the maid of honor. Of course, Rashida and I had to toss a coin for that honor. We wore pink sleeveless, floor length dresses with scoop necks and pink cocktail gloves and the groomsmen wore tuxedoes with tails and had pink corsages in their lapels. When the wedding march began, Sidney came marching down the aisle, she was a vision. Her bridal gown was made of yards and yards of pure white lace and satin. Her head piece was made of extra material to create a full rich look. They said their vows that each of them had prepared themselves. Sidney was so happy and so beautiful. There were some very well to do folks in attendance and one could tell they reeked of money. We were stepping in high cotton now which was evidenced by the limousines, Rolls Royces, and Mercedes Benz' parked outside the church. We were tasting the high society life of Philadelphia. It certainly gave me something new to shoot for. Rashida and I hung around for two days after the wedding. Since David and Sidney were off to the Caribbean for the honeymoon, we took in a few of the sites. We took the opportunity to catch up with each other and inevitably I dropped her off at the airport as I began my trek to Cincinnati. We parted, vowing not to be apart for so long again.

When I got back to Cincinnati, I had a lot of soul searching to do . I needed to determine what I wanted to do with the rest of my life. Cincinnati had too many bad memories for me, so I really needed a change of scenery. First the horrible relationship with Brandon and then the death of Roy reinforced my resolve to leave. I wanted and needed to get a fresh start. Several months passed by and day by day I simply existed, living like the walking dead. I was just going through the motions of life. I knew that I was much too young to be feeling this way and had to do something about it. Even more weeks passed by as I continued to sink further into depression. I decided to check into moving from Cincinnati to either San Francisco, Los Angeles or Atlanta. I had heard great things about each city. While going through my process of elimination, I thought about the fact that California was too far away from my parents, so I looked closer into moving to Atlanta. I setup a plan to go visit Atlanta in a few weeks. I had heard that Atlanta was a very progressive place and there were lots of opportunities for Negroes. It couldn't be any worse than Cincinnati, since this was mostly a white city which had a rich German history. It would be great to walk down the streets in a city where you see your own kind in charge or that's what I felt that it would be like.

Ruby Green, a girl that I met through Bobby, and I, decided we'd drive to Atlanta and spend a four day weekend there. My mom and dad said they would keep the boys for the weekend. Ruby told me that Danny, the older boy from Lincoln Park Drive had moved to Atlanta with Dora, the girl he rode around in the trunk of his car. She said they had been there for almost a year and we could hook up with them to get the lay of the land. It sounded like a good idea to me, especially if it would get me out of Cincinnati for a while and I could see some new scenery.

This was the first time I had actually been out of the Cincinnati or Northern Kentucky area. I was excited about this trip. I packed some sandwiches and chips along with some pop for the ride. Since it was Ruby's car, I figured I would show some initiative by preparing the snacks. Along the way we talked, sang and listened to the radio in each city that we went through. We stopped four times for restroom breaks and to stretch our legs. The ride took us about nine and half hours. I was really ready to get out the car for a long time, I started dreading the ride back even before we got there. But, that all went away when we pulled into the outskirts of the city. It was beautiful! The mere fact that there were so many Negroes there really blew my mind. When we got near the downtown area I noticed so many Negroes walking up and down the street, Negro bus drivers sporting big afros, Negro mailmen delivering the mail, Negro shop owners, Negro business men dressed in business suits and white shirts with ties. Wow, I was really impressed! At that very moment, I realized that the potential change was good, at least that was what I had heard all of my life and now I had proof. I thought, this is the reason that Sidney and Aaron had left Cincinnati and now it was my turn. Although I knew I had to think logically, I knew that I had to make up my mind fast. My heart was racing with anticipation.

We made our way to Danny's apartment in Southwest Atlanta, off Campbellton Road. He lived in an A frame apartment called Bent Creek, the likes of which I have never seen before. We parked the car and got out. As we were walking towards his apartment, we ran into a couple of black guys getting out of a BMW. These guys were slick looking and as fine as any men I had ever seen. I knew at the moment that I was moving here and it wouldn't be long before I did. We got to Danny's apartment door, knocked and Dora opened it. She was shocked and looked relieved to see us. She motioned for us to come in. Danny had some loud music playing. It was so loud that I couldn't hear what Dora was saying. I hollered at Danny asking him to turn it down some.

He said as he walked toward the stereo system to decrease the volume, "You come in my house and order me around?"

I said, "I'm not ordering you around, it's ridiculous that we can't even hear each other. It's a matter of common courtesy."

He said, "You are the only woman that has ever gotten away with talking to me like that."

I said, "I wouldn't speak to you or anyone else in a manner that is disrespectful, because I demand respect myself. My conversation was for clarification only. Besides you know me and I know you...right?"

He said, "Whatever, you're all right with me!"

I said, "I thought so, so can we move on now?"

In the back of my mind I was thinking that there was something going on when we walked in because I noticed how Dora was looking when she opened the door. She looked scared to death. Why was she still with this creep? Was there this much love in the world? What power did he have over her to make her stay? It was all beyond me. Danny had been beating up on Dora again we found out later but she was used to it. She told me that he had bruises on her arms and shoulders as well as her legs and thighs. I thought she was a fool to stay with someone that treated her this way.

We checked into the only Negro hotel in town, Paschal's on Hunter Street. Danny allowed her to take us around to show us what she knew about Atlanta early the next day. We were out for about five hours just riding around experiencing the city. Atlanta turned out to be a very interesting place. I wanted more than ever to live in Atlanta now. Ruby and I were on our own the next day and early in the afternoon on Monday we packed the car and headed back to Cincinnati. On the ride home, I made plans in my head about how I would accomplish my move and when. I refused to stay in Cincinnati any longer than I had too. I wasn't sure how I would pull it all together, but I would have to make a way somehow.

Two weeks later I packed all of my belongings in a U-HAUL truck and paid a friend of mine to drive it for me. I purchased a Greyhound bus ticket for him to get back to Cincinnati. I knew I had to leave now before I lost my soul, my hopes and all of my dreams to the sad memories of the past. I believed that second and in some cases third chances were available to us if we would only take them. When we pulled away from the front door of my parents house, my mom and dad stood their stunned. Their shock revealed on their faces and in their body language said it all. They couldn't believe that I would actually leave them and live so far away. It was heart wrenching to them . I tried to tell them that I had no choice and that I simply had to do it. They wanted me to at least leave the boys with them until I got settled, but I just couldn't. I felt that where ever I went they had to go too, because I was responsible for them and I knew deep down inside that all three of us would be all right. The restless drive that I had inside me was as strong as ever and I just knew I would make it happen for me and my boys. I drove my 1968 Cougar and Harry followed me and we slowly continued down the road to my freedom.

When we got to Atlanta, I set up shop in the same complex as Danny and Dora. Of course it helped me that Dora was the property manager in the complex and assisted me in securing the apartment. I didn't have a lot of money left and knew that it was imperative that I find a job as quickly as possible. So, I remembered seeing several HELP WANTED signs when I was in Atlanta two weeks before. Being the proactive person that I am, I wrote down some of the phone numbers. I used Danny's phone to call each place to see if the jobs were still available. On my fourth try, I called a real estate company about ten minutes from where I got the apartment. They had a position open as a secretary. I setup an interview and four days later I got the job. I wasn't getting paid for two weeks so, I had to leave the boys in the apartment alone which was very difficult. They were both still very young, but what choice did I have? In that two week period, I was called home three times to address some problems that my youngest had gotten into. School would be starting again in five weeks and that would solve some of the challenges I was facing. Little by little it would all work out for me. Dora, however was not so lucky.

One evening when I returned from work all hell had broken out in the complex. Police were everywhere. Dora had gotten up enough nerve to try to leave Danny with the help of Bernie, a new man in her life.

Danny and Bernie were involved in a shootout over Dora. Danny tried to keep her from leaving, but she was determined to go. The police intervened before anyone got hurt. When the dust settled Bernie and Dora ended up together. Danny was left alone. He deserved it from the way he treated her all these years.

CHAPTER TWENTY

Rashida had bitten off more than she could chew. She was in over her head, but somehow getting the hang of her new life. Wahsef was a handful to say the least. No wonder he didn't appear to be like the other Muslims. He wasn't like them at all, but he was still good to her. He treated her like he really loved her! So much so that he was possessive and vigilant about her at times. He was involved in so many secretive activities. How reminiscent of Evan. He even dealt in marijuana. Over the past year he had become really involved in selling it and no telling what else. Ever since she had to live in that rooming house with Evan she was suspicious of anything having to do with drugs or the secretive activities of a man. Rashida thought she couldn't win for losing.

It was the spring of the year. Rashida had had so many problems with her female organs that her doctor had scheduled her for surgery in a few days. She was to go into the hospital to get a hysterectomy. She had suffered from heavy menstrual periods and cramping for well over three years, which was ever since she had her son. She suspected it was because she wasn't able to get any medical attention or go to the doctors for care during the pregnancy. Because she would be in the hospital for a week or more she wanted to make sure that Ryan, her ten year old daughter would be okay, so she sent her back to Cincinnati to stay with her grandmother on Evan's side of the family. Rashida accepted the fact that Ryan would only have to miss a couple of weeks of school, but there wasn't much more she could do because she had to have this surgery done now. Avery could stay with Wahsef since he doted on him so much. They were wonderful together...just like father and son!

Wahsef drove her to the hospital and got her checked in. The surgery went well and he was there when she woke up from the anesthesia. The doctor said she'd be up and around in no time at all even though she had to stay there for a few days. Rashida was in the hospital for six days recuperating. Wahsef really missed her terribly and visited her everyday. He brought Avery along, but because he was under five years of age, the hospital rules stated that he couldn't be brought into the ward or on the floors where the sick patients were. It had something to do with immunizations. Wahsef left him in the car with the windows rolled down to make sure he had fresh air. Wahsef felt he would be safe, while he ran up for a quick visit with Rashida. He parked the car in a very visible spot where Rashida could look out of her hospital room window and wave to little Avery. That was the only way she could see her baby. All five days while she recuperated, Wahsef repeated the same ritual during his visits. Both she and the baby could see one another from the same window. She felt that Wahsef was being very thoughtful and appreciated it immensely.

On the day that she was to be released from the hospital Wahsef was delayed. He was usually a stickler for being on time. He finally came for her over an hour later than they had agreed upon. In between packing her things she peered out of the window a couple of times to see if she could see the car with little Avery waiting to wave at her. She was still sluggish and a bit tired from the operation, so she tried to minimize the trips from her bed to the window. When Wahsef walked into the room, she was fully dressed and laying on top of the covers on the bed looking up at the ceiling. She smiled at him as he crossed over the threshold.

"Hi Wahsef, I'm happy to see you and I'm pleased to be going home."

He had a faraway look in his eyes as he sauntered toward her to kiss her on the forehead.

"Hi baby, I'm glad to see you too. I was up late last night taking care of some business and didn't get a lot of rest," he explained, "sorry I'm late."

"I'm ready to go," she said, "will you walk out to the nurses station to let them know that

I'm ready for my wheel chair now?"

"Sure," he responded.

She thought to herself that there was something that was not quite right. It was just a feeling she had, but she brushed it off.

When he returned to the room, he helped her up to swing her legs over the side of the bed while they both waited for the nurse. Two minutes later, the nurse hurriedly entered the room with the wheel chair and they both helped Rashida into the seat. Over the last five days he had parked in a spot at the edge of the front entrance. She hadn't seen the car this time since he was late today, but hopefully, he was parked there again so they could get to the car quickly and she could see her baby. As she was pushed in the chair, Wahsef and the nurse walked behind her. They exited through the automatic doors onto the front drive. She looked to the right and saw the head lights of the car. She was excited about seeing Avery again. The closer they got to the car, the more excited she became. She immediately became alarmed because she didn't see Avery's little head moving about.

She looked back at Wahsef, "Where is he?"

He said, "Maybe he is laying down in the back seat."

They were just about to the car now and Rashida leaped from the wheel chair only to find out that her baby wasn't there at all. She looked back at Wahsef in horror as she screamed, "WHERE IS HE?"

"Maybe he got out and wandered away...let me look around," said Wahsef appearing concerned.

Rashida cried and cried. She became hysterical. Her tender condition was deeply affected by this horrible feeling that something was desperately wrong here. Wahsef came back to the wheel chair to announce that he couldn't find the baby. He ushered Rashida into the car and while he was doing so, commented to the nurse that they would go home and call the police to help in locating the child. The nurse looked confused and bewildered. She took the empty wheel chair back toward the hosiptal entrance while glancing back at Rashida and Wahsef several times. In her heart she knew something wasn't quite right.

Rashida cried all the way home. When they arrived at the apartment, Wahsef called the police. It only took about twenty minutes before they arrived. There were three car loads of them. They were given a description of Avery and what he was last wearing. An **All Points Bulletin** was put out on the police radios and scanners. The entire city was searching for this kid. The neighbors came to offer any assistance. They were on special bulletins every thirty minutes on television. A command post was set-up in the house in case there was contact from kidnappers. Twenty-four hours went by with no reports from anywhere.

Rashida was becoming more and more frightened for her child. In the meantime, in the middle of everything, Wahsef disappeared on different occasions.

It was after almost three days of the police searching that a childlike girl, who appeared to be lacking good judgment, turned herself into the police and confessed to having knowledge of what happened to young Avery. She told the police headquarters that she and Wahsef were getting high on cocaine and having sex at his home. During the eight hours that the young girl was there, the baby kept crying from obvious hunger and neglect. Wahsef's patience quickly faded while he was under the influence of the drugs. He struck the baby trying to put enough fear in him to stop the crying. He consequently hit him too hard. She reported that both she and Wahsef thought the kid was only sleeping, but after he was so quiet for such a long time, they tried to wake him up only to find that he wouldn't respond. She said they panicked and in their drugged state, they buried the baby in a shallow grave in the nearby park agreeing to say that Avery wandered off, while he was at the hospital picking up Rashida. The manhunt turned to Wahsef and he was hauled off to jail.

Rashida was devastated. This was dreadful. The man that she had hoped to spend the rest of her life with was charged with the murder of her son and had tried to cover it up. He was to be arraigned in four days. The immature girl was to be prosecuted as an accomplice to the crime, but was told that she would get a lighter sentence, if she testified for the prosecution.

The day of the arraignment, Rashida could barely make it to the court room. She was still reeling from her operation and now mourning the loss of her only son. She called both me and Sidney to fill us in on what had happened and to ask us to come to Detroit to be with her. We dropped everything and made our

205

way there. Sidney and I were with her ever step of the way. I had to drive to Detroit and on my way there, I dropped my boys off at my parents house in Cincinnati, got a good nights sleep and continued on the next morning. Sidney could fly for free, since she worked for the airline, so she took a flight in and was there when I arrived. We walked with her through the arraignment and the opening days of the trial. Wahsef declared his innocence to the bitter end. Inevitably, he was found guilty of involuntary manslaughter and was sentenced to twenty-five years. The girl was also found guilty and sentenced to five years. Rashida wasn't sure if she could go on. She had endured so much for so long. Where would she find strength? She only knew that she had to try mainly because of Ryan, but she had to admit that it would all be uphill from this point on.

PART II

Sidney was having a great time in her new marriage. Her new husband David was the toast of Philadelphia and he was very much in love with her and was extremely good to her. He was around all of the colored stars in the New York area. His career as a model had opened the door for him as a promoter of plays and concerts which he had thrown himself into heart and soul. His career had now taken off. She had a live in maid and was working on her second baby. They were the proud parents of a beautiful baby girl. Both Sidney and I were kinda sad and blue about what Rashida was going through and we left her with the assurance that if she needed us, we would always be there for her. We had deep feelings about what Rashida should do next, but that had to clearly be up to her. But for now, Sidney was appreciating all that God had given her. Her relationship had blossomed with her famous father and he was in and out of Philadelphia to visit while he toured the country performing in concert. Things had worked out well for both she and David. They hosted lavish parties at their home. He bought her mink coats and all the fineries that go with the lifestyle they were leading. Through it all, she kept her job at the airline, which made sense...no point in spending money to fly to Europe and other parts of the world, if they didn't have to.

Mrs. Celeste was still caught up in her own personal misery. She visited Sidney on many occasions with the thought of still trying to run her life. We all supposed that she just couldn't help herself. When she was visiting, Sidney and David could count on Mrs. Celeste trying to tell the maid what to do. She also wanted to run their marriage and interfered both in their personal conversations and their decisions that they had to make regarding the running of the house. She really interfered in the care of her new granddaughter. When both Sidney and David were fed up with the meddling, they sat her down and told her how it was going to be from that point on. Mrs. Celeste was pissed and flew back to Cincinnati that same day to retreat. Mrs. Celeste thought, "How dare they!" She said all she was trying to do was help. As far as Sidney and David were concerned, they didn't need or want that kind of help.

PART III

The job that I had was not at all what I wanted to do for an extended amount of time. I knew I had to keep it for now, but I needed to make more money for me and the boys. The real estate broker and president of the company had set his sights on me and was not to be denied. He was married and swore to me he was separated from his wife and going to get a divorce. He said he had her situated in a house that he used to live in with her and their two children. He told me that he had a small place of his own now and wanted to have a relationship with me exclusively. He was a fairly decent looking man who was hard working and I thought that if he could help me, why not? I knew that I wouldn't become emotionally attached to him because of my ambivalent feelings about relationships since Roy passed.

So, he wined and dined me and helped me out financially. He eventually assisted me in securing a little two bedroom brick house for myself and the boys in Decatur. One night late, while he was there with me we had just finished having sex, his wife came to my door crying and about to beat the door down. I went to the door and when I opened it my heart sank and , I felt really bad because she had these two little children with her and they were crying for their father. Well, needless to say that was all she wrote for me and him. I hadn't realized how difficult it would be to break it off with him, but it was . He hounded me for weeks. Eventually, he got the message.

Nine months later, Kelly moved to Atlanta and stayed with me until she got a job and on her feet.   By that time, I was fully indoctrinated into the city. Kelly and I really did the town together a lot. I showed her all that I had learned. In those days, I was responsible for so many people from the old neighborhood moving to Atlanta. A year and a half later Bobby, his wife Lisa, Curtis my little brother and Carey my baby sister had all moved to Atlanta. As a matter of fact, I remember walking in the Greenbriar Mall one Saturday afternoon and seeing so many people that reminded me of the people back home. Could it have been them?

As time marched on, I got my real estate license to sell under the direction of a new real estate broker. Obviously, I couldn't continue to work at the same company. I had a lot of luck in listing and selling houses. My first full year I made almost forty-five thousand dollars. That was enough money for me to buy a larger house especially in light of being able to use my commission as a down payment and the sale of my Decatur home. The boys and I moved to Southwest Atlanta. It was an upscale neighborhood and I was excited to own a house that was so nice. I was also able to buy a new car. Bobby went with me to look at the Cadillac Sevilles. He already had a Cadillac DeVille and knew a lot about cars. I loved those new Sevilles and that's what I had my heart set on. When we walked out of the show room, I was the proud owner of a "brand new" rust colored Seville. I was stepping in high cotton now!

Things were really going well at this point. Mr. V's Figure 8 was the happening spot for all the Black Urban Professionals (or BUPPIES) in Atlanta. I frequented the club every Sunday and Thursday nights and eventually so much that I had my own seat at the bar. I had never had that much money in my life and I was enjoying every bit of it. I had to save part of my earnings for Uncle Sam and income taxes, because in real estate there was no automatic deduction for taxes to come out of anyone's commission checks. We had to pay on our own. Many times I spent part of what I should have set aside for tax time and would have to scrape up money when it was time to pay my taxes, but I always managed.

After working in real estate for two and a half years, the market started to dry up. It was difficult to sell houses because of the interest rate hikes and no one was selling because it would be much too expensive to make subsequent purchases. In order for me to maintain my life style, I had to find a real job. I put in applications all over the city and finally after two months of looking, I got an interview at Zerox. Then a second interview and a third. I was hired as an administrative assistant. God was looking out for me! It was difficult for me there. The white managers there were very critical and not supportive at all. Even though the money was real good, I didn't believe that I could endure this for the next twenty years. It was tough to stay because of the opposition from some of the white managers and my inability to take glaring disrespect, but through it all I got promotion after promotion because I was a hard and thorough worker, which made it even tougher to leave. I realized after five years on that job, that it wasn't for me. These people were cruel to their employees and brow beat them for every little thing and that wasn't my nature. I vowed to work there until I could find something else. Something that was more who I was. But, after making that kind of money it wasn't easy. I began the painstaking task of looking for a new job. Everything that I ran across was less than half of the salary I was currently making. I figured out that I would have to take a huge cut in pay in order to start over again. But, I was willing to do that to be happy.

PART IV

In the late seventies I started my new job at America Banking in downtown Atlanta. I was excited about this new industry, and knew I had to once again work my way up to make any money. I was fine with that but, I also knew how it was for black people and that it wouldn't be easy. Besides having no money, I had no personal life at all. It was work and home again for months. I really missed Mr. V's. While I had a lot of fun there, I also ran into a lot of people that brought me nothing but problems.

One afternoon after work, I stopped by Bobby's out of shear boredom, to see what was happening. There were a couple of cars right in front of his door that I didn't recognize. He was entertaining four new friends of his. They were Sonny Pazallio and three of his cronies. Sonny was a very handsome man. He and Bobby had become good friends recently and as Bobby put it "ran together" often.

He was six foot four, medium dark complexion and great to look at.

Besides his name alone was exciting! He had attended college here in Atlanta and appeared to be very intelligent. In the following months, I was in his company several times, while he and Bobby were together. We started spending some time together independently. And as time went by, I was introduced to several members of his family and a couple of his friends that he grew up with. We drove by the area where he grew up and he familiarized me with parts of Atlanta I hadn't been made aware of since I moved to town.

The male members of his family were as good looking as he was and all except two of them had what I would call a slick demeanor about them. It appeared to me that most of them wanted to be so called *players* tough guys and womanizers, if there were such things. I thought long and hard about getting caught up in this kind of crowd, but I had a lot of adventure in my soul, so I went for it. I have never been the type to be afraid of anything, or so I thought. We went out to dinner a few times and had long walks hand in hand and talks about everything under the sun before we decided to become an item. I honestly felt that there was no game in this new relationship. We were really into each other. I believed that this man was possibly my destiny. It was what I wanted for so long. I never thought I could feel this way again especially since Roy's death. One thing lead to another and we were all going out together.

Several weeks later we had come in from a very nice party and Sonny brought out some cocaine. He was tooting it right there in front of me. I asked him, "Why are you doing drugs?"
He said, "Why not, here try it"?
I said, " I barely drink alcohol, why would I want to use drugs?"
He said, "Don't be such a big baby, go for it, it won't hurt you !"
He was very convincing, and being tired of being called a baby, I moved closer to

him, willing to give it a try. He separated two lines for me and gave me a straw from which to inhale the substance into my nose. At first I messed it up. I exhaled when I should have been inhaling. He then prepared another line for me and this time I did it right.

I said to him after a minute, "I don't feel a thing, you mean people pay all their money for this and there is no feeling?"

He said, "give it a minute and you will.

A couple of minutes later, I felt like I had energy to burn and everything was as clear as a bell. This was very new for me so I asked for another toot. Before I knew it I was asking him if he had any cocaine all the time. He gave it to me whenever I asked for it. Sonny let me in on some of his dealings. I thought that as long as they didn't affect me, what did I care. A month later five of us went to Tuskeegee to take a kilo of cocaine to a well known singing group there. Sonny wouldn't let me know who it was The ride was fun because we tooted all the way there. When we got there I never got to meet the actual customer. They transacted the business and before I knew it we were back on our way to Atlanta. But, I didn't care because I was as high as I could be. When we returned to the area of my house, we noticed police cars all around beginning three blocks from my house. Sonny and his brother got out and told me to drive to my house and check out what was happening. I was too stupid to say no or to question why. The police were all over the place. When I drove into the drive way, they all rushed my car holding up their badges and a few of them even had their guns drawn. I was scared to death. What had I gotten myself involved in. One would think that Sonny was Al Capone or worse. They barked orders at me to get out of the car and let them in. They had a search warrant so I had to do what they said. They said they had been told that my house was Sonny's headquarters operation . They also told me that they were going to search my house from front to back and top to bottom.

All the coke that I had snorted had simply disappeared in the wake of all of this. I began to think straight in the midst of this madness. It seemed as if I was plagued with first one thing then another. Would it ever stop? It was a good thing that the boys had gone to Cincinnati for the summer with my parents. This was terribly embarrassing, police everywhere and the neighbors standing on the outside watching it all and whispering. After they finished searching, they asked me a battery of questions. None of which I had the right answers. They told me that they were searching for him and that they had a warrant for his arrest. Finally, they left warning me to stay away from him, because he was dangerous. Of course, I immediately got in touch with him and helped to find a place to hide him out. A friend of mine Tanya, who happened to be white and liked black men, was more than willing to give Sonny shelter.

I met her at Mr. V's several years before, where she was always under one black man or another. We took him to her house. He got settled in and I went to see him everyday after work. For a long time, I was paranoid that the police were following me everywhere. I would ride for miles and miles out of the way to make sure I wasn't taking the cops directly to him. When Bobby found out he hit the ceiling! He and Sonny got into it over my being involved. Bobby threatened me and promised that he would kill me if I ever took drugs again. Both Sonny and I gave our word that I was out of this environment forever, as of that moment.

Things got a little strained and strange for quite some time, but eventually even more truth came to light. Tanya and Sonny had become an item. That sneaky son of a bitch was bedding her after I introduced them and all that I had done for him. And, I found out almost six months later that he was involved in a host of other illegal activities too and of all things, that he had killed two people! Was every black man in the world caught up on doing wrong? As a matter of fact, I also found out that Randall, his very best friend, turned up murdered three months ago and Sonny was implicated in his death. Could he have really been this cold hearted? Was my ability to detect this kind of behavior in someone so far off? And, to add insult to injury, we found out that he killed a girl that he brought to my door not two months later, asking me if she could stay with me and the boys for a few days. I said, "Absolutely not!" I wouldn't dare have a strange woman or anyone else that I wasn't familiar with staying in my house with my boys. No way! Man, when I said that to him, he blew up. He was pissed with me because, as I found out later, he had never had a woman say no about anything to him before.

Later in the week the woman's picture flashed across the television screen. She was found dead in a ditch alongside the railroad tracks in Union City. A feeling of fear overcame me, one that I cannot describe if you paid me a million dollars. I immediately picked up the telephone and called Bobby. I had to let him know about it. Bobby told me he had just seen the news too and that he was sitting there in shock with his mouth wide open. He told me that Sonny had the girl at his house about three days before. This was weird! Out of all that we had all experienced in life, we never interacted with or knew a murderer!

As the weeks progressed, we knew that Bobby would be called as a witness, because he and Sonny were hanging partners. We believed that the police would never accept the fact that Bobby didn't have a hand in this mess. Thinking logically, I talked to Bobby about it and encouraged him to just tell the truth about everything. He got a lawyer and told his lawyer all the details from beginning to end. He was very detailed and went into every aspect of how they met and ran together through to the time he found out about the murder. He said that the last time he saw the girl was when both Sonny and the girl left his apartment. The girl had threatened to tell the police that Sonny was involved in a murder of a lady that was found dead in her apartment six months earlier in which the police suspected was a drug related robbery. The girl was upset with Sonny because he wouldn't give her the cocaine that she wanted. When Sonny and the girl left Bobby's apartment, after letting her out of the door first, he leaned back inside the door and whispered to Bobby that he was going to squash this hoe. The next thing we knew, she was dead.

From that point on, I was afraid of my shadow. Anytime I heard that he was in the neighborhood, I was shaking in my boots. This time it was much worse than the time when I was afraid of Juanita Mathis in elementary school. That couldn't compare to this, at all. For the next few weeks, I was very careful about every move that I made making sure to keep myself and my boys safe.

The trial was a long one. The Atlanta District Attorney had had the FBI watching Sonny for two years and they had been trying to get the goods on him. They had wanted to put him away for a long time. In the opening arguments, the District Attorney told the jury that the State wanted to give him the electric chair, if the jury found him guilty. There were thirty-seven witnesses for the prosecution testifying against Sonny. Thank God Bobby was never called to testify, even though he was in the courtroom every day of the trial. The district attorney's office checked out Bobby's story from beginning to end and found out that he was telling the truth, so he was no longer under scrutiny. During the trail, I was the topic of conversation to so many people. How could she be with someone like that and not know it? What could she have been thinking about subjecting her children to a man like that? What was she thinking to allow someone like that to get her hooked on drugs? Everywhere I went I heard comments like this. I must admit, I was weak for a handsome face. I guess after

Roy's death, I was starved for affection. I wasn't really hooked on drugs, but I certainly did use them. And, I liked using them. It really started me to thinking.

To make bad things worse, Roy, Jr., my youngest son, told me a story of when he was riding with Sonny one day to run some errands for me, Sonny stopped by a man's house about fifteen minutes from where we lived, to pick up a package. He told Roy, Jr. that he would be right back and to stay in the car. Roy, Jr. said that Sonny was in the house so long that he decided to get out of the car to see what the holdup was. When Roy, Jr. knocked at the door, there was no answer. So, he walked around the side of the house to see if they were in the back yard. He saw Sonny was standing poolside with a gun in his hand. There was also a man climbing down the pool steps with all of his clothes on. Sonny had obviously given the man an order to get into the pool. As Roy, Jr. tip-toed closer, he heard Sonny say to him,
"Either give me my money or drink all of the water in the pool...NOW!"
The man pleaded for his life and kept saying,
"Man c'mon, you know I can't drink all 'dis water and I don't have your money yet, please give me another day or two!"
After standing there for thirty seconds, Sonny pumped him full of holes. Roy, Jr. said he couldn't believe what he saw and flew back to the car, got in and shook from head to toe, while he prayed to God to just let him get back home safely. That was horrible for a thirteen year old boy to have witnessed.

Sonny was found guilty and was led to the Atlanta city jail for the sentencing phase of the trail which was five weeks away. Bobby felt that he turned his back on Sonny, but the first law of nature is self preservation and to me it was very prudent for him to do what he needed to do to keep himself out of this mess. As for me, I don't wish anything bad on anyone, but of all the people in the world that I could have met, I had to meet someone who cared so little about human life, not even his own. A month after the trial Sonny got life without parole. What a waste. One of those victims could have just as well have been me or one of my boys, but God wasn't ready for us at that time.

CHAPTER TWENTY-ONE

Reality sets in...

Sidney's dream life was starting to fade away. Times weren't so good for David since his work had begun to dwindle. The concert business had been taken over by mega-companies which made promoting concerts for small outfits difficult. The artists' fees were skyrocketing due to huge artist contracts and only the mega-companies could afford these fees. The costs of the arenas and amphitheaters that were being built all over the country, where most of the concerts were held, were also getting too high. The venues were partially owned by the same mega-companies. This helped cut the costs to the mega-companies doing business in these venues. These venues were for the most part brand new and they could hold more patrons enabling the mega-companies to make more money. As time marched on this pushed smaller operations out of business.

The makeup of the audiences was also changing. With younger artists coming on line, the potential of the musical tastes of the people who had frequented David's shows was changing. This along with crime in the country on innocent individuals simply out for a good time, created a big gap in the type of audiences who felt safe to come out to enjoy the shows that David once put on. It seemed like more mature audiences were finding entertainment in what they considered safer venues like jazz clubs or other smaller places or even just entertaining at home. The money wasn't rolling in for David like it had been before. And to make a bad situation worse, now their daughters were growing up and in need of more money for their school activities, ballet and music lessons and other expensive things. Their lifestyle had already been set when David was the man. David and Sidney argued more and more about finances. In the months that followed they had to let the maid go and this was really putting a cramp in Sidney's lifestyle. She was so used to Miokayi taking over all of the household duties like cooking, cleaning, ironing and even being a nanny to their children. Life was still tolerable for them, but not nearly the same as what they had become accustomed to. A split was inevitable.

In the following months Sidney sunk more and more of her time into work, which was difficult for her to do, since she was used to spending so much time with the girls and loved them so much. David, with the time he had on his hands, was at home more with the girls. Sidney planned for this to keep she and David from bumping heads and it also kept impending arguments to a minimum. This was definitely all right with her. They went on like this for eight or nine months.

Because she was at the office for longer hours and ultimately doing more work, her efforts were recognized. The shear volume alone had come to the attention of her direct supervisor. This was working out in a number of ways for her. A top level manager, Mr. Nolton, also noticed her job performance had improved drastically, which was adding more to his bottom line and making him look real good to the board of directors. Mr. Nolton asked Sidney's immediate supervisor to set up an appointment so they could discuss her career with the company. He wanted to meet her face to face in an effort to congratulate her on a job well done and to also offer her a promotion.

Three weeks later she walked to the twenty-eighth floor of her building for the requested meeting. Mr. Nolton's secretary escorted her into his office and asked her to take a seat. She was advised that Mr. Nolton would be in before long. As she sat there waiting for him, she reviewed the office area that she was in. Things were a bit different, but she remembered that she had been here before. This was the office where she had her second interview, so many years ago. The people occupying the offices were of course different, but she'd never forget this area.

Mr. Nolton entered the office and spoke with a deep white man's voice. He asked, "How are you today Mrs. Bernard?"
"Oh, just fine Mr. Nolton" she replied.
She wasn't quite sure why she was there.
"Let me get straight to the point. I have been reviewing your files over the past couple of weeks and I want you to know that I am very impressed with your work over the years. Your steadiness and your production, your punctuality and attendance, your ease with the passengers and co-workers have all been excellent. And the more recent contributions over the past four months have been outstanding. Now I think it is time that we look at putting your very considerable talents to better use for the company. Are you interested?"
"Well, of course I am!"
"Well, you look like you are in shock!?"

"To be totally candid, I am. It's just that I never thought that anyone noticed, to be honest," she said.

"Well we have noticed and we want to work with you on a new position beginning Monday. I have put all the plans in motion and you are to report for training in your new responsibilities on Monday of next week," he reported.

She asked, "As what?"

"Director of all city ticket offices in the Northeast. As she stood to her feet with a huge smile reflected in her entire body, she extended her hand to him while uttering a well poised, " Thank you very much!"

She turned to walk out of the office and felt the urge to turn to him once again and say

"Thank you so much for noticing my efforts, I really love what I do and it evidently showed, so thanks so much!"

He said, "No thanks necessary, you earned it!"

As she walked through the big double doors back to her office it was extremely difficult to contain herself. It was as if she was dreaming. She planned to make the very best of it and continue on with her career. She wanted now to make plans for her next move in the corporation and now she knew what it took to get there.

When she got home she was thoroughly thrilled and it showed! She gave David the good news, but he was less than excited. His impending downfall at his job was gloom and doom for him and she was hitting the high road on hers. Although he was happy for her, to think that his wife would now be making more money than he was, was very deflating to his ego. His attitude pissed her off as their relationship tumbled a few more feet that instant. The arguments became more and more frequent and got to be louder and longer. Eventually, she knew that she had to move on with her life because this wasn't working out. She looked around the townships that were close by to try and find another place to live, keeping it a secret from David. Eventually, she purchased another house, which was in a different township and moved out. She wanted to make sure it wouldn't be easy for him to pop-up at anytime to bother her. She said, the further away the better. She convinced herself that she had to make this break and start fresh.

Part II

Rashida was making plans for her future. She was still reeling from the murder of her son. The fact that her husband was charged with the murder was beyond belief! How bazaar! She knew it would take her a very long time to get past this, if she was ever able to get past it at all. She had made so many new and good friends at the mosque, she got assistance from all of them. They were with her night and day for months. As the time passed, she was making plans on how she wanted to move forward and get beyond this nightmare. Several months later, she moved back to the Cincinnati area. She purchased a brownstone in Covington, Kentucky and tried to get herself and her daughter settled in there. Her plans were to be close by her remaining family. She also had so many former schoolmates and friends in the Cincinnati area, she knew she would be all right in time.

Once Rashida got settled into her new home, she started on her job search. She knew that she would have to start all over again and wanted to keep busy to try to free her mind from the tragedy. She picked up a newspaper to survey the want ads. She saw a few interesting ads and went out to put in applications, place after place. In the listings on the third week of her search, she noticed there was a secretarial position at the Northern Kentucky Community Center. She had begun to run short of funds and called to see if the job had been filled. The young lady answering the telephone said it had not, so she scooted over there to put in an application in person. When she got there, the director took her application and asked her to wait while he reviewed it.

He said to her as he walked back to his office, "We really need someone fast, so bare with me please, I'll be right back."

Thirty-five minutes later he returned to the reception area and told her that she had the job, if she wanted it. He explained all of the job responsibilities and told her what the position paid. He asked her if she could report the following morning. She said she could be there and they shook hands. Rashida thanked him for the opportunity. She glided out of the door and as she drove home, she had a strange feeling that this was the new beginning that she had prayed for.

The next morning, she reported to work not knowing what to fully expect. When she arrived she was given a desk and a telephone with no clear instructions on what to do. When the telephone began to ring, she answered and fielded questions from the individuals on the other end, as much as possible. She used common sense on most of the issues and researched information, when time permitted, on the rest. This went on for several weeks. The director, Mr. Hayes, came to her at the end of that time to let her know that she was only expected to type and take messages, referring the calls and whatever situations they presented to the social workers. At the same time he congratulated her on fielding the calls and helping the people in need better than the two sorry social workers that he had working for the Center. Two additional weeks passed and he decided, after many counseling sessions, to let social workers go. They had been hanging on by a thread for over ten months anyway. The director admitted to himself that he kept them on only because he had no one else. He felt at the time that they were better than nothing, but not by much. When Rashida came on board, she really showed the other ladies up, by the way she handled the calls, the people and the situations. So, Mr. Hayes decided to combine their jobs and give Rashida a shot at it. He realized that she had no formal training in social work, but felt that she could do it especially in light of what he had seen over the past thirty days. Rashida thanked Mr. Hayes for the confidence he had placed in her and promised not to let him down.

For the next few months Rashida threw herself into her new job. She was thrilled to have something to put her heart and soul into, to help her forget what had happened to her baby. She and the director began to become friends. They worked very closely for a lot of long hours together and it helped that they had a mutual respect for each other.

Rashida felt that it would be smart for her to start taking some night college courses to assist her in being even more prepared for her new field of work. She felt that she had found her niche and wanted to make sure she was well equipped in every way. She was gratified that she was back in the Cincinnati area, surrounded by family and friends that would pitch in to lookout for both she and her daughter, while she got settled into her new home and job. It looked like she was getting another chance and that it was all working out for a change, but with all that had happened, she wasn't about to let her guard down, not at all. There was too much that had happened in the past. She kept each incident in her mind and she knew what her role in each one was and vowed that she wasn't going to let it happen to her ever again.

PART III

I had to pull myself out of the proverbial mental gutter from this point. How could I have been fooled by someone like Sonny? I was still using cocaine. I really liked it and didn't see anything wrong with it either. I kept my use of drugs from my boys and continued to go to work everyday, so I thought I owed myself a little fun.

Keeping pace with my Mr. V's activities every Sunday and Thursday, I often ran into a lot of people who also used. So, I found it very easy to get cocaine from any of them, if I wanted it. I used the excuse that after all I had been through, it was all right. There were always so many fine men there too, so having a good time was secondary. I met a tall, very light skinned brother there one Sunday night. I had just parked my car and was walking in to hook up with Kelly. I had on a deep pink and black spandex dress which was skinned tight and some black sling back pumps. My hair was in long braids down my back and I was HOT by anyone's standards. He parked his car as I passed. It was a white Mercedes. I had his undivided attention. I was glad he didn't see the jaloppy that I had gotten out of, I thought. I whispered to myself, "I have to get a new car somehow." I had to represent myself a lot better than I was when I cruised in the car I had.

He stepped out of his car and loudly cleared his throat. I was about fifteen steps in front of him and continued to walk, as if I hadn't heard a thing. I got to the club entrance and, of course, there was a line of people waiting to get in. I walked straight up to Butch, the regular guy on the door, he unlatched the stanchion and held it back in order for me to go right in. I heard several people in line make some snide remarks, but what did I care...I was a regular there and I made it work for me. I walked up the staircase and took my regular seat at the bar, which was where Kelly was sitting. Slim, the bartender was aware that I had gotten there and poured me a Hennessy on the rocks. The music was loud and the club was packed. The dance floor was really crowded and more and more couples continued to make their way to dance. The club was jumping and the atmosphere was nice as usual.

I took a sip of my drink and began to take a look around to see who was there. My normal course of action was to scope the room to see what I could see. You would think that I was a twentieth century robot, the way my head went from one side of the room to the other, missing nothing or no one. After all, I didn't want to miss anything good. I got settled in for the evening. A few minutes later, I noticed the tall guy from the white Mercedes. He was standing at my left engaged in conversation with several other men. They were all looking directly at me. I wondered what that was all about?

I had a stash, so I told Kelly that I'd be right back. I went to the ladies room and waited in line to get into a stall. Once I got into one, I took the cutoff straw out of my handbag and parted the little plastic coke bag to get me a "one in one," which turned into a "two in two." Man, that lifted me right up! I was sailing and felt great! I slinked back to my seat getting attention from all the men along the way and I loved it. To my surprise as I approached the area where we were sitting, I saw the guy from the Mercedes standing at the bar talking with Kelly. As I got closer, Kelly smiled and introduced me to him.

"Taylor, meet Eric Dunn," she said.

I responded as I slide back into my seat and held out my hand, "Nice to meet you."

He had the same old look on his face that most men have when they are trying like hell to pick someone up. There was a slow song playing in the background and I bet that was his cue to ask me to dance.

He held out his hand, "Would you like to dance"?

I said, "Sure, why not," as I thought this is so predictable.

We walked to the dance floor hand in hand. When we got there he looked at me as if he could eat me alive.

I thought to myself again, "You'll get none of this tonight mister."

We danced closely as I really got into it. This guy was both good looking and light on his feet. We talked small talk about him and where he worked and he declared that he was very attracted to me. I looked up at him and smiled, saying nothing. When the record was over, he escorted me back to my seat and asked if he could see me again. I told him that I hardly knew him and that I'd hopefully see him again here at the club and maybe from there we could get to know each other.

I must have met at least ten guys at the club that I had interest in. Peter,

Daniel, Tony Louis, Jimmy, and others. They all had cocaine and were willing to share it for their right reasons. Periodically, they would give me a little, but Eric had something to prove. He really wanted me, so he gave me all I wanted. Finally, I invited him to my apartment, and we did the wild thing. I was glad that the boys were gone for the summer. It was not the sex I wanted, but his mind. After I gave him the ride of his life, he would give me anything I wanted. He had been with Delta for many years and was making a pretty decent chunk of change each week. I knew I could use the help, especially if I wanted a new car and other things. Besides, how many times has a man used a woman? Right or wrong, I was paying one of them back for what so many of them had done to so many sisters!

PART IV

Sidney was coming to Atlanta to get away from David. They had hit a couple of rough spots in their relationship and she needed a break. She came down two weekends a month to relax. We hung out at the club or went shopping or just chilled out. As we were getting dressed for the evening on the second weekend, I introduced her to cocaine. She was prudish at first, but she tested it as I had in past. She couldn't feel too much that first time, but after a few times, she began to like it too. We just sat around and periodically, in between topics of conversation, took a hit. But this particular weekend, I was invited to a major party.

Tony Sobito from the club was having a party at his house in Decatur. Sidney and I went. We were looking and smelling good when we finished putting on our party duds. We were both careful to have our makeup on to perfection. I had on a skinned tight spandex striped purple and black striped dress which had a very wide black patent leather belt to accentuate my incredibly small waistline, with black seamed stockings and black patent leather sling pumps. Sidney wore a slinky black oriental spandex dress which had red oriental trees at the breast area and black pumps and plain stocking. Her lips and nails were blood red to match the red trees in the dress. We looked delicious and were as hot as we could be.

When we pulled up to the house, the street was lined with fine car after car. Tony's house was all light up and surrounded by all of his vintaged cars. He had a strong flare for the dramatic and you could even tell it in the way he dressed and the ruckus that cropped up when he came to the club. It was as if he was the man all the way around! It all reminded me of Al Capone movies. It was truly exciting! Tony was a smooth talking, cute light skinned little fellow who was as sharp as he could be, with tons of money and everyone knew it. When we walked in, we got all of the attention. Tony stopped what he was doing and rushed over to me to escort us in. He had several of his women there but he dropped them instantly when we walked in.

It was a HOT party! All the latest records. He had all kinds of food, alcohol and even cocaine too. Tony walked us to the bar and told the bartender to take care of us and to make sure we had everything we wanted. He then disappeared into the crowd with the promise to return shortly. The bartender poured us a shot of our requested Hennessey on the rocks. After I was handed my drink I walked about five steps away with the objection to stand at the rear of the room to see all that was happening. Sidney got her drink and joined me there. I noticed, directly to the right of me a small mound of cocaine on a table right next

234

to the bar. One the same table to the right of the mound, someone had set up line after line of the cocaine as if they were waiting on which ever of the guests interested in partaking to so at their leisure. I elbowed Sidney and forced her to notice the goodies laid out for any of us. After standing their just to see who indulged, she and I walked over to the coke and did three lines apiece. It went straight to my head. Afterwards, Sidney wandered off and onto the dance floor with a dark skinned gorgeous looking guy who approached her to ask her to dance. A slow record was playing and she was just about invisible in his arms. He was really a big guy and his body appeared to have swallowed her whole.

Tony reappeared a few minutes later and asked me to join him in the other room. I said of course. We walked in there and he motioned for me to sit. He took a seat next to me as we began talking. He was a class act. I was thoroughly impressed with him. He was nothing like he appeared to be while we were in the club. In the distance, I heard the end of the song that Sidney and her new friend were dancing to come to an end. A few seconds later Sidney and her partner appeared at the door of the room where Tony and I were. As couples, we talked and kissed and drank and tooted coke for about thirty more minutes. We were definitely in to each other. Tony broke free and asked us to make sure not to leave, explaining that he and his friend had to walk through the house to make sure everything was going okay. We assured them that we would be there after everything was over to spend some quality time with them. When they left she and I talked and tooted some more. We agreed to get out of that room to walk around to see who all was there and to see what else was going on in the house.

The party was all over the house, in every room. We visited room after room. In one of the rooms, we walked into seven or eight people were naked and playing sex games. We immediately closed that door and continued on. There was even a little room in the basement where they were smoking cocaine. We went in there and just stood watching that activities and talking to each other and eventually conversing with some of the fine men who were there also smoking. Neither me or Sidney had smoked this stuff, but we were high enough to try anything once. In the room there were eight women and three guys. One guy was cooking some coke in a small bottle, carefully measuring baking soda to add to the coke. As he cooked it, the mixture solidified and then he drained the water off and broke up the big rock into small pieces. He sat a small pebble on top of a glass pipe, lighting it with a contraption made of a piece of coat hanger with cotton wrapped on the end of it. The cook took the first hit, inhaled it and obviously enjoyed it. He then told the first girl in line to pull from the pipe and to hold in the smoke as he did. When she did, the bottom of the pipe became filled with white smoke swirling in it and the girls eyes rolled back in her head. When she let the smoke out and she screamed that she was feeling better than she had ever felt in her whole life! My heart began to race, I couldn't wait to do it! Sidney tried it before me. She did the same thing as the other girl and then it was my turn. It was better than sex! We did it a couple of times again and then it was over. My heart was racing, I was sweating and I wanted to have some more. Tony came looking for me. As he entered the room everyone became anxious because everyone knew that he was the man and that his entering the room meant more drugs for all of us. He gave the cook some more and all I could think about, like everyone else was getting high.

Hours later, when we finally came out of that room everyone was gone. It was five o'clock in the morning. We stayed there all night and half the next day doing nothing but getting high. Tony's objective, as he said to me, was to get some pussy from me and I like a fool fell into the trap and gave it up. He had a huge dick which I surprised me. He was a little fellow, but carried a big stick. He

236

did it to me over and over again continuing to tell me that he had dreamed about fucking me since he first laid eyes on me. He was erotic. He insisted going down on me, giving me oral sex too. I had never even thought about this act, but it was very sensuous. It was an eye opener for me to say the least. Sidney and her new friend were obviously having a good time too because I heard her moaning and groaning in the next room. Finally it was over. I got up, took a shower and fell back into Tony's bed exhausted.

When we left there the next afternoon, I was embarrassed and thoroughly spent. What had I done? Sidney and I had sex and hadn't started out to do that. We both felt dirty. She had a flight to catch because she had to get back to work the next morning and so did I. When we got back to my apartment, the first thing that I saw when we walked through the door was my answering unit flashing. Eric had been calling and had called at least ten times. He sounded mad as hell, but I didn't care.

Sidney and I both painstakingly cleaned ourselves up and she got packed. I drove her to the airport, hugged her and then she disappeared into the terminal. I got back into my car and drove back to the apartment and crashed. I slept and slept hard. When I was awakened by my alarm clock the next morning, it was difficult to get up. I dragged myself in to take another shower with the hopes that that would wake me completely. I was mistaken. It was as if I was still walking in a fog.

When I got to work, I was dragging. All of my co-workers had one comment or another about my appearance. They said I looked worn out. If they only knew! As hard as it was, I made it through the day only to get back to my apartment and go straight to bed. It took me three days to get back to my normal self.

Sidney came down again two weeks later and we went right back to Tony's house. When we got there this time, we were introduced to a whole new crew of people. A girl of no more than sixteen or maybe younger was there with her father. They were smoking cocaine together. Sidney and I couldn't believe it! We didn't smoke this time, we only tooted the coke. Neither of us wanted to feel the same way that we felt two weeks prior.

We watched as the girl was sent out in the middle of the night three times by her father to the instant banker to get more money. How could he do this to his own child? When she got back the last time, her father was so high that he didn't know where he was. He was standing in the middle of the floor grinding the air. He began to run hands around his private area, acting as though he was having sex all by himself. Jeanna, his daughter, took a toke of the free base pipe and as her eyes rolled back in her head she appeared to have zoned out all together. When she levelled off, she slinked over to her dad and began to gyrate with him. He was rubbing on his own child in her private areas and her breasts, right there in front of all of us. That was disgusting! Drugs will make anyone do anything it seemed! We were so turned off that we made some lame excuse and left. On the ride back to my apartment, we agreed that the scene we had just witnessed gave us a wake up call. We talked about it in detail. How could we be a part of something so morally unacceptable? Was this where we were headed? After all that we had been through, how could we allow this to be? This was plainly a matter of the soul. Could we allow all of our hopes and dreams go up in smoke? On this topic, we definitely saw eye to eye! This scene was enough to make us swear off doing drugs period. We were better than that and besides, that wasn't really what we were all about anyway. I thought about our plans as we sat on the high school steps all those years ago and this was not part of the plan.

Saturday we spent trying to make sense of what had happened to us over the last two weeks and to all of us in general. We were so happy being together when we were kids. The old neighborhood and the high school steps were a safe haven for us. Day by day, week by week and month by month our lives turned into one delicate situation after another. Sidney's mother's abuse, Don's possessiveness, Aaron's problems with Evan and then Wahsef, my challenges with Brandon and then Roy and his obsessive actions about me and then his death. What was happening to us? We had to get to the bottom of it.

We decided later that afternoon that we had to get Rashida on the phone so that all three of us could talk about it. When we reached her, we told her all about the drugs and what we had witnessed. We talked for over an hour discussing everything in detail. I declared that I was swearing off men period. They both chuckled and went on with the conversation. That's when we decided that we needed to be with each other more often. We promised that we would all get together soon and often. We put together a schedule and pledged not to go more that a year to a year and a half without coming together. We scheduled our first mini reunion at the next Taft High School class reunion which was in six months.

CHAPTER TWENTY-TWO

We all gathered again in Cincinnati! It had been a long time since we were all together at home. We set a time that we would all meet at Rashida's house so we could make our rounds together. Later in the afternoon of the second day, one by one we arrived at Rashida's house. It was wonderful to be together again! We marveled at the changes in each other and discussed incident by incident what all had transpired over the years. Trevor suggested that we drive over by the high school just to see what it was like now. We jumped at the thought of it!

We road over the Cincinnati/Kentucky Bridge toward downtown Cincinnati. So many things had changed. As we road through the old neighborhoods we discovered several of the streets had even been made one way. Even though it had changed, nothing could keep us from getting to where we needed to go. A few seconds later, we found ourselves on John Street right in front of the high school steps. There was really no where to park but we sat there with the lights of Rashida's car blinking indicating to any other cars coming in that direction to pass us. Many thoughts ran through all of our heads as we gazed at the steps, but as quickly as we pulled up there for a moment we were off to look at the rest of the neighborhood. What a wonderful feeling it was to be back again!

The next night it was time for the reunion. The unique thing about Taft's class reunions was that it enabled all past students to come together whether or not it was a particular individual's fifth, tenth, fifteenth, twentieth anniversary or whatever. The theme of each years reunion was the five year increments, but many of us came just to see the people that meant so much to each other during our youth.

Our normal course of action was to arrive late in order to make our grand entrance. We did and it was fabulous! We could never understand why everyone remembered our names while we didn't remember all of theirs. Many of the young ladies' heads were together as we came in and their tongues started wagging about us. We looked good! We hugged a lot of people and mixed and mingled for the next hour. It was magnificent!

Then, low and behold, I saw Phillip! He was even better looking than before. He had matured nicely and I couldn't take my eyes off of him! A few records later he approached me about a dance. I melted inside. Time actually stood still for me. I mentally went back to the days when we were at St. Joseph's auditorium and he and Beverly were dancing cheek to cheek. We had wasted all this time, I thought. We walked onto the dance floor, hand in hand, as I imagined we should have done so many years ago. It was like he had always been mine and I had always been in his arms. After the dance, we stepped to the side off to ourselves and began a light conversation. I asked what he had been doing and where his wife was? He told me that his main course of action over the past two years was playing softball and working because he and his wife had divorced. He said it was a bitter divorce because she ran away with one of the other boys from Taft. He told me that it was as if Paul Kranter had her in a trance. He bragged that he was still very close to their four children. I thought to myself, four children later, she runs off? What could this other guy have had? I know that if I had been fortunate enough to have had him as a husband, I would still have been there with him. Not wanting to look as though I was too eager, I told him that I should get back with my group. He said okay if we could get together later. I said sure. I really didn't want to blow this now by appearing to be too anxious.

Sidney and Trevor were at the other end of the Topper Ballroom when I found them. They were surrounded by seven of the guys from Sidney's class. All kinds of flirting was going on. A few seconds later Anthony Jerrod, who was one of the seniors when Sidney first started Taft, came in. Sidney and Anthony had always had the hots for each other and had been good friends since the fall of 1962, so they were happy to see each other again even though they had stayed in touch by phone over the years. This reunion was turning into a huge event for us. There happened to be many more of us there this time than in the past. It was wonderful getting together again and we didn't want this night to ever end!

About thirty of us wound up in the same circle discussing the past and what the future held for each of us. Mr. Waterfield entered the room and all of our attention turned to him. He hugged each and every one of us as tears formed in his eyes to see us all grown up and most of us looking so successful. He also informed us that Mr. Starfal, Mrs. Childron, Mrs. Andrews and several other teachers were seated to the right as you went toward the dance floor and threatened us that we'd better make it that way soon. We got a real charge out of the threat because it instantly mentally put us back in high school when he used to do it all the time.

We all walked over to the teacher's area and surprised Mrs. Childron and the others. They were so happy to see us and proud of the way that we all turned out. We hugged and hugged and hugged. What a superb group of human beings!

Many of our former classmates and others who attended the school saw all of the activity on that side of the ballroom and heard all of the commotion. They came over to the area to get a closer look. Several of the onlookers were some of the pretentious former seniors, the so-called pretty people. They joined in on the activities too. Claudia, Darnella, Cameron. Mary Jane, Kayla and Aysia all of the schoolhouse snobs weren't so pretty now. The years hadn't been very kind to them. Most of them had begun to get fat and from the looks of things hadn't faired too well so far. I thought to myself, that's how it goes, individual physical looks will diminish, but a good person with a kind heart will always be accepted. It can also help to define who you are in the long run. Being the kind of people that the sisters were, we welcomed everyone who wanted us to, with open arms.

Phillip couldn't stay away. He stood just to the left of the group watching me as I mingled with everyone. Our eyes locked a couple of times, but I was determined to keep my cool and not to appear overly interested even though I was. We all began to make plans for an after party. There were several suggestions thrown in the air. Butch, one of the former athletes suggested his house in Evanston. He had a pretty large house that his parents left him when they passed away some years ago and we felt that everyone could fit there, so it was on to Butch's house. As we enjoyed the last moments of the reunion, Phillip appeared once again to ask me to dance. He was everything that I could have hoped for all of these years and now, here he was.

I rode to the after party with Phillip. He was driving a new dark blue Cadillac. He was dressed nicely too and I had noticed his expensive but understated jewelry. To sum it up he was doing well for immediate practical purposes. I wondered what type of man he really was? When we arrived at the party, he got out to open the door for me. Hmmm,
that was a nice touch. We walked into Butch's house hand in hand. The girls all rode in Aaron's car along with Anthony and pulled up just before Phillip and I reached the front door.
Trevor called out, "Hey Taylor, wait for us."

We stood to the side to wait for them so we could all go in together. That night, I became more and more in love with Philip. Was this the Phillip of the moment or the Phillip of the past? I had to find out. About four a.m. it was time to go home. I hugged the girls, letting them know that I'd see them at the picnic the next morning. I alerted Aaron that Phillip had offered to pick me up at my parents house and take me to the picnic. They taunted me about getting with Phillip after all this time.
I was stimulated.

On the drive to my parents' home, we continued to hold hands. I asked him about the school days and even that of the Neighborhood House when we saw each other. He told me that he thought that I was always a pretty girl, but he had been strung out over Beverly and couldn't explain it. He said that had been over for a long time and wanted to know if we could work something out.
I asked him, "How would that work? I live in Atlanta now."

He responded, "You could possibly find a job here in Cincinnati?"

"I'll have to see," I said.

I thought to myself, I know my parents would love it if I moved back, but I love Atlanta and it was better there for black people now, so I wasn't sure about this at all. We arrived at my parents' house and pulled into the driveway. He looked deeply into my eyes and I was drawn to him as we kissed a long, wet, seductive kiss. I was in heaven. All of the years that I had waited and wanted. It was everything that I had hoped it would be. I was still in love with him! He whispered, "I'll see you in the morning about ten, okay?"

I whispered, "Okay," as I moved to get out of the car. He asked me to sit still while he ran around to the other side to assist me. He walked me to the door and gave me a light peck on the cheek. He walked down the steps, turned around as I opened the door with my key and went in. I heard his car start and watched as he backed out of the driveway and started on his journey home. What a night it had been!

PART II

Phillip was at my door the next morning at nine fifty-five a.m. He was dressed in a pair of navy shorts and a white pullover short-sleeved golf type shirt with tennis shoes and socks. I hadn't realized that he had big hairy legs. He was really a lot of man and I was falling for him all over again. I was dressed in a red plaid short skirt with a red blouse and white tennis shoes and socks and was ready to go when he arrived. The mood was light hearted with a touch of uneasiness. Where were we going with this new relationship that was twenty years old? Did we really still have a chance to be happy with each other?

We arrived at Mt. Airy for the reunion picnic. I became very nervous and couldn't figure out why. It was a gorgeous morning and the cars were streaming in. There appeared to be a whole lot more folks at the picnic than the dance the night before. The 'Sisters' were already there. They had staked a claim on one of the picnic tables right in the center of the action. Rashida waved while jumping up and down for me to see where they were sitting. Phillip and I sauntered over to them. Music was playing, food was flowing and guys were drinking beer at eleven in the morning, but I guess that was cool because it was reunion and everything. We all danced some of the old dances from our era. It was a blast to do the uncle willie, the monkey and the cha cha again and to be doing it with the people that you danced with when they first came out was outstanding! We danced for seven records straight. Then, because I needed to rest for a moment, we headed back to our table. That's when I saw him. It was Scoopie!

I hadn't seen him since he and Raymond took me to this very park all those years ago and tried to have their way with me. I was pissed. I broke free from holding Phillip's hand and went up to him and began to curse him out. That was why I was so nervous when Phillip and I first entered the park. Deep in my mind, I went back all those years remembering those two boys and the fact that they tried to rape me.

Phillip couldn't believe that I was acting that way, but I didn't care. Scoopie deserved this and more! I rationalized in my mind that I had to do this to free my soul. While I was cursing him, he looked up at me to display that he was in a drunken stupor. His wife came to his rescue and in a soft spoken manner, explaining that he was an alcoholic and that he didn't have much longer to live. She told us that he had serosis of the liver, because he had indulged for so many years. My hostile attitude changed to one of pity. I came to tears. Earlier in my life, he was such a good friend and then he tried to take my virginity and now this. I took him in my arms and hugged him telling him that I forgave him for what they did and wished him well. Phillip took me by the arm and led me back to our table consoling me as much a possible. Neither Aaron nor Bo had prepared me for this. All of this put a damper on the rest of the day for me. I sat at the table watching Scoopie as he sat there drinking and drinking. I wondered if what they tried to do to me was the beginning of the end for him?

The next day Phillip came to pick me up. We were headed to his apartment in Kennedy Heights. It was a well appointed bachelors pad. He was a very neat man which was impressive. He prepared lunch for me while I browsed and we chatted . We ate, while having general conversation. He wanted to know about Atlanta and all that I had been doing since I moved there. Naturally, I couldn't tell him any of the off the wall stuff that had happened, but I did tell him the truth about all of the good stuff. He wouldn't want to be bothered with me if I had told him what I did with Tony or Sonny. But, I was sure that he was no saint either.

After we finished eating, we relaxed in the living room to watch television. We teased and played with each other just having fun. One thing led to another. He put one of those heavy kisses on me just like he did two nights before and there we were in the heat of passion. He expertly unbottoned my blouse and then unsnapped my bra, sliding the straps down my arms, while sweeping me up in his arms and slowly carrying me into his bedroom while he kept his tongue down my throat. Oh, how I have wanted this for as long as I could remember. He laid me on the bed while he virtually tore his tee shirt off. I helped him to get ready by unzipping his jeans. He slid them off. I was laying there completely naked when he began to kiss me from head to toe while tenderly caressing my complete body. It was the most sensuous moment I had ever been involved in my entire life. He did his job working me up to the point of an orgasm, when he opened my legs and enter my body with a penis as hard as Stone Mountain in Georgia. He made sweet love to me nonstop for the next hour and a half which resulted in at least four big orgasms for me. I had never felt so good. He was all that I had waited for and more. When we were done, we both laid there holding each other in the afterglow of making love and fell off to sleep.

We were awakened by a knock on the door. He laid there just listening for a few minutes and then jumped up and asked me to stay put and be quiet. I was confused. Why didn't he get up to answer the door earlier? Who was it that he was hiding from? Whoever it was, had begun to beat on the door hard, knowing that we were in side. It was a woman because she started calling his name in first a whisper, then yelling as she beat the door continually, rapidly and hard. I was becoming quite alarmed.

He got up, went to the door looking out through the peephole. He rushed back to the bedroom to put on his jeans and house slippers in a hurry. He left the bedroom again with a look of concern on his face, closing the door behind him. He opened the front door to the apartment. A raging woman, who was incensed that she had to go through all of that to get in, entered the living room. She interrogated him, asking him who was in the apartment and wanted to know why it took so long for him to answer. He told her that he had company and that she should leave and stop making a fool of herself. She started for the bedroom as I jumped back hoping she wasn't coming into the room where I was. I wasn't prepared for this. They began to tussle when he told her that she was not welcome there any longer and not to come back. She called out two names, "Beverly ??? Karen???? He is no good! He'll do you the same way he did me in the end," she shouted. He shoved her to the other side of the door asking her to leave or he'd call the police. Twenty minutes later after she stood around outside talking loud and obviously hurt about the whole thing, she left. He returned to the bedroom asking me to please forget this incident. I asked him how I could just forget it? I wanted to know who Beverly and Karen were. He didn't want to get into it. Apparently, there was something that he was hiding? No more lies or secrets. I just couldn't take anymore, I had been through enough with men over the years to last me a lifetime.

The rest of my visit with him was quiet. I became very reserved and wanted to go back to Atlanta to think about all of this. He dropped me off at my parents' house around four o'clock. The girls and I were to get together at six for dinner for our farewell. I met them at the Coach & Six downtown. We reviewed the weekend and agreed it had been spectacular!

We made our plans for the next mini reunion with just the four of us. It would be in New York in 1986 at Trevor's house. I left to catch my nine p.m. flight. The next morning , the boys and I went shopping for their school clothes. It was time for them to get back to the books and for me to get back to work. We had to get back to our normal routine.

Phillip and I stayed in touch after that. We met in Tennessee once a month, which was the midway point between Atlanta and Cincinnati. Kelly stayed with the boys on the weekends. She was a big fan of Phillip's. If our relationship was to survive at all, we had to spend time together. The last time that I met him, he suggested that he drive to Atlanta to stay a week with me and to see what the attraction was about Atlanta. I was glad because the four hour drive every month was wearing thin and I couldn't see where this was headed.

Three weeks later he came down. He and the boys and I had dinner at a fancy restaurant. They needed to get to know him too. The boys were very protective of me much like Bobby and my dad had been when I was younger so there was a lot of tension in the air. There was no point in my thinking that Phillip could sleep in the same bed with me while he visited. It was a good thing that the boys were always at my parents' for the summer when I was having my escapades with Tony and the others. Phillip's trip didn't fair too well. I know that if we had started out of the gate together years ago, my children would have been his and we could have made a good life together but now it was too little too late.

PART II

    Sidney got back to Philadelphia with one thing on her mind which was the opening of an executive position at her job. She knew she was being considered for it, but she also knew that she was up against two white boys. She knew that she was the best candidate for the job but understood that this was still America and run by white males. She had worked hard for this chance and wasn't going down without a fight. The board was voting on the three candidates in the next two weeks. She wanted to continue making the strides necessary to get their attention. When she got back to the office, she was low keyed and determined. She listened intently to the office chatter and evaluated all of the comments she heard. Everyone knew what was at stake and watched with bated breath as the days leading up to the two weeks came and went. The Board voted for Tom

Jenkins. He attended Harvard, had a degree in business and was a white mans perfect image. He was about six foot four with an athletes build and a deep voice. He wasn't necessarily the best person for the job but he fit the description. Sidney was upset but took it in stride while she was in the office. She thought to herself, she'd get her chance to make them sorry. Tom became her boss and taunted her at every opportunity because he knew that she was the best person for the job. He wanted to make it as difficult for her as possible hoping that she would quit. Sidney wasn't about to let that happen no matter how difficult it was to work for him.

The weeks rolled by and some of the tasks of Tom's new job were brought to the surface. He was having a difficult time completing these tasks. He had to ask for Sidney's assistance in completing these tasks. Sidney did just enough of the job to let Tom get in a Board meeting and have him where he was not able to adequately answer the questions that were asked of him regarding the specific tasks. This occurred time after time. Finally the Board recognized that Tom wasn't right for the job and offered it to Sidney. Her plan was for six months down the road and she accomplished all her moves in ninety days. Tom was out!

Trevor got back to New York with the idea that she needed to move from Queens to Manhattan to make her pilgrimage easier to her office each day. Her daughter had become an adult and gotten married so the house was no longer necessary. She moved in the city the following week. She was closer to the night life that she liked. Her marriage to Robert hadn't faired well and they had been separated for the past year. He moved to Yonkers and she was totally on her own. She knew that one day she'd move back to Cincinnati to be around her remaining family and all of her friends.

Kelly got back to Atlanta on Tuesday morning, She had married a butcher who was a very strange little guy. They separated, but she kept the house. She was working at the Amoco Oil Company key punching. So she went back to work hoping to determine what her next move would be. When she got to work that afternoon, she learned that she would be faced with either moving to Kansas City or finding herself without a job. What a shock. She would have to make a huge decision in a few weeks and it wasn't going to be easy.

Rashida and her new boyfriend, her boss Bob Hayes were working out great. She had learned through all of her other relationships not to expect too much too soon. Bob was well thought of in the city and had served in the service returning to Kentucky a hero from the Viet Nam War. He and Rashida were billed as friends, but their relationship was exclusive. He understood what a jewel he had found in her and she in him. They had a great deal of admiration and respect for each other. They went everywhere together. He spent some weekends with her and she with him. They were totally satisfied with this arrangement. Each of them had a daughter and even the daughters liked each other.

Rashida was so good with the job that he had hired her for that Bob recommended her for some outside projects. When these projects were completed, one of them ended up on floor of Congress in Washington. The congressman from the state of Kentucky was pointed out on the floor of Congress as being the representative from the state that had a profound view on record, which was now being considered becoming law. He had to meet this woman who put this project together. Congressman Tinger contacted Bob Hayes to set up a meeting for the introductions and from that point on Rashida climbed the business ladder and climbed it fast. Her upbringing in that small apartment in the Lincoln

Courts and the drive that she was born with to win had ultimately taken her to where she deserved to be. She was now really on her way.

Two weeks later we were called back to Cincinnati to attend the funeral of Trevor's first husband and her daughter's dad. He was a good friend and an ex schoolmate of ours. We would miss him terribly.

CHAPTER TWENTY-THREE

A change was at hand for me. I had driven my car so hard back and forth to Tennessee that a few weeks later it died on me when I was on my way to work. The boys had left for the bus stop and I was finishing a couple of items then I would be off to work. I bopped down the steps and got into my car only to find out that it wouldn't start. I got out to raise the hood to try tinkering with it to see if I could get it started. I couldn't. I gave up and went back upstairs to my apartment to wash my hands and head for the bus stop.

After waiting about ten minutes, the bus came and I climbed aboard. On the ride downtown I noticed the bus driver. He was remarkably good looking and I noticed that he wasn't wearing a wedding band. I observed him closely on the ride to downtown. When I was getting close to my stop, I got up and walked down the aisle to the seat closest to the front door. He turned to look at me which was my intent. I turned my head not to notice. I rung the bell to get off. I stood up as he approached my stop. I turned to him to say thank you and stepped off the bus. I waited for the bus to continue on as I proceeded to cross the street to the bank.

I thought about him all day. How could I get to know him? I had to concoct a plan of action. The rest of the week I was late in order to ride his bus. I was certain that I would marry this man and wanted to finalize my plan on how I would make this happen. The next morning I boarded his bus with a huge smile on my face. I sat next to a young lady on the front seat. She was holding an in-depth conversation with him as we rode to the downtown area. I sat there riding along as people got off and on through the next six stops wishing she would get off. She was making a move for him. She was impacting my plan. I wasn't sure at all how I was going to manage this situation. I only knew that I had to do something. Perhaps her stop would come up before mine. I prayed that it did. Twelve stops later she was still there and still talking. The bus driver was eating up her conversation. He asked her what she was doing tonight and my heart sank. She said, "Nothing much, I don't do a lot during the week."
He said, "Do you feel like company?"
She said, "Sure," as she handed him her phone number.
I was ready to throw up. I knew that I didn't stand a chance now.
Her stop came up and she got off. I wanted to talk to him about it, but didn't know how.
When she left, he turned to me and smiled.
He said, "Did you enjoy the show?"

"What show?" I remarked.

"The show that I staged especially for you," he said.

He continued, "I had never seen you until this week on my bus and was attracted to you from the moment that I saw you. I don't usually respond to the women who get off and on my bus and believe me there are a lot of them, but you were different. I noticed you right away."

"How do I know that is not just a line you are giving me?" I asked.

"Well, I guess you don't, but I hope I have time to show you that it isn't. What's your name?" he asked.

"Taylor," I responded. "And yours?"

"Morgan Canfield, and I really want to see you again."

I had my home number already written down and planned to give it to him at the end of my ride that day, I proceeded with my plan. I was excited all the rest of the day. I couldn't wait to get back home. I hoped he was being sincere because I felt something this time. It wasn't like all the other times. He called me later that night. We talked about this and that, which was basically chit chat. We were both a little tentative probably because we both wanted to be safe. He told me that he hadn't had a real relationship in quite some time because he felt that most women these days only wanted someone to take care of them. He said I appeared to be different, very self reliant and full of confidence. We made plans to see each other on the weekend. On Thursday night he called again to make sure that we were still on and to verify the time. He also wanted to get the address.

When he arrived that night I was ready to go. He knocked on the door and I answered with my heart fluttering. He stepped inside the apartment while I ran to the bedroom to pick up my purse. We walked down the stairs and he opened the door for me to get into his late model dark colored Toyota. It was a small economy car, but it was freshly washed and smelled like incense inside. He was neatly dressed in a pair of dark slacks and a colorful silk shirt and some nice expensive shoes. I had a special way of telling a lot about a man. I immediately checked out if he had good hygiene, looking to make sure his teeth were clean and fingernails were also clean and neatly trimmed. I also noted the type of shoes he was wearing. If a man passed all of these tests we could advance further.

He was extremely handsome with his almond shaped eyes and full mustache. We went to 200 South, a jazz spot off of Campbellton Road. We had a very pleasant evening and while the mood was romantic, he didn't come on too strong. It was as if he felt that he had nothing to prove and I liked that. He took me back home and walked me to the door. We stood there talking and making plans to see each other again. He leaned over to kiss me, that's when it was sealed. He had the perfect kiss. It was just right. I knew this was it.

Morgan and I started dating regularly and that was the best thing that ever happened to me, besides my family, my boys and the 'Sisters.' He visited me regularly. I wanted to make sure that this was the right thing for me to do. I had jumped into so many relationships over the years and most of them had been very wrong for me. I had to be as cautious as I could this time. The boys would have to get along with him if I was to have a relationship with this man. I thought he was nice, very nice, but I had also thought that about Brandon and some of the others too, so I needed to be as sure as I possibly could before diving in.

We went to movies, to the park, I even spent a whole day just riding with him on his bus route to see exactly what he did everyday. It was interesting with all the different types of people that he encountered everyday and I got a good feel about him especially how he handled strangers. Female after female got on and off. Some flirted with him some didn't and he handled them expertly.

Eventually, I met his mother and father who were divorced but had remained very good friends. I also met his grandmother who was a nice little lady too and his sisters one of which was a real bitch, but she was young and I hoped that she'd grow up one day and become a better person. The older sister was nice and kind of gullible. She had a family too. Her husband was an executive with a computer company and they had three children, two boys who were older and a girl nine. They were a sweet family and I was happy about possibly becoming part of it.

We got married three months later. When he moved in with me we feuded day after day. I guess it was the getting to know you stage. He was used to being in control of his family or at least that is what he told me about his first wife. They had two children together and she never worked or contributed in any way. She had sat on her ass and gotten fat and expected him to do it all. Since their divorce, she had turned their two children against Morgan telling them that he was no good and both his children have denounced him as their father. How sad that any woman had to go to such lengths to get back at someone who didn't want them any longer. She was as much the blame as he was that their marriage had gone awry. She should have been the right type of wife, while she had the chance.

I, of course, was a totally different type of woman who believed in doing my fair share and wouldn't by any stretch of the imagination be told what to do by any man. We could discuss it and agree to disagree because that was fair. The other way just wasn't who I was. If anything, it would be fifty-fifty. So, after we learned all about each other, we settled in and have been by each others side everyday since. He has been a strong arm of support for the past fifteen years in every way and I have been there for him to. He has aided me in each step of my way to the top of the banking industry which is what we agreed to in the very beginning. Day by day, we have learned how to work together, putting the past behind us and moving on with our future.

Bobby had settled down in Illinois after having a number of health problems related to that dreaded sickle cell anemia, but he has a wonderful third wife, Erin, who is with him every step of the way. He just had a kidney transplant in which she and I went four days together not knowing if he was going to live or die. Thank God he made it and I for one am profoundly grateful. He studies the Bible religiously and spreads the word of God wherever he goes. He has carried a lot of baggage from his pasts with him into today and will into the future. He has demonstrated himself, in my opinion, to be a loving brother whose first acts as a brother when we were kids let me know what it felt like to have the protection of a man in my life. We should all be so lucky and blessed to have such a strong protector around us who is willing to love and keep us from daily harm. He richly deserves happiness. We are still an intricate part of each other's lives today.

Sidney and David recommitted themselves to each other as David has ventured off into other lucrative endeavors, while assisting Sidney in her rise to the top. Their two daughters have both graduated from college and still live at home with them and have begun to work on their careers. They managed to rehire Miokayi and their family is back to the happiness that they once knew. Sidney is now a vice president with the airline and is looking to setting new records in the next few years.

Rashida is still the tough talking, hard hitting person that she was when she and Sidney ran that first race in the late fifties. She has mellowed some, but she is still as driven as the pure white snow that often falls in the Cincinnati area.

She has lost much in her life, but she has grown immensely from all the pain. She cherishes all that God has given her and appreciates the blessing of close family and friends. While she is wealthy in terms of money, she relishes in the fact that she is dedicated to helping others who are not so fortunate, which is why social work has helped to bring her through. She is very concerned about her future because Wahsef is due to get out of prison soon and she wants him to stay away from her, but she is not sure that he will.

Trevor has retired early from the insurance industry. She had a hard travel schedule training all over the country and was burned out early. She has purchased a small house in the suburbs of Cincinnati in order to once again be near her family and the host of friends in the area. She is still looking for the right man.

Kelly is currently married to her second husband. She has not been successful in business but she continues to try. She realizes that she is older now and that the young kids with many prepared skills will beat her out in moving ahead in most cases, so she remains at the housing agency as a receptionist. But she has found the love of her life and is living happy now.

I heard that Danny was now running from the law. And, after all the horrible treatment he has given so many women over the last twenty years, we learned that he is **gay** of all things. We spoke about his torture of women and wondered what had driven him to be such an abuser. The fact that he was fighting the internal feelings he had inside made him hate women. How sad.

Dora, Danny's record shop employee and part-time girl friend, is still with Bernie. After the shoot-out at the top of the hill next to the A framed apartment in southwest Atlanta, they have been together every since. It was a difficult road for them though. Bernie got involved in selling drugs and had to do some hard time in the federal pen in Atlanta. Dora looks like she is fifteen years or so older than the rest of us. She has led a hard life. She looks very old and worn because of the abuse she suffered at the hands of Danny, but she can rest in the fact that what goes around comes around.

Mrs. Celeste married again but that didn't work either because of her controlling personality. She is now divorced and living in a senior's home in Cincinnati. Sidney and her family go to visit Mrs. Celeste and she visits them too, but they have to be short visits because Sidney is emotionally scarred from her years with her mother and will be for the rest of her life.

My mother and father have a little home in Forest Park and he has just retired from twenty years with the post office. We talk every Saturday morning to catch up. My brother Curtis and his wife still live in Cincinnati. My sister Carrie and her family lives in Atlanta about twenty minutes from me and my baby brother Joshua and his family lives in Oklahoma. He is studying to become a minister.

Jay Ballard is still alive and performing in the oldie but goodie shows all over America. His relationship has flourished with Sidney and since she and Jay met and developed their bond, Sidney found out that she also has a half brother and sister with whom she has also developed strong ties.

As for me, I have been happily married to Morgan for fifteen years now. He is a wonderful man with which God has richly blessed me. My boys Rodney and Roy, Jr. are both married and living on their own in the Atlanta area with their families. I have been blessed with three beautiful grand children, two boys and a girl. Shay, the girl, is the spitting image of me when I was a kid back in the Barracks in Lincoln Heights. Life does really come full circle. All the mistakes, the lewd behavior, the drugs, the murders and deaths that have happened, were all part of becoming who we are today. When it's all said and done, we evaluate our choices and what is really important in life. Through it all Morgan and I found each other and for that we are eternally grateful.

Growing up poor and in the *projects* was for all practical purposes all we knew at the time. If any of us had gotten spooked during the rough days of our lives, we could have lost out on what the future had in store for us. Instead, we chose to take it at face value and make the best of it having a little fun and a lot of heartache along the way. We all had to learn not to develop any preconceived notions about our lives and let the chips fall where they may. As we got older, we learned to let go of the bad memories of the past and to forgive others as well as ourselves. We realized that this was essential to our survival.

Many people go through life as if they see no good in it at all. We agreed that we wouldn't live everyday as if we are only living because we have an axe to grind. We have to keep our eyes on God, which was the way we were taught when we were raised as children in the church. It is clearly up to us to determine who we could become. We had to remember that advances came little by little and as we advanced, first to one stage and then another, we had to learn to reward ourselves along the way, so that we could continue striving. We reminded each other over the years that we had to all keep moving forward and not let what had happened to us take control of the rest of our lives. But, through it all, we were there for each other at every turn. Sometimes, we appeared to be in the middle of a three ring circus, but together we decided that we had to permit ourselves to look beyond that to our tomorrow. We couldn't avoid reality. We had to reach deep, deep inside and overcome any of the obstacles along the way. We always reminded each other that we had to remember that society had divided us along the lines of race, gender and class. But, be that as it may, we could always get what we needed if we wanted it bad enough.

Being raised in the *projects* could have been an advantage for us if we chose to look at it that way. Many of the people born with so called silver spoons in their mouths have no idea what it means to be as tough as we were forced to become. This alone could have more than prepared us to be able to endure anything and everything that we encountered. I feel that is why we did not perish in the wake of the devastation that we experienced. The difference between the haves and the have nots are the ones that believe in themselves no matter what their humble beginnings and will never lay down or give up without giving the fight all they have inside. We remembered to keep our circle of influence small, because there are some dangerous people out there. They don't want happiness or peace and they are not capable of respect or love. Our circle of influence was small and full of wildly charismatic people who genuinely loved each other. The bond that we were able to build early in our lives made us inseparable and we always knew that no matter what the circumstance, we were there for each other. We held onto each other through thick and thin and these same people along with our families are the sole reason for our survival and success.

We were lucky and blessed by the Lord. So, either way you look at it...success or the lack there of is directly tied to the past and everything that you are deep inside of you.

Look for the next novel by Mikki Rogers in the fall of 1998:

* * * * * * * * * * * * * * * *

$236.52 Every Two Weeks...

Corporate America the Real Story

The story of 4 Black and 3 White Americans in their personal lives and the work place.